JOIN THE CLUB

FOUR KINGS SECURITY BOOK 3

CHARLIE COCHET

CONTENTS

ACKNOWLEDGEMENTS

Thank you to all the amazing folks who've helped me get Lucky and Mason's story out into the world. To Poppy and Amy, whose help, love, and support means the world to me. You may not be my sisters by blood, but that doesn't mean you're not family.

To my parents for the risks they took and the sacrifices they made when they left their country, home, and families behind so their children could have a brighter future. I was small and don't remember the perilous journey across stormy waters, but we embarked on a new and frightening adventure together. I will never forget where I came from, or the love that's allowed me the chance to forge my own path. Thank you.

FOUR KINGS SECURITY UNIVERSE

WELCOME to the Four Kings Security Universe! The current reading order for the universe is as follows:

FOUR KINGS SECURITY UNIVERSE

STANDALONES
Beware of Geeks Bearing Gifts - Standalone
(Spencer and Quinn. Quinn is Ace and Lucky's cousin.)
Can be read any time before *In the Cards*.

FOUR KINGS SECURITY
Love in Spades - Book 1 (Ace and Colton)
Ante Up - Book 1.5 (Seth and Kit)
Free short story
Be Still My Heart - Book 2 (Red and Laz)
Join the Club - Book 3 (Lucky and Mason)
Diamond in the Rough - Book 4 (King and Leo)
In the Cards - Book 4.5 (Spencer and Quinn's wedding.)

FOUR KINGS SECURITY BOXED SET
Boxed Set includes all 4 main Four Kings Security novels:
Love in Spades, Be Still My Heart, Join the Club, and
Diamond in the Rough.

BLACK OPS: OPERATION ORION'S BELT
Kept in the Dark - Book 1 (Standalone series can be read
anytime)

THE KINGS: WILD CARDS
Stacking the Deck - Book 1 (Jack and Fitz).
Raising the Ante - Book 2 (Frank and Joshua)
Sleight of Hand - Book 3 (Joker and Gio)

THE KINGS: WILD CARDS BOXED SET
Boxed Set includes all 3 main The Kings: Wild Cards
books: Stacking the Deck, Raising the Ante, Sleight of
Hand, and bonus story In the Cards.

RUNAWAY GROOMS SERIES
Aisle Be There

SYNOPSIS

Eduardo "Lucky" Morales is a fighter, from his childhood days in Cuba to his time as a Special Forces Green Beret. Scarred by the wars of his past, Lucky has learned nothing lasts forever. Guarding his heart is second nature, and getting emotionally involved is not an option. As co-owner of Four Kings Security, Lucky works hard alongside his former brothers-in-arms and fellow Kings, but he also plays hard. Flirting with sexy Texas cowboy and detective, Mason Cooper, is too much fun to resist, until Mason turns the tables on him.

Mason Cooper may not be a soldier, but he's fought his share of battles as an openly gay cop and now a detective for Major Crimes. Mason has no idea when things changed between him and Lucky, but the gorgeous, fiery Cuban has turned his world upside down. When a mistake leads to his suspension from the force, Mason turns to the least likely person for help: Ward Kingston.

Determined to keep Mason at arms' length, Lucky is surprised to find the man at Four Kings Security. The

Florida nights might be getting cooler, but the heat between Lucky and Mason burns hotter with every passing moment. Working private security can be dangerous and unpredictable, but so can falling in love.

ONE

IT'LL BE OKAY.

Lies.

It would *not* be okay. *He* wasn't okay.

"Fuck. *Fuck.*" Lucky tightened his hold on the mini-ape handlebar grips of his Harley-Davidson Road King Special. He knew better than to drive when pissed off, so he forced himself to focus on his bike and the road instead of his anger. Ace was probably annoyed with him. Definitely worried. His cousin worried about him too much. His family was always concerned about him for one reason or another.

Tienes que calmarte, Eduardo.

How many times had he heard those words from his parents, from members of his family? As if by them telling him to calm down, he would somehow change his ways. Make him less... him. There was nothing wrong with him. It had taken him years to realize who he was and longer to accept himself. Did his family not see that their blood ran through his veins? They were all as dramatic and hotheaded. But he refused to play by the rules, always had, and that made him *problemático*. Difficult. He was *not* difficult. Complicated, yes. Certainly that. His life was especially complicated now, thanks to a certain blue-eyed, fair-haired cowboy.

Lucky clenched his jaw at the memories of that sinful son of a bitch. He still felt Mason's touch on his hand, those calloused fingers pressed gently against Lucky's palm, his thumb stroking Lucky's skin. Soft expressions of comfort had slipped from Mason's full mouth, the words unexpected, the gentleness more so.

"Look at me."

Stupidly, Lucky had.

"Well, damn, aren't you pretty. I know the timing is for shit, but how come I never noticed before?"

Lucky shouldn't have listened. Why didn't he get out of the car? He should have gotten out of the car. The padding of his motorcycle helmet against his jaw had his brain conjuring up the memory of Mason's thumb on his cheek before it slowly traveled lower to Lucky's bottom lip. All Lucky had to do was part his lips. What would Mason have done? Would he have slipped his thumb inside Lucky's mouth? On instinct, Lucky ran his tongue over his bottom lip. Mason had leaned in, but Lucky managed to get ahold of himself. More like fear had taken hold of him and forced him to take action.

Few things frightened Lucky, but at that moment, he'd been terrified of the gorgeous cowboy and the unexpected feelings the man stirred up inside him, feelings he'd managed to avoid just fine until then. Forever was not a word he associated with relationships. Family was forever. His brotherhood was forever. Everyone else in his life came and went like the tide.

Fuck Mason Cooper.

And fuck this heat! Florida in August was *un infierno*. Ninety-two degrees, but the humidity made it a hundred and five. With his motorcycle moving, it was fine, but every time he stopped, the sweat dripped down his back, making the Balmain jersey T-shirt beneath his graphite Mojave motorcycle jacket stick to his back. He might have thundered away from the café like a bat out of hell, but he wasn't stupid. Not even his temper could make him ignore safety. It was ingrained into him. He approached riding his motorcycle like he did sex. No matter the circumstances, he didn't ride without protection. First chance he had, he'd pulled his jacket and gloves from his saddlebag and slipped them on. He'd worn his DSquared2 Blue Simplice city biker jeans and his Bowery distressed leather boots from Frye.

In the right saddlebag, he carried his Kings equipment, including a locked compartment with his Glock, and in the left saddlebag, he had a wardrobe change and a small cooler with two bottles of icy water. He'd planned on hanging out with his brothers, but that plan went to shit fast.

The sudden appearance of a moving object to his right had his adrenaline spiking and his body reacting on instinct. He swerved into the empty oncoming traffic turning lane to avoid getting plowed into by a silver BMW. Lucky hit the brakes, turned off his engine, and lowered the kickstand before he pulled off his helmet. The driver skidded to a stop beside him, and the window slid down to reveal a white-haired man, somewhere in his midfifties, in a business suit. He glared at Lucky as if *he'd* been the one to fuck up.

"You need to slow down, buddy."

"What?" The balls on this guy. "I wasn't speeding, and *you* ran the stop sign." He thrust a finger toward the unobstructed red sign the man had clearly ignored. "That's how innocent people die."

"Yeah, well, maybe you should learn how to speak English."

The fuck? Lucky straightened. "What does how I speak have to do with anything? And last time I checked, I *am* speaking English." *Tienes que calmarte, Eduardo.* Okay, this would be one of those times where he did need to calm down. Assholes like this weren't new to him. Take the high road. That's what King always said. Be the better man.

BMW Douchebag looked him over, his lip curling up in a sneer. "I can barely understand you."

"That's your problem, not mine." Maybe his accent was thick, but he always did his best to speak as clearly as possible, and it was rare someone didn't understand him. English wasn't his first language, and it didn't help that he'd started learning the language fourteen years after everyone else his age. It hadn't been easy, and even now many words and phrases confused him, but he continued to learn and improve because America was his home. His country.

The man snorted. "Um, no. You're the immigrant."

"Excuse me? I'm an American citizen." Lucky didn't call the guy an asshole, but his tone implied it. He was *not* in the mood for this.

"Yeah, but you're not a real American. You don't belong here."

"You almost killed me, and you're going to come at me with your racist bullshit?"

"I'm not racist."

Lucky's eyebrows shot up near his hairline. "Um, yes, you are."

"I don't think I like your tone."

Lucky couldn't help but laugh. "Oh shit, is this guy for real? Are you for real right now?"

"Go back to Mexico," the guy spat out. "You're not welcome here."

"One, I'm fucking Cuban. Two, you're a racist piece of shit."

"Mexican, Cuban, Puerto Rican. It's all the same shit. You should all go back to your countries and stop fucking up ours."

Lucky peered at him. "Are you high right now?" He held up three fingers. "Tell me, how many fingers do you see?"

"What?"

Lucky put down two, leaving the middle one up. "How about now?"

"Fuck you!" The guy hit the accelerator, flipping off Lucky as he tore down the road.

"¡Vete con la puta madre que te parió, pendejo!"

The car skidded to a halt, then started to reverse. If the asshole wanted to start something, Lucky was in a damn good mood for it. He got off his bike, and marched toward the car, pulling off his gloves as he went. "You want a piece of me, motherfucker?" Seeming to have second thoughts, the guy burned rubber and took off.

Lucky's cell phone rang, and he removed it from his pocket. "¿Qué mierda quieres?"

"What do you mean what the fuck do I want?" Ace growled. "How about we start with you not snarling at me, bro."

"I'm sorry. I just—it's been a shit day, you know?" A police siren broke the silence, and Lucky grinned. BMW Douchebag had been stopped the next block over. When the police officer got out of the car, Lucky's grin widened, especially when BMW Douchebag poked his head out of the window, took one look at the very large white man in uniform, and a smug grin came onto his face. He'd clearly taken one look at Officer Murphy and like any judgmental prick, made assumptions. He was about to learn a thing or two about assumptions.

"What's going on?" Ace asked.

"Let me call you back. Two minutes," Lucky replied before hanging up, his attention on Officer Murphy and BMW Douchebag, who started talking and pointed at Lucky. Murphy looked over, and Lucky waved, earning a smile and wave in return from Murphy. Karma was a bitch. You put nasty shit out into the world, and that's what you got back. Lucky would bet his Harley that Mr. BMW thought he was about to get himself out of a ticket, but he didn't know Murphy. Lucky did.

Wait for it.

BMW Douchebag grinned, and Lucky didn't have to be within hearing distance to know he'd just spouted some racial slur against Latinos, because the way Murphy's body went rigid, his expression darkened, and his jaw clenched tight enough Lucky saw it from where he stood, said it all. BMW guy laughed at his own words until Murphy murmured something, and BMW Douche turned gray. The color literally drained from his face. He said something— most likely an apology—held his hand out for the ticket, took it when offered, then drove off.

Murphy shook his head before making his way over to Lucky. He held out his hand, and Lucky pulled him into a hug.

"'Ola, hermano."

"Hey," Murphy replied, still tense, and why wouldn't he be after someone obviously insulted his wife. Martina Murphy was Mexican, a stunning and valiant woman who'd fought tooth and nail to escape the horrors of her life in

Tijuana. The fight continued when she reached America, and one day she found herself in St. Augustine. She'd been serving tables at one of the Old Town bars when some drunken asshole groped her. Murphy happened to be there on his night off and stepped in, unaware the guy wasn't alone. The asshole's equally drunken friend rushed Murphy from behind, a knife in his hand, only to be knocked off his feet by Martina and the serving tray she'd swung at his face with far more strength than anyone would believe a tiny woman barely over five feet tall would have. Murphy had set out to save Martina, but it was Martina who'd ended up saving Officer Murphy.

Lucky loved hearing the story. How in the middle of all the chaos, men brawling, and glass flying, Martina smiled up at Murphy and that was it for the big Irish man. He'd lost his heart that night, and they married not long after and had two girls, who'd grown into young women as beautiful and fearless as their mother. Lucky felt for Murphy. The man had no hope of ever getting his way. All his girls had to do was bat their lashes, and he was done. He loved his girls. God help the poor bastard who tried to hurt one of them.

Lucky met Murphy's family at the beach back when Ace and Mason dated. Mason had invited the Kings to a charity event on the beach hosted by his precinct. They'd met all of Mason's fellow officers and superiors, the event cementing a bond between the Kings and their local law enforcement.

Not wanting Murphy to dwell on that asshole's words, Lucky smiled at him. "How are the girls?"

Murphy groaned. "Estrella has a boyfriend."

Lucky barked out a laugh, quickly covering his mouth at Murphy's scowl. "I'm so sorry, bro. I know this is very painful for you."

"I'm trying not to be an overbearing, overprotective Neanderthal, but she's my baby. How is she dating already?"

Murphy's pout was too cute, and Lucky patted his huge bicep in sympathy. "Estrella is a smart and strong young lady. She won't take any bullshit, you know it."

"Yeah, I know," Murphy said with a sigh.

"Hey, it could be worse," Lucky teased. "She could be dating a guy like me."

Murphy narrowed his eyes at Lucky, making him laugh. "Sir, did you know your motorcycle is illegally parked?"

Lucky threw his hands up. "Okay, okay. I'm going." He pulled his gloves back on and returned to his motorcycle. "Have a good day, Officer Murphy. Say hello to the girls for me."

"Stay out of trouble, Morales."

"No promises," Lucky called out, his phone ringing as soon as he was astride his motorcycle. "¿Sí?"

"Where are you?"

"I'm fine, Ace."

"That's not what I asked you. Where are you?"

Lucky sighed. "Not far. I need to decompress."

"You do that. Be safe."

"Always." Lucky hung up, and once his helmet was on, he turned his bike around and headed in the direction he'd come. Mason would be long gone by now, but there was always a chance Lucky would run into him if he wasn't careful. Why the hell did they both have to live in the same fucking city, and one as small as St. Augustine Beach? He decided he'd done enough thinking about Mason, but that lasted only as long as it took him to reach the parking lot behind the pier.

They'd flirted that day. It was no different than any

other day. Lucky never hid what he thought, and anyone could see what a gorgeous man the cowboy was, from his long powerful legs to his broad chest and huge biceps. He had large hands, which Lucky loved, and his low gravelly voice with his Texas accent sent delicious shivers through Lucky, but all Lucky did was flirt. It meant nothing. Mason would grumble at him, flip him off, bitch at him about his motorcycle or the cost of his designer clothes. It had been fun. Then something changed, and Lucky had been unprepared.

Once his jacket and gloves were secured in the saddlebag of his parked bike, he headed for the pier. The beach was busy, and a few people sat on the old wooden boards of the pier, legs dangling off the sides, but the very end was usually empty. He was far from everyone else, so he did what he'd done many times.

After stripping down to nothing but his black boxer-briefs, he inhaled deeply and closed his eyes. Mason's voice filled his thoughts, and Lucky let out a low growl. He was so stupid. *Idiota.* Letting himself get worked up, angry. It wasn't their first argument, by any means, but it had been their first real fight. It hurt, and he couldn't get Mason's words out of his head.

"Damn it, Lucky, wait." Mason had grabbed Lucky's arm and jerked him around to face him.

No. Not this time.

"Fuck you, Mason. 'One and done. It meant nothing.' That's what you said about Oscar, no? And when did you say this? Less than a week after all the bullshit you said to me in the car, after you almost—" Lucky shook his head in disgust. "Then I go to the club, and there's Oscar on his knees with your dick in his mouth. You are a lying piece of shit." He was so fucking stupid. Stupid for letting

Mason's pretty words get to him, for making him even consider....

Mason thrust a finger in Lucky's face. "Better a liar than a goddamn cock tease. You're the one giving mixed signals. One minute I think I know what you want, the next you're ready to stick your dick in whatever hot piece of ass shows up. You want to talk about what happened in the car? Let's talk about how the second we're outside you're flirting with the first potential fuck you see. What the hell am I supposed to think?"

"Not 'let me go find someone's mouth to fuck.' Yes, I flirted, but that was all it was. What you said came out of nowhere, so excuse me if I needed time to make sense of what the fuck was going on. I'm not a replacement for my cousin."

"No shit. Ace was never this fucking exhausting."

Lucky flinched. He recovered quickly from the blow and shoved Mason away from him. "Yeah, well, I don't make a habit of going after my cousin's sloppy seconds."

Screw Mason Cooper. Screw his beautiful face, sad eyes, and enticing mouth. Cock tease?

"Fuck you, Mason." Lucky jumped off the end of the pier, his arms wrapped around his knees as he hit the water.

The darkness surrounded him as he sank, eyes closed, legs crossed, and arms at his sides. He welcomed the silence, the calm, the nothingness. The world around him ceased to exist, leaving only him and the quiet. He'd been doing this since he was a kid. Back in Cuba, he'd go swimming either alone or with his friends in the Bay of Cojímar, not far from the little village where his parents lived. He'd jump off the rusty old dock, arms wrapped around his bony knees, and sink, letting the water silence his thoughts and hungry belly. It was a lifetime ago, and yet it felt like yesterday. He thought it funny how he had more nightmares about being back in Cuba than he did of his time in the military.

Lucky stayed beneath the water for as long as he could, which was longer than most people. Part of his Special Forces' training. His mother had cried when he'd declared he was joining the military along with Ace. Their mothers argued over it, Lucky's mother blaming Ace for Lucky wanting to join, but the outcome would have been the same had it been Lucky's idea. The two of them had done everything together. Lucky didn't want to be left behind in Miami while Ace was on his own who knew where.

When Lucky arrived from Cuba, he'd been afraid of his own shadow. Everything had been too big, too loud, too much, but he'd never had to worry. Ace protected him like a big brother, even though they were only a year apart. He'd taught Lucky how to defend himself, helped him with his English every day, and paved the way for Lucky coming out. Ace announcing he was gay during his sixteenth birthday party gave Lucky the courage to come out as bisexual a few months later.

Of course, when Lucky came out, his family believed he was confused. While they found it hard to understand Ace's attraction to other men, they didn't question his declaration because Ace was confident, strong, and always knew what he wanted, even at a young age. When he got something in his head, no one could deter him. With Lucky, his family came up with many excuses for his sexuality. Some of his family believed he was trying to be like Ace, while others thought he would pick one or the other. It had been frustrating and led to many arguments, because if he could choose, then why not choose only women? It had been infuriating.

One day during a Special Forces training, in the tenth

hour of a twelve-hour hike carrying heavy sandbags, it hit him. His body screamed in pain, his head pounded from dehydration, and he was ready to collapse from exhaustion, but his mind became clear. Why was he trying to please everyone? Maybe it was time he did things for *his* happiness.

Lucky broke the surface and smiled as he wiped the salty water from his face. He felt Ace's presence before looking up confirmed his cousin was there, sitting on the edge of the pier.

"Feel better?" Ace called down.

"Maybe." In truth, just having Ace around made him feel better. "Where's your man?"

"Colton's in the car, where there's air conditioning and he won't spontaneously combust from being exposed to the surface of the sun. His words, not mine."

Lucky laughed. "Your man is very dramatic."

"Says the guy who jumped off a pier in his underwear because he got into a fight with my ex-boyfriend."

Lucky wrinkled his nose. "Why do you have to always remind me he was your boyfriend? You have a new boyfriend. Who you love, by the way."

"Yes, I know. I remind you because you need to understand what you're getting yourself into. How many times did I come to you about the problems we were having?"

"I'm not getting myself into anything, especially not Mason. Can we not have this shouting conversation with me down here and you up there?"

"Good point. I'll bring your clothes and meet you down there."

"Thanks." Lucky swam beneath the dock toward the shore. By the time he got to shallow waters, Ace was waiting for him with a towel and his clothes. Making sure no one was watching, Lucky ditched his wet underwear and quickly pulled on his jeans. He waited until he was off the sand to pull on his socks and boots, then followed Ace to the black SUV. With a grin, he tapped on Colton's window, chuckling as the window was lowered, revealing a scowling Colton.

"Hello, Colton."

"Get in the car. It's disgusting out there. Look." He pointed to his fogged-up sunglasses.

"You act like this is your first Florida summer."

"Just because I live in Florida doesn't mean I enjoy the August sun's attempt to set me on fire. I'm rolling the window up now. Talk inside."

With a laugh, Lucky opened the back door, then climbed in. The air conditioning did feel good. Ace sat in the driver's side, and he turned in his seat to look at Lucky.

"You want to tell us what happened back there?"

Lucky shrugged. "What happened is that Mason Cooper is a lying piece of shit and an asshole."

"Lucky, Nash calling Mason about Oscar doesn't mean they were going to get together."

"Like I care." Lucky crossed his arms over his chest, his gaze out the window.

"Don't give me that bullshit. The second Bibi confirmed it was Oscar, you were out of that chair so damned fast you almost gave me whiplash. I know you, bro. There's you pissy, pissed, and then *pissed*. What happened between you two? What changed?"

"How do you know?" Lucky asked, as if his cousin had all the answers. Even now as a grown man, Lucky always turned to Ace for reassurance.

"How do I know what?"

"That he wasn't going to hook up with Oscar?"

"I don't know. How do *you* know he was?"

Lucky moved his narrowed gaze to Ace. He hated when Ace was right. Not that he would tell Ace that. "Why wouldn't he? They already hooked up at Frank's. Why not now?"

"Maybe because he cares about you," Colton offered gently.

"Bullshit."

Ace let out a heavy sigh. "Come on, Lucky. If he didn't give a shit, he'd still be hooking up with Oscar, and he certainly wouldn't have gone after you at the café when he saw you were upset. Tell me what happened?"

Lucky and Ace talked about everything. They were each other's confidants. Now that Ace was with Colton, Colton had become one of Lucky's closest friends as well, mostly because he balanced them out. Colton was the best thing that happened to Ace. He was the reason Ace took fewer risks, which Lucky appreciated. Ace had a terrible habit of thinking he was invincible. He still did, but at least he was more cautious now and thought things through before jumping into the fray. Most of the time.

Giving in, Lucky told them everything, from what happened in Mason's police cruiser the day Laz was shot at, up until earlier that morning when Lucky left Mason standing in his dust.

"Shit," Ace muttered.

"See? He's an asshole."

"Lucky, I love you. You're the brother I'd always wanted," Ace said, meeting his gaze and holding it. "I say this with all the brotherly love I possess."

Lucky peered at him. Waiting.

"Get your head out of your ass."

"This does not sound like brotherly love to me." Lucky

looked to Colton. "Does that sound like brotherly love to you?"

Colton shrugged. "I wouldn't know. I'm an only child. Maybe?" Amusement danced in Colton's gray eyes.

"You are not helping."

Colton laughed. "Lucky, I think what Ace is trying to say in his very Ace way of saying things, is that Mason clearly does care about you, and it's obvious you care about him too. I think that scared you both, and you're looking for excuses to lash out at each other in order to get back to that safe place, except there's no going back. You need to think about what you want from Mason and then figure out your next course of action. You know we're here if you need us."

Ace tilted his head at Colton. "What he said." He kissed Colton's temple. "You're so smart."

Colton shook his head in amusement. "Thank you, love. Lucky, why don't you come home with us?"

"I'm not a stray puppy," Lucky mumbled. Just because Colton was right didn't mean Lucky had to admit it.

Ace reached out to pinch Lucky's cheek. "Aw, but you're as cute as one."

"Fuck off, bro." Lucky swatted his cousin's hand away. "I will bite you."

Ace cackled. "Meet you at ours."

"Yeah, yeah," Lucky grumbled, getting out of the car. He waved goodbye before heading back to his bike. Some time at Colton's with Ace would be good for him. He could hit the beach and forget about Mason for a while, or at least try to.

Lucky's phone rang, and he checked the screen, his heart skipping a beat. Fuck, he hated this. His finger hovered over the screen, but instead of answering, he returned his phone to his pocket, letting the call go to voicemail. As much as he wanted to hear the man's voice—and when the hell had *that* happened—he couldn't talk to Mason right now. If he did, he'd end up making things worse. After grabbing his jacket and gloves from the saddlebag, he pulled them on before securing his helmet, then got back on the road.

As much as Lucky hated to admit it, Colton was right. He needed to figure out what to do about Mason because there was no going back. Even if nothing had actually happened between them, what *had* almost happened changed everything. With only one sentence, Mason had stirred something inside Lucky he hadn't even known was there. As if their relationship hadn't been explosive enough.

As Lucky got on A1A northbound for Ponte Vedra Beach, the wind whipping around him and the open road in front of him, he felt much better. Time and distance. That's what he and Mason needed. The rest would sort itself out. Yep, that's all they needed. Maybe the next time they met up, they'd have both forgotten why they were even pissed off. Who knew, maybe things between them had changed for the better.

TWO

"FUCKING HELL."

Two months. It's been two months. Get your shit together.

Mason rolled over with a groan. Hadn't he just gone to bed? How was it time to get up already? Sitting up was like moving through molasses, and his head pounded like someone had taken a jackhammer to it. He rubbed his hands over his face, but that did nothing to relieve the drowsiness. Another night of tossing and turning. Perfect. He ran a hand through his hair and stood, then started toward the bathroom but stubbed his toe against the bed.

"Fuck!" He dropped onto the mattress and checked he hadn't lost a toenail. With everything intact, he hobbled into the narrow hallway to his tiny bathroom. As he washed his face, he asked himself yet again why the hell he didn't get a bigger place. He asked himself the same question every time he bumped into something in his small one-bedroom apartment. His answer never changed. *You wanted to be near the beach, and a bigger place means using* his *money.* No way on God's green earth was he going to use that bastard's money.

Until he saved up enough to put a hefty down payment on a nice beachfront house, this would have to do. Just a few more years.

The apartment was silent, like always, the only sound coming from his razor as he shaved. He rinsed the foam from his face and dried off, then paused long enough to scowl at himself in the mirror. Jesus, when had he gotten old? Not that forty-one was ancient, but these days he felt older than his years. His fair hair had gray strands at the temples, and the corners of his eyes had gained additional lines in the last few years.

"You're not getting any younger, Mason."

The hell with this pity parade. He'd done fine for himself. He had friends he could count on, a nice retirement fund saved up, and after years of fighting the homophobic bullshit that came with being a gay cop, he'd finally earned a place of respect among his peers. As of two months ago, he'd been promoted to detective for Major Crimes, and although he still came across assholes, he'd managed to educate and enlighten a few minds throughout his law enforcement career, making his presence easier to digest for those perplexed by his masculinity, because after all, weren't gays supposed to be all "limp-wristed and feminine"?

When he'd heard those words, it had taken Mason a moment to look around and acknowledge that no, he hadn't somehow been thrown back to the year 1950. He'd put an end to that nonsense right then and there. For one, being feminine was not an insult, nor should it be treated as such. There was nothing wrong with being feminine. And two, there were more than two types of gay men, none of which were going to be the butt of anyone's jokes, not while he was around. It probably didn't hurt that he tended to outmuscle and outweigh everyone he'd ever worked with. No one wanted to fuck with a six-and-a-half-foot Texan. In his youth he'd accepted a lot of shit from people, but as he got older—and more ornery—he'd discovered the marvels of just not giving two fucks what people thought.

After finishing up in the bathroom, he got dressed in charcoal gray slacks, a deep blue button-down shirt with matching tie, and black boots. He'd have the sleeves of his shirt rolled up his arms by the time he reached the office, but first, coffee and breakfast. It was roughly a twenty-minute drive to work with an added two minutes to get to the little café on US-1. Being close to the St. Johns Sheriff's Office, the fire station, and a host of other facilities meant the café was always busy.

With his holster and Glock secured to his belt, his phone in his pocket, and his badge hanging from the chain around his neck, he grabbed the duffel bag containing his workout gear, an extra change of clothes, water bottle, and some protein bars before he realized he didn't have his keys. He was usually more organized than this. Checking his duffel bag, he finally found them in one of the outside pockets. He locked up and was halfway to the elevator when he realized he'd forgotten his wallet.

"Goddamn it. Get your head outta your fucking ass."

What the hell was wrong with him? There had to be something. It couldn't be him hung up on a guy. He didn't get hung up on anyone. No, that was a lie. He'd had a lot of sleepless nights when he'd been with Ace, and part of that had been down to the fact he'd known early on that things wouldn't work out between them, no matter how much he wanted them to.

Anston "Ace" Sharpe was an open book. He wore his heart on his sleeve and expected full disclosure from everyone close to him. The man co-owned a private security company, and before that he'd served in the military as Special Forces. His whole life revolved around trust, about being able to put his faith in the people around him. If having a man like Ace and losing him wasn't bad enough, Mason had to go and screw things up with Ace's cousin, who also happened to be ex-Special Forces.

What the fuck was he doing even considering getting involved with another one of these guys, and Lucky of all people? The guy left a trail of men and women wherever he went. Mason didn't give a shit that Lucky was bisexual, or that he'd had more sexual partners in a month than Mason had the whole of his adult life. What Mason did care about was Lucky's aversion to sticking around. Even if Lucky was a one-guy or gal type of guy, Mason's relationships *always* fell apart. Why was he torn up about all this?

"Fuck this. You're thinking way too goddamn much before coffee."

Breakfast was good, as always. He had his coffee and another to go. It was time to get to work. At least he could lose himself in his job and not have to think about those long lashes, hooded brown eyes, and pouting lips.

Yeah, good luck with that.

Mason greeted his coworkers as he headed to his desk. He'd just sat down when one of his fellow detectives, Erikson, took a seat on the edge of his desk, his expression grim.

"Looks like someone fucked up."

Mason's head shot up. "What?"

"That asshole from IA is here," Erikson muttered, nodding toward the commander's office. Mason turned in his chair, his frown deepening at the sight of Internal Affairs Officer Malley. He seemed like a nice enough guy, but the fact he was IA was enough to mark him as an asshole because his presence meant someone was about to lose their job or embark on an epic journey of fuckery.

Malley smoothed out his tie before stepping into the bullpen. Shit. Mason hoped the guy would keep walking and head out the door. Instead he stopped in front of Mason.

"Mason Cooper?"

Mason narrowed his gaze and slowly stood. "Yeah?"

Malley handed him an envelope, and Mason's stomach dropped. No. This couldn't be right. His blood turned to ice, and the thin envelope in his hand suddenly felt like it was made of lead. The room plunged into silence, all eyes on him.

"What the fuck is this?"

He'd been a cop for almost two decades, and yeah, he'd been investigated by IA for shit he hadn't done, thanks to some of the homophobic assholes he'd worked with over the years, and although those times had been stressful as hell, he'd *known* without a shadow of a doubt that he hadn't done anything wrong. The difference was, at the time, those complaints against him hadn't come as a surprise because of who he'd been dealing with. Now? He had no idea what the fuck was going on, because as far as he knew, no one had a problem with him. Not that they all wanted to be his buddy, but as long as he did his job right, they didn't concern themselves with what or who he did in his bedroom. He'd been a detective for Major Crimes two and a half months, and everything he did was by the book. He was meticulous. His fellow detectives liked to tease him about having a hard-on for paperwork. In truth, he liked things to be done right the first time.

"I would recommend contacting your union rep immediately."

Mason tore through the envelope, frantically trying to grasp what was happening. His brain sifted through every case he'd worked on, every conversation he'd had, anything that might shed light on what the fuck he'd done wrong. He read the letter over and over, his heart in his throat, the words in front of him starting to lose focus until only a few remained vivid and clear, burning a hole through the page.

Drug test.

Positive results.

Investigation.

Suspended.

"Oh fuck." Mason sank down into his seat. *Fuck, fuck, fuck.* Holy shit, he'd done it now. "I can't believe this."

"Cooper?"

Mason lifted his gaze to Erikson. "I fucked up." There was no time for further explanation, and he hated the questioning look in Erikson's eyes.

"Please come with me," Malley instructed.

Mason stood tall as he followed the guy through the bullpen. He was the new guy. They'd put their faith in him. Jaw clenched, he tried not to think about the questions going through their heads, questions that had gone through his own head whenever he saw someone led away by IA. Were they dirty? A rat? Was he losing his shit? Was it an alcohol problem? Domestic violence? Was someone fucking with the gay guy? This time, there was no outside force. He'd fucked himself over.

Inside the commander's office, he was asked to take a seat.

Commander Haynes had Mason's file open in front of him. The guy had a reputation for being ruthless when it came to the law and the conduct of his people. He was firm but fair, and from what Mason had heard, he hated bad PR. This didn't look good.

"I've heard nothing but good things about you, son. What happened? If you have an addiction, we can help—"

"I don't have an addiction, sir. I have never partaken in any illegal drug use." Mason shook his head, unable to believe his stupidity. "It was cough medicine. I had a bad cough a few weeks ago. You can ask any of the guys. They kept telling me to get it checked out before I dropped dead and became one of their cases. I went to the doctor, and he prescribed some cough medicine that cleared it right up. I forgot all about the damn thing, which is why I didn't list it. I remembered the Tylenol and the Claritin, but not the damn cough medicine with the codeine."

"If you'd like to appeal, you're entitled to speak with your union rep."

Mason's jaw clenched, and he nodded. Damn right he was going to appeal. He couldn't lose his job over this shit.

"Your gun and your badge, Detective."

Mason swallowed the bile rising in his throat. He removed the badge hanging from the chain around his neck. The sense of loss hit him immediately. He placed it on the desk, followed by the Glock tucked into his holster. *Breathe.*

"We'll be in touch."

Mason gave a curt nod before standing and leaving the room. He had to go back out into the bullpen to get to the locker room, not that he planned on avoiding his coworkers. He'd fucked up and he'd own up to it.

As soon as he got to his desk, Erikson was there waiting. He didn't mind. Erikson was a good guy. Even if he did gossip like a schoolgirl.

"What the hell is going on?"

"I forgot the fucking cough medicine."

"Shit." Erikson shook his head, his lips pressed together in a thin line as he squeezed Mason's shoulder in sympathy.

"I need to go. I have to call my rep."

Erikson nodded. "Just take it easy, man. Don't let this drag you down."

"Thanks," Mason replied, doing his best to smile. "Don't go solving too many cases without me."

"Are you kidding?" Erikson waggled his eyebrows. "This is my chance to shine, buttercup."

Mason chuckled. "Asshole."

"No, seriously. Enjoy the time off while you can."

"Sure." Like that was going to happen. This could take weeks to sort out. What the hell was he supposed to do? He was officially suspended with pay, but if he was found guilty of lying, they'd take the pay from his vacation days and that was it. The end of his career.

First things first. He needed to make a few calls, and he'd rather not do it from here. Saying his goodbyes, he picked up his bag from the locker room and headed out to the parking lot. He'd been about to unlock his truck when something moved in his peripheral vision. Turning, Mason expected to find Erikson there. Instead, he saw nothing but parked cars. The breeze picked up, ruffling his hair and rustling the leaves of the palm trees around him, making the shadows dance. Man, he needed to get a grip. The last thing he needed was to be jumping at shadows. A flier on his windshield caught his eye, and he snatched it off. He'd been about to crumple it when he saw what it was. He let out a humorless laugh.

"Fucking Kings." Every damn day a flier for Four Kings Security ended up under his windshield wiper. Since when did the Kings use fliers? If he hadn't seen them on some of the other cars, he'd have thought the guys were fucking with him.

Once inside his truck, with the AC blasting, he called his union rep. He apprised her of the situation and got contact details for one of the union lawyers who had a solid reputation. After thanking her for her help, he called the number she'd given him. Thankfully, Terrance Jones was available. He was a no-bullshit kind of guy who didn't sugarcoat things or make promises he couldn't keep, which Mason appreciated.

"Do you have proof?" Terrance asked him once Mason had given his story.

"Yeah, I do. I've got the prescription from my doctor."

"Good. I'll arrange an interview with IA, and you'll be investigated. In this situation, you do not have the right to remain silent. I'll provide a Garrity statement."

"Am I going to lose my job?"

"It was an honest mistake, Detective. You didn't lie. If they're looking to terminate you for some reason, they'll need to prove you're guilty of what they're accusing you of. Once the investigation fails to discover enough evidence to prove the allegations made, you'll receive a letter of Not Sustained and can go back to work. You'll most likely be required to do a drug awareness class or something similar. As you know, this is going to take time. It can be anywhere from a couple of weeks to a month."

"Great."

"I would recommend taking it easy."

Why did everyone keep telling him that? He was being investigated. His career was on the line. He'd fucked up. Again. "Thank you, Terrance."

"Don't thank me yet. We have a lot of departmental bullshit to wade through. I'll be in touch."

"I appreciate it." He hung up and took a moment to just breathe. What was he supposed to do now? He needed to work. Sitting at home pretending everything was going to be okay was not an option. Being alone with his thoughts for that long was out of the question.

He made to start his truck but spotted the balled-up flier on the passenger seat. After unlocking his phone, he opened his contact list, and his thumb hovered over the call button. Closing his eyes, he took a deep breath, then tapped the screen. A deep, gruff voice answered on the second ring.

"Hey, it's Mason."

Pause. "Mason," King greeted. "What can I do for you?"

"You, um, you got a few minutes to talk?"

"I answered my phone."

Smartasses, these Kings. Every last one of the them. "I meant, can I come in and talk to you. Face-to-face."

Another pause. "I'm at the office."

"I should be there in about fifteen minutes."

"I'll be in my office. Security will be expecting you." With that, King hung up.

"I can't believe I'm doing this," Mason grumbled as he drove out of the parking lot. Maybe he was losing his mind. After all, he was on his way to talk to Ward Kingston. He couldn't think about it because if he did he'd head straight home instead of King Street. Maybe he should call Ace or Colton? The thought made him smile. Mostly because he pictured Ace's scowl every time he was reminded Mason and Colton were friends.

Mason had lost his chance with Ace; he'd screwed it up. Why would he be a dick about it? Ace was a great guy, which was why they were still friends. Why would Mason begrudge Ace happiness with someone else? Ace finally found someone who gave him everything he needed. Who was able to give all of himself, unlike Mason.

Before Mason knew it, he was parking in a visitor's spot in the Four Kings Security parking garage underneath the office. He'd been here enough times to meet Ace when they'd been seeing each other. After taking the elevator up to the reception area, security greeted him cheerfully and handed him a visitor's lanyard that he hung around his neck. He was shown to the executive-floor elevator, where security swiped a keycard for him. He tapped his fingers against his thighs, his pulse soaring, not because he was on his way to see King, but because he might run into Lucky, and that was the last thing he needed right now.

The elevator pinged, and he stepped out after taking a deep breath. He made a left and headed down the hall, greeting folks as he went. Outside King's office, Jay, King's executive assistant, smiled warmly at him. The guy was cute—one of those guys who looked younger than he was—with blond hair in a trendy cut, a pinstripe slim-fitting button-down shirt with flamingos on it tucked into slim navy slacks. He had big blue eyes and plump pink lips, which were pulled in a wide smile.

"Hello again, Mr. Cooper. King's just on a phone call. He'll be with you in a moment."

"Thanks, Jay. Cute shirt."

Jay did a little shimmy and batted his lashes. "Aren't you sweet."

"You've been working for King a long time, haven't you?"

Jay nodded and pursed his lips in thought. "Going on eight years now."

"Wow. And King hasn't driven you nuts?"

"King?" Jay blinked at him before laughing. He leaned

forward, his voice low. "Don't let that growl fool you. He's a big, soft, squishy teddy bear." He sat back and preened a little. "Besides, the man would be lost without me. Technology is not his friend. I swear he's jinxed when it comes to computers."

Mason laughed. The computer part he saw, but the "soft, squishy teddy bear" part? Nope. There was nothing squishy or cuddly about Ward Kingston. Speak of the devil....

Jay's phone beeped, and he picked up with a knowing smile. "Yes, sir? I'll send him right in." Jay hung up and motioned to the door on his right. "Good luck."

"Thanks." Mason stepped into King's office, waving a hand in greeting. "Thanks for seeing me."

King nodded. "Close the door and have a seat."

Mason sat in the plush black chair in front of King's sleek black desk as King resumed his seat, pressing a button on his phone.

"Jay, hold my calls, please."

"Yes, sir."

King sat back and waited.

"Fuck. This was a bad idea."

"Why don't you tell me what the idea is, and then I can tell you if it's a bad one or not."

Cocky bastard. Well, it was now or never, and never wasn't an option. "I got suspended."

King narrowed his eyes, but he didn't say a word.

"I was called in for a random drug test at work, and I failed. Not because I'm on drugs, but I failed to list the cough medicine I'd taken a few days earlier. It was a prescription."

"Codeine?"

Mason nodded. He sat back with a sigh. "I feel fucking stupid."

King was quiet again, but that was hardly a revelation. When he spoke up, he could have knocked Mason over with a feather. "It was a mistake. Don't beat yourself up over it."

Wait. Was he hearing right? His expression must have given away his shock because King rolled his eyes.

"I don't dislike you, Mason. You're a good man."

"Am I dreaming right now? Is this a dream?"

"Should I be concerned that you dream about me?"

"This conversation is turning all kinds of awkward. Thankfully, I don't dream about you at all." The only King who occupied his dreams and waking life was in the form of a temperamental Cuban with a mouth that should be illegal. "I meant I must be dreaming because in what reality do you tell me I'm a good man instead of busting my balls?"

King arched a thick blond brow at him. "I tend not to look fondly on those who break the hearts of people I care about."

"It was never my intention to hurt Ace."

"Ace is familiar with heartache. He can deal with it. Besides, he has Colton. He's in love and happy. That's not who I was talking about."

Lucky.

"We got into a fight. I didn't break his heart."

"Lucky isn't like Ace. For all his blustering, he's... easily hurt. You can't just exchange one cousin for another."

"Fuck you, King," Mason spat, sitting forward. "That's not what this is."

"Then what is this?"

Mason ran his hands through his hair. "Fuck. I knew this was a bad idea."

"You haven't told me your idea yet."

"I didn't come here to talk about him."

"Then why are you here?"

"I need to work."

King's brows shot up near his hairline.

"Well, I'll be damned." Mason was stupefied. In all his years of knowing the Kings, he had never witnessed such a reaction from *the* King. The man was like one of those damned Easter Island statues, his expression stoic and unmoving. "I can't just sit around waiting, wondering if it's the end of my career. I'll lose my mind. There's gotta be something you can give me to do." Four Kings Security employed plenty of ex-soldiers and ex-cops. Mason had an entire law enforcement career he could put to use for the Kings.

"You want to work with the Kings?"

"Yes. Temporarily."

"The people we hire at Four Kings Security have undergone a lengthy vetting process, conducted personally by either me, Ace, Lucky, or Red. It's then followed by an even lengthier review process, followed by an intense training schedule. Few freelancers are hired, and we do not do busy work. We're talking about people's lives and businesses here. Our reputation is on the line."

"I understand that."

"Do you?"

"Yes, I fucking do," Mason growled. Who the hell did King think he was dealing with? "I wasn't suggesting you give me busy work. When I said I need to work, I meant work. Whatever you give me, I'll give it my all, and you know it. Just like you know I'm the least likely to go off script."

King sat forward. "What are you insinuating?"

"I'm not insinuating anything. I'm telling you. You

Kings don't exactly play by the book. You can't. Not when you've got a couple of mavericks like Ace and Lucky."

"They might not play by the book, but they know what's at stake. Hope for the best, prepare for the worst. That's how we do things." King sat back in his chair again, a large man who'd once led a unit of Special Forces Green Berets. He was an intimidating, no-nonsense kind of guy, but he was a good man who looked after his family. Mason couldn't blame him for being cautious. "This job can be as dangerous as anything you've faced in your career."

"I'm aware."

"And you think you can work alongside your ex-boyfriend and your current... whatever he is to you?"

"Friend," Mason replied through his teeth. Were they friends? They had been before he'd gone and made a mess of things.

"Sure. Let's go with that."

God, the man could be such a dick. "Yes. As a professional, I can behave in a professional manner. Can the same be said of certain individuals?"

"Don't worry about Lucky."

I worry every damn day. "I have a condition."

King's bark of laughter startled Mason. "You have some balls, I'll give you that. Okay. What are *your* conditions for working the job *you* asked *me* for?"

"If I have to work with Lucky, he rides in a damn car with me. He can ride that death machine on his own time."

"Well, shit, Cowboy. Why don't you just ask for the moon? You know how attached he is to that thing?"

"I want my only worry to be the job, not him on that wreck waiting to happen."

"Lucky's been riding motorcycles since he was a kid. He's also proficient in defensive driving."

"He's not the one whose driving skills I question."

King shrugged. "Fair enough." He drummed his fingers on his desk, his gaze on Mason. Who the hell knew what was going through the man's head. Of all the Kings, King was the hardest to get a read on. Mason had never seen the man in action. He'd seen him defuse situations, but he'd never seen King anything but calm, cool, and collected. "Okay." King stood and leaned over his desk, his hand held out to Mason. "Welcome to the family."

The words felt off. Like the meaning behind them was different. Mason couldn't put his finger on what exactly made him feel that way, so he brushed it aside. Their gazes met, King's blue eyes filled with warning.

"Don't underestimate him, Mason. Lucky might be an emotional wreck at times, but at heart, he's still a Green Beret."

"Once a soldier, always a soldier, huh?"

King released his hand and nodded before resuming his seat behind the desk. He pressed a button on his phone. "Can you come to my office?"

Why had King warned him about Lucky?

"I'm on my way," the voice on the other end of the phone responded, the smooth, thickly accented voice sending a shiver through Mason.

THREE

LUCKY WALKED into King's office and froze. His heart pounded in his ears, and the butterflies in his stomach made him queasy. He hated it, hated that he had no control over his body's reactions to this man. It wasn't just the size of him, but his presence. Lucky didn't have to see him to *feel* him. Then there were his fucking manners. Despite what King said, Lucky and Ace had been raised with manners, but Mason was on a whole other level. He was chivalrous, taking off his hat when greeting someone, opening doors for people, saying "yes, ma'am" or "no, sir." It was ingrained into him, and he did it because it was the right thing to do. That pretty much summed up Mason Cooper.

Mason stood when Lucky approached. He held his baseball cap in one hand and tapped the fingers of his other against his thigh. Lucky refused to let his gaze linger there. Under normal circumstances, Mason would have given Lucky his hand to shake, but awkward did not do their situation justice.

"What the hell is he doing here?" Lucky asked King.

From the corner of his eye, he saw Mason's lips pull into a smirk.

"Well, good afternoon to you too, Eduardo. How are you doing this glorious day?"

Lucky crossed his arms over his chest, his eyes not moving from King, who sat back in his chair, his expression unreadable as usual. "I'm not talking to you, asshole."

"You're talking to me right now."

"You're not cute."

"I'd have to disagree with you on that, darlin'. I'm downright adorable."

Lucky let out a snort. "Oh, I'm most certainly not your darling."

"But you agree I'm adorable."

"I didn't say that." He was *not* going to smile. Arrogant. That's what Mason was. Not cute. Arrogant. *Atrevido.* Handsome with... large hands. He had very large hands, but then he was a large man in many ways. Hm, was the rest of him—*¡Ya basta, Eduardo!*

"You didn't *not* say that."

Lucky flipped him off. "What the fuck is he doing here?"

"Mason, could you excuse us for a moment?" King motioned to the door. "There's an employee lounge down the hall on the left. Help yourself to some coffee."

"Thanks." Mason turned to face Lucky, but Lucky didn't move. If he moved, he might smell more of Mason's cologne or be tempted to look into those bright blue eyes. "Good to see you."

"Still not talking to you," Lucky called out over his shoulder as Mason headed for the door.

"Still are."

The door closed behind Mason, and Lucky let out a

frustrated growl. "¡Señor, dame paciencia con este hombre porque si me das fuerza, lo mato!"

King arched a brow at him. "Did you really just pray to not kill a man?"

"No, I prayed to God for patience with *that* man because if God gives me strength, I will kill him, and by him, I mean Mason."

"Yeah, I gathered that." King motioned to the chair in front of him, and reluctantly Lucky sat. Why was Mason here talking to King, of all people? The two of them never talked unless it was to say something they knew would annoy the other. As much as Lucky enjoyed King ruffling Mason's feathers, Mason was in Lucky's place of business. It was disconcerting.

"Why is he here? What's going on?"

"Mason's going to be working with us for a while. I need you to—"

Lucky leaned forward. "*¿Que?*"

"Did you not hear me, or do I need to give you some time to process this information?"

"Screw you, King. I'm *not* working with him." It was horrifying enough running into Mason at Four Kings Security, but to work together? Absolutely not. No way.

"Oh, but you are, and you're going to be an adult about it."

"Fuck you. I'm an adult." And as an adult, he could pout if he fucking wanted to.

"Clearly."

"I'm not working with him. I don't care what you say."

"You telling me you don't care that you're the reason he's in this mess to begin with?"

Lucky sat up. "What?"

"Mason gave me permission to share some of the details

of his current situation with the rest of the Kings, Joker, and Jack. No one else needs to know why he's here, only that he's here because he's doing some freelance work for us."

Lucky waited. With King, there was often a good amount of waiting. It drove Lucky crazy. He loved King, but sometimes....

"Mason was suspended. He's currently on paid leave while Internal Affairs investigates him."

That had Lucky jumping to his feet. "IA? Why are they investigating Mason? If they think he's dirty, then that's bullshit." The thought boiled his blood. "No one is more squeaky-clean than Mason. The guy won't even jaywalk." Mason reminded him of the cowboys in his father's favorite Westerns from back in the day. Flawed men who fought for what was right even if it meant their demise. In Mason's case, a beautiful, flawed man who carried a heavy burden on his shoulders and in his heart. Not that Lucky cared. Mason Cooper's heart wasn't his problem.

"He failed a random drug test, but his failing the test isn't why he's being investigated. It's because he forgot to list the prescription cough medicine he'd taken prior to the test. As far as they're concerned, he lied. He may not have meant to, but he did, and now they need to investigate."

"Fuck." That was very unlike Mason. To forget something *so* vital, something that could cost him his job? The man was meticulous in everything he did. Like Lucky, he was a big believer in doing things right the first time.

"Yes."

"What does this have to do with me?"

"Have you looked at Mason lately? Really looked at him?"

Lucky shifted uncomfortably. These days he was trying

his best *not* to look at Mason. Looking at him led to thinking of him, and that led to all kinds of problems for Lucky.

King let out a heavy sigh. "Whatever happened between you two is obviously eating away at him. You both need to work this shit out, but do it off the clock. You still have a company to run, just like the rest of us. However, this investigation is only going to get tougher on Mason. He needs to know he has friends who've got his six." King stood and walked around the side of his desk, then took a seat on the edge of it in front of Lucky. "He came to *me* for help. What does that tell you?"

Shit. It was bad. "Yes, okay. I'll try very hard not to punch him in the face."

"I'm sure Mason would appreciate that very much."

"But I'm still pissed at him."

The corner of King's lips twitched as if he wanted to smile. "Of course you are. I'm sure you have every reason to be. Why don't you get him set up? Jay should have the contract ready. Have Mason read it over and sign. He can use Manolo's desk since it's still empty."

"No new applicants?"

King stood and walked around his desk to resume his seat. "Oh, plenty of those, but none of them a good fit."

One of their team leaders had moved out West to be closer to his family, and despite the many, *many* applicants, none had made it through their second interview. The hiring process at Four Kings Security was intense, starting with all four Kings needing to approve an application before the person was even contacted. Multiple steps were involved, but they weren't prepared to rush things and hire anyone, even if it meant having a vacant spot for several months until the right person could be found. It wasn't just about hiring the most qualified—though that was part of it too—but whoever they hired needed to have the right attitude. For some reason this time around, it was taking forever, and they couldn't seem to agree on one applicant. If the three of them happened to agree, King ended up vetoing it.

"I should have a job for you two soon as you've got him set up."

"Sure." Lucky left the office and headed for the lounge, running into one of his favorite security officers who also happened to be a good friend to him and Ace, Graciela Cortéz.

"¡Oye, Graciela!" Lucky threw his hands up. "¿Hasta cuando, mijita?"

Graciela rolled her eyes as she walked over to him. "Stop being such a baby."

"No, you promised me your abuelita's flan de coco, and when she makes it, you bring it in, and what happens? You give it to Cavallero? You simply give away my flan?" He clutched his chest over his heart. "How could you betray me like this?"

"I didn't betray you. Come on, Lucky. The guy's divorce was just finalized. You should have seen him in the break room looking like a puppy who'd been tossed out in the cold."

"Puppy? The man is almost as big as Red!"

Santos Cavallero was an ex-Navy SEAL who Lucky considered a good friend. At least until the bastard went and ate his flan.

"You know I have a soft spot for big burly dudes with soft squishy hearts. He needed the flan more than you did."

"What he needs is to find himself a new woman."

"Or man," Graciela offered.

Wasn't Cavallero straight? He arched an eyebrow at her, and she gave him a pointed look.

"Remember William?"

"Damn, how can I forget? Mm, the things that man did to me...." Most certainly not things a straight man would do to another man. So many lovely filthy things. Graciela was right. Lucky could easily think of two or three men he'd met over the years who'd claimed to be straight and by the end of the night were begging him to fuck them. Lucky had happily obliged. One of those men had been the supposed straight boyfriend of a woman Lucky picked up at a bar a couple of years ago.

Lucky never got involved with anyone who had a partner or was married, but the beautiful redhead had been upfront about wanting to try something new and asked him if he'd mind her boyfriend joining them in the room to observe. Lucky had no problem having the stunningly beautiful black man watching them. By the time Lucky was naked and had the woman moaning and gasping as she writhed beneath him, the boyfriend decided he wanted a taste as well.

A taste of Lucky.

It had been one hell of a night.

Graciela let out a very unladylike snort. "Yeah, straight my ass."

Lucky shrugged. "You're right. Especially when I get my hands on them." He waggled his eyebrows, and she shook her head at him.

"You're insatiable."

"What can I say? I have a healthy appetite." He headed to the employee lounge, making sure to call out over his shoulder. "Don't forget my flan." She cursed him out in English and Spanish, making him laugh.

Lucky found Mason in the employee lounge, sitting at a table, a cup of coffee in his hands as he gazed out the window. The lounge was bright and homey, resembling someone's kitchen and dining room rather than a work environment. When it came time to design the interior of Four Kings Security headquarters, they'd all agreed they wanted their company to feel like home. After all, if they weren't out on a job, they'd be at the office. The Kings were family. Those who were trusted to become a part of Four Kings Security were treated like family, and it reflected in the environment around them.

The white door to the lounge led into a small hallway that opened up into a large space with vinyl flooring resembling wood. To Lucky's right were two round tables in a lighter wood color with chocolate-colored bases matching the four brown chairs around each one. Next to it sat a matching coffee table, and across from it two comfortable lounge chairs with a taller coffee table in between. Positioned beneath the large double window was a plush cream-colored couch with throw pillows, and against the far wall across from it, a large mirror hung on the wall above a sturdy wooden bench. The white door beside the bench led to a bathroom.

The table Mason sat at was long and white, with four yellow chairs on each side, and behind that was a full kitchen, with white cabinets, stainless steel stove, and full-size two-door refrigerator. Potted plants added color, as did the sunny yellow canvas paintings on the white walls. The room was immaculate. Cleanliness was not optional at Four Kings Security. Even Joker, the messiest of them, led by example, making certain to always clean up after himself when at the office.

"It's kinda strange being here in your territory and all."

How did Mason know Lucky was there? He hadn't made a sound or walked in far enough for Mason to see him. Not to mention that getting into places undetected was something he'd been trained to do. Lucky entered the kitchen and took a seat opposite Mason.

"How did you know I was there?"

Mason shrugged. "A feeling."

"What happened at work?" Lucky wasn't about to comment on Mason's words.

"Didn't King tell you?"

"I want to hear it from you."

Mason sighed, long and weary. It squeezed Lucky's heart. King was right. Mason looked terrible. His bright blue eyes—which were still focused on the window and not on Lucky—seemed tired, and Lucky missed their usual sparkle.

"I fucked up. I got picked for a random drug test at work and forgot all about a prescription cough medicine I'd taken a few days before. I didn't list it. When my test came back positive, I got suspended."

"Why?"

"Why what?" Mason moved his eyes to Lucky. "Why did I get suspended?"

"No. Why did you forget to write down the medicine?"

"Oh, I, um...." Mason cleared his throat and averted his gaze again. "I've been having trouble sleeping, but you know how it is. That's the job, right?"

"So, what you're saying is you weren't sleeping because of your job?"

Mason worried his bottom lip between his teeth.

"Mírame."

Mason did as Lucky instructed, lifting his gaze. Fuck, why did Mason have to be so damned handsome? It wasn't like Lucky hadn't had plenty of good-looking men before, but Mason Cooper was different. Every rugged inch of him was mouthwatering, from his chiseled jaw and sinful body full of rippling muscles, to his huge biceps, thick neck, and long legs. His hair was long enough to tuck behind his ears, but did he? No. He let it fall over his brow, taunting Lucky. It cascaded forward when he looked down, the soft strands calling to Lucky. His fingers itched to touch.

"Lucky?"

"¿Que? Oh, I want the truth from you."

"Okay."

"Always." Lucky tapped the table for emphasis. "From this moment on, always the truth."

Mason hesitated. He opened his mouth to reply, then closed it, nodding instead.

"The reason you weren't sleeping, was it the job?"

"No."

"What was the reason?"

"You. But my fuckup is on me. I shouldn't have let it interfere with my job. What I did was stupid, and now I have to deal with the consequences. I'm not here to make your life difficult, I swear."

"How long will the investigation take?"

"A few weeks, a month, who the hell knows? Your guess is as good as mine."

The room plunged into silence again. Having Mason here threw Lucky off-balance, but King was right. *Carajo.* He hated when King was right. Normally, Lucky wouldn't have any remorse for Mason. Everyone was responsible for their own actions, but Mason wasn't just anyone, and as much as Lucky hated to admit it, he cared. Before he could speak, Mason stood.

"Listen, I understand if you don't want to work with me.

I was a real asshole and said some shit things. I lie awake thinking of all the words I should have said instead, what I might have done differently."

Lucky wanted to ask what words Mason would have used instead, or what he would have done differently, but it was best he didn't. If he kept his distance from Mason, they might make it through this unscathed.

"This was a bad idea. I'm sorry I troubled you." Mason turned toward the sink, his back to Lucky as he washed his cup.

"It's okay," Lucky said, standing. He walked around the table. "We're two professional adults. Besides, if we don't do this, then one of us will have to tell King, and that won't be me."

Mason finished washing his cup and placed it on the dish rack before wiping his hands on the small towel. He turned, his lips curled up in a smirk as he leaned back against the sink, his arms folded over his chest making his biceps stretch the material of his button-down shirt within an inch of its life.

Never had Lucky wanted to lick someone so badly. Lick, nibble, do all kinds of terribly naughty things. That sparkle of mischief was back in Mason's eyes, and it took everything Lucky had not to march up to him, take hold of his face, and kiss him until they were both weak in the knees and gasping for air. What would Mason do then? Would he retaliate? Spin Lucky around, bend him over the table, and shove his pants down to his knees? Wonderful. Now all he could picture was Mason fucking him.

"Well, I sure as hell won't be the one to do it. I've asked him for enough, and I ain't the begging kind."

Lucky grinned wickedly. "You'd be surprised what a man is capable of when faced with the right motivation."

Mason pushed away from the sink, his powerful, sleek body moving with unexpected grace as he stalked forward, like a lion hunting its prey. He stopped so close to Lucky their bodies almost touched, sending Lucky's temperature soaring. Mason's lips pulled into the kind of smile that promised wicked things, and he tipped his head to one side in observation. His bright blue eyes darkened, and he dropped his gaze to Lucky's mouth as he brushed those calloused fingers down Lucky's jaw. Refusing to show Mason how his touch affected him, Lucky remained unmoving, even when Mason slid his fingers beneath Lucky's chin and tipped his head back so their eyes met. "Cuidado, Cariño. You keep playin' with fire and you're gonna get burned."

Oh, this motherfucker did not just speak Spanish to him *and* call him sweetheart. Lucky would never *ever* admit it, but he loved hearing Mason speak Spanish. Loved that every time they spoke to each other, Mason had learned to say something new. It would be easy for Lucky to fool himself into believing Mason was learning for him—since Lucky was the one Mason always tried his new words out on instead of Ace—but it was more likely down to the fact Lucky spent more time speaking Spanish than Ace. Also, Mason had lived in Florida for years now. As a member of law enforcement, it made sense he'd want to pick up as much of the language as possible.

Mason's fingers trailing down the side of Lucky's neck snapped his attention back to whatever madness was happening right now. If he didn't do something, the rising inferno inside him was going to erupt, and he couldn't have that.

"But then you like playing with fire, don't you, Querido?" Mason murmured, his voice a low seductive rumble.

Lucky parted his lips, his eyes on Mason's tempting mouth. He held back a smile when Mason's breath hitched. "I don't play with fire," Lucky whispered, leaning in. "I *am* fire." He flicked his tongue out, licking a trail over Mason's lips from bottom to top, then walked away, smiling at the sound of Mason's growl.

"Where the fuck do you think you're goin'? Get your ass back over here."

"Sorry, Mr. Cooper. We're on the clock now."

"Little shit," Mason grumbled with a huff. He caught up to Lucky, his pout endearing. "You're not sorry at all."

Lucky chuckled. He was most certainly not sorry. Maybe working alongside Mason wouldn't be so bad. At the very least it would be entertaining.

They headed to Jay's desk, and Lucky thanked him for the contract before heading to the elevator. The top floor of the building housed the executive offices belonging to the Kings, Jack and Joker—who headed their own departments —along with the executive assistants, the human resources department, conference rooms, and an impressive reception and waiting area.

Their first stop was to the security office on the ground floor near the entrance of the building so he could add Mason to their security system and have a badge and key card made for him. Everyone who worked for Four Kings was in their system, and a key card was required to access nearly every room in the building. Each key card varied in the level of security assigned. Only the Kings, Jack, and Joker were cleared to add or make changes to personnel on the system, one that had been designed by Jack himself. The kind of client information in their possession was worth billions, and they took the responsibility of looking after that information incredibly serious.

Once Mason had his ID clipped to a lanyard that hung around his neck, they headed back upstairs, where Lucky showed Mason to the desk he'd be using.

"You can use this desk in the meantime. Here is the contract. Take your time reading it."

Mason nodded and took a seat. He started reading it when he noticed Lucky was still there. "This has several pages."

"I know. I helped create it."

"Do you want to come back? I can grab you when I'm finished."

Lucky shrugged as he leaned against the desk, his arms folded over his chest. "You're going to have questions."

Mason frowned. "Uh, okay." He went back to reading, and Lucky waited patiently. Employees always had questions regarding the contracts. Not because they were opposed to anything, but because they had trouble believing what they were reading. As expected, two minutes into reading the contract, Mason frowned. He looked up at Lucky, his brows furrowed. "It says this includes gym membership. Is that deducted from the salary?"

"No. Certain positions are physically demanding, which means staying in shape. We don't expect our employees to have to pay for something that is a job requirement. Gym membership is included along with all your equipment, weapons, and uniforms."

"Meals are included?"

"While on the job, yes. Keep your receipts and submit them to your boss."

"Who's my boss? King?"

Lucky shook his head, his smile wicked. He laughed at Mason's wide eyes.

"You?"

"Sí, señor."

Mason opened his mouth to reply, then seemed to think better of it. He went back to reading the contract. "Wait, canine insurance?"

Lucky chuckled. "Yes, that was Joker. We have several bomb sniffing dogs on staff. Joker said they need benefits too. There's a canine perks package if your job includes your furry friend."

Mason flipped to the next page, his eyes lifting to Lucky's. He craned his neck, then lifted up as if searching for something, his eyes narrowed.

"What are you doing?"

"I'm looking for the halo."

"What?"

"You fellas created your own charity?" Mason dropped back down into his chair. "If I didn't know you all as well as I do, and the fact you're all a few pickles short of a barrel, I'd have thought you were a bunch of saints."

Lucky squinted at him. "Pickles? I don't like pickles."

"Forget the pickles. Tell me about this charity."

"There are many excellent charities for military veterans and their families, but we would rather have the money go straight to the soldiers and families who need it, without any overhead, executives to pay, or fund-raising expenses. We created our own very small nonprofit charity, which generates very large donations from clients and employees—the employee donations we match at the end of the year—and every penny goes to support military veterans, retirees, and military families. Our accountability and transparency are one hundred percent."

Mason looked thoughtful. He nodded before returning to the contract, and Lucky smiled, waiting for the next question he knew Mason would ask as it was the same one all new employees asked.

"It says here there's no vacation or paid time off programs."

"No. We expect the best results from our employees, and that is how performance is measured, not by how many hours you work. Employees are free to take time off as needed. No guilt. You need a day to go to the doctor or get your car fixed, just speak to your boss. You need to take a week to relax at the beach, just ask for it."

"Just like that?"

"Just like that."

"Don't people abuse the system?"

Lucky arched an eyebrow at him.

"Right. Like someone would be stupid enough to try and take advantage of King."

"We have the best employee perks and benefits in the state, but our employees work very hard, and the job is not without risk."

"Gotcha. Work hard, play hard." Mason signed the contract, then handed it to Lucky. "Well, I'm all yours."

Those four little words hung in the air between them, and Lucky forced himself to look away from Mason's penetrating gaze. He moved from the desk and cleared his throat. "Follow me."

They stopped by Jay's desk, and Lucky handed him the signed contract to file, and then they headed into King's office. Lucky smiled at Jack. "Hey, look who it is."

"It's not my fault."

Lucky peered at his friend. "What's not your fault?"

"I've got a job for you two," King said from behind his desk. "Jack has to take off with his team to Clearwater for a complete overhaul of a client's security system."

Lucky's brows shot up near his hairline. "Something's wrong with one of your systems? Are you broken?"

"No, ass. The client thought he'd save money by having someone else install a cheaper system than the one I installed in his corporate headquarters at one of his other businesses, and holy fuck, what a disaster. The alarm goes off at all hours." Jack ran a hand through his black hair, his gray eyes narrowed. "The guy who installed it is an asshole, and he clearly has no idea what the fuck he did or how to fix it, and instead of bringing someone in to help, he's blaming the security guards, saying it's their ineptitude that keeps fucking things up. The client finally called me." Jack's smile was huge. "The ass-kissing wasn't necessary, but I didn't want to interrupt him while he was telling me how amazing I am. So, I need you to take my CTSCM job downtown."

"Fuck, bro," Lucky said with a groan. "Can't Red or Ace do it? You know how much I hate your corporate surveillance cases. Why would you send me to do this?"

"Because it's important, and there's no one else. I know you hate all the cyber stuff, Lucky, but we've been planning this for months, and this is the first real shot we have to bring this fucker down. I need a King on this job, so it's you. I'll be in your ear the whole time in case you need me."

"Fine. It's not like I have a choice." Lucky enjoyed technology as much as the next guy, but he wasn't big on figuring out how it all worked. That's what he had Jack for. Though Lucky wasn't as bad as King. No one was as bad as King. His friend had a serious aversion to technology and hated social media, which was probably a good thing. Too many stupid people online, and that didn't mix well with King and his inability not to tell people what he thought of them. It was in everyone's best interest he not have access to them.

Jack reached into his pocket and pulled out a set of keys. He held them up to Lucky, but when Lucky reached for them, he snatched them away. "You treat her like a lady and not one of your dates, you hear me? No making a mess of her only to leave her wrecked for the next guy to worry about."

Lucky put a hand to his chest. "Sir, I am a gentleman."

"You're a cad."

"A cat? Is that like a Tom cat?"

"A *cad*."

Lucky whipped out his phone and googled it. He frowned at Jack. "Fuck you. I'm not dishonorable."

"You're a player." Jack tossed him the keys, and Lucky swiped them out of the air before shoving them into his pocket.

"I'm a lover," Lucky argued, glaring at Mason when he scoffed.

It quickly turned into a cough, and Mason shook his head. "Sorry, um, throat's still a little scratchy from that cough I had."

"Mm-hmm. Let's go, Cowboy." Lucky left the office with Mason in tow. He gave Mason the side-eye as they got into the elevator. Is that how Mason saw him? As a player? Lucky had many sexual partners, but he never played anyone. He never took advantage of anyone, pretended to care about them, or be interested in more. From the moment they met, he let them know he was only interested in a night of hot sex. Lucky never lied. He hated lies. What was the point? In the end the lies would catch up with the liar.

"What's CTSCM?" Mason asked as the elevator doors opened up to the garage beneath the building.

"Corporate Technical Surveillance Countermeasures."

"Which means?"

"Sitting in one of Jack's surveillance vehicles for hours hoping some corporate asshole fucks up so we can take him down."

"Corporate espionage?"

"Yes." Lucky headed for the end of the garage and the truck parked near the exit. Mason stilled, his eyes going huge.

"Holy fuck! When you said surveillance vehicle, I was expecting a van or something, not a thirty-foot truck."

"Not quite thirty, but almost."

Mason's expression was uninspired, and Lucky laughed.

"Go big or go home, Cowboy. That's how we do things." Lucky climbed up the steps at the rear of the truck and unlocked the back door. Before they left, he needed to take stock of everything. Not that he expected the truck to be anything but immaculate, but there were procedures that needed to be followed. "Jack's in charge of Cyber Security and System Installations at Four Kings. He has his own team of security agents. They handle very big complicated jobs. Mostly large corporations, military bases, and very wealthy clients. There's a separate security team for the smaller installations." He climbed in and picked up the iPad tucked into the black leather pocket attached to the wall.

"They must be pretty smart, huh?" Mason asked as he climbed the stairs. Once inside, he let out a whistle. "I'm in the wrong business. The only thing I have during surveillance is AC and a cup of coffee, and I consider myself lucky. You're looking to ruin me for future jobs."

"If we're going to be the best, we should have the best. Most of Jack's team are former military, their MOS similar to Jack's." He powered up the tablet and opened the software he needed to take inventory. The truck was immaculate as usual.

"MOS?"

"Military Occupational Specialties."

"Right. Ace said you were both weapons sergeants. All the Kings were sergeants, right?"

"Sergeant First Class. Except for King. He was a Warrant Officer 1."

"I'm guessing by the 1 that there's more than one? What's the difference?"

"King was appointed to Warrant Officer 1 after a warrant was approved by the Secretary of the Army. Chief Warrant Officers, such as Warrant Officer 2, are appointed by the President." Lucky moved his gaze to Mason who'd taken a seat in one of the plush black leather chairs in front of the security console.

"Is it weird taking orders from King at work? I mean, I know he was your commander and whatnot in your unit, but you all own Four Kings same as him."

"We've found a way to avoid the whole too many cooks in the kitchen thing. Each of us is in charge of a department that plays to our strengths. Jack is in charge of Cyber Security and Systems Installations, Joker is in charge of Canine and Special Events, Red is Vulnerability and Risk Assessment, as well as Unarmed Security, Ace is in charge of Armed Security and Defensive Driving, I'm in charge of Media and Entertainment, King deals with Executive Protection and Military contracts. We have teams and personnel within each department, along with team leaders. There are also certain areas where we will all be involved, such as hiring, training, emergency and crisis situations. Depending on our availability and the cases, we sometimes work in a department that is not our own, like now."

"But King seems to be the one in charge."

Lucky considered Mason's words. "At times, yes."

"And you're okay with giving up that kind of control?"

"I'm not giving up anything. None of us are. There are times when one voice is needed, and that voice is King's. He's a leader. It's what he does, and we're happy to have him lead us. He knows exactly how to handle every situation, what to do, when, and how. Who else's orders would I follow? Ace?" Lucky scoffed before moving his eyes back to the tablet. "Remember the models at the beach?"

Mason shuddered. "Point taken. King just seems.... I don't know. Like he's got a stick permanently inserted up his ass."

"He's very reserved." Lucky finished up, saved the document, then turned off the tablet and returned it to its pocket. "But you will never know a better man. If King has your back, you know whatever the outcome, it will be the best it can be."

Mason nodded. He pointed to the counter beside Lucky. "Is that an espresso machine?"

Lucky looked from Mason to the espresso machine and back. "Yes. Doesn't it look like an espresso machine?"

"Don't look at me like I can't ride and chew at the same time."

Lucky squinted at him. "I... I don't know what that means. Ride and chew what?"

"Ride a horse and chew tobacco."

"Chewing tobacco is disgusting. My tía chewed tobacco. Que Dios, la tenga en su gloria," Lucky said, crossing himself. "You shouldn't chew tobacco or smoke. Very bad for you, you know?"

"Agreed. I don't chew tobacco or smoke." Mason shook his head. "Why are we talking about tobacco?"

"I don't know. You're the one who brought it up."

"No, I brought up you looking at me like I was an idiot because you have an espresso machine in your surveillance truck. Who the hell has an espresso machine in their surveillance truck?"

"We do. Surveillance means many hours and lots of coffee."

"You boys ever heard of a coffee pot or a thermos?"

Lucky gasped, his hand flying to his chest. "Don't you ever say those words in my presence again. Are you trying to kill me?"

"The thought has crossed my mind on occasion."

"You're not funny. We have an espresso machine because it makes real coffee, not the coffee-flavored water you fill your thermos with. I'd rather drink water from the Everglades."

"Why don't you tell me how you really feel, sweetheart."

"Stop calling me your sweetheart. I'm not your sweetheart."

Mason turned around, mumbling to himself. "It's like putting socks on a rooster."

Lucky had no idea what the hell Mason was talking about. He closed the back door, locked up, and then took a seat behind the wheel. He buckled up and started the truck, expecting Mason to stay in the back, but he didn't. He maneuvered his large, muscular body between the front seats and turned to face the passenger seat, sticking his ass right in Lucky's face.

Leaning quickly away, Lucky was forced to press his lips together and placed his fists on his lap to keep from reaching out, grabbing Mason, and taking a bite out of him. He should, just to teach the bastard not to go shoving body parts in Lucky's face. Mason dropped down onto the passenger seat and fastened his seat belt. He sat back with a sigh and a shit-eating grin on his face.

"Well, come on, darlin'. We're burning daylight."

With a curse under his breath, Lucky put the truck in Drive.

So much for entertaining.

FOUR

THIS WAS GOING to be a long night. Lucky felt it in his bones.

Once they were in downtown Jacksonville, Lucky pulled the truck into the parking lot of the bank across the street from the skyscraper they'd be watching. Jack had acquired the perfect spot near the lot entrance in case they had to move quickly, and a small team of security agents were parked in the Central Station parking lot, waiting for word from Lucky. With the engine turned off, Lucky unbuckled his seat belt and climbed out of his seat at the same time Mason did. Lucky reeled back in an effort not to bump into him, the back of his knees hitting the seat. He flailed, throwing an arm out, but he needn't have worried. Mason wrapped an arm around his waist and caught him, bringing him up against his hard body.

"Easy there, darlin'," Mason murmured quietly, their lips only inches apart. "Don't want you hurting yourself."

Lucky swallowed hard. He felt Mason's warm breath against his skin. "You're stepping on my shoe."

Mason frowned. "You're worried about your shoe?"

"These boots are Guiseppe Zanotti."

"Am I supposed to know what that means?" Mason asked, releasing Lucky.

"It means they cost almost a thousand dollars."

Mason stared at him. "Why the hell are you wearin' thousand-dollar boots to work surveillance? You know there are kids out there starvin'?"

"Yes, I know," Lucky spat, pushing Mason away from him. "I was one of them. Now excuse me. We have work to do."

At least Mason had the decency to look mortified.

"Shit, Lucky, I'm sorry. I didn't—"

"Forget it," Lucky muttered, taking a seat behind the console to log into the security system. "I don't need to explain myself to you. Just sit down and pay attention."

Mason took a seat beside him, his expression solemn. Thankfully, he didn't speak. Lucky didn't need his apologies or his permission. In Cuba he'd spent most of his time barefoot because the shoes given to him were either beyond salvation or he grew out of them so quickly they hurt his feet to the point he couldn't walk. Now he could afford all the shoes he wanted, and if he wanted to spend money on designer shoes, no one had the right to make him feel like shit for it. He wasn't stupid. His savings account was solid, and his retirement account was one of the first things he'd set up when he got his first job. He spent *a lot* of money, but he also saved money because he knew what it was like to have nothing. He was never going back to that again. Never.

A building came into view on one of the large flat-screen monitors. He pointed to one of the floors marked on the screen. "That is Techu Technologies. It's a multibillion-dollar company. Jack believes this man is a corporate spy. Dirk Grant." He pointed to the second monitor and the profile of a man in his midthirties. "Techu Technologies spent millions of dollars and several years developing a new medical smartwatch, but a month before launch, a rival company launched their own medical smartwatch that used the exact technology with minor changes. It's not the first time this kind of thing has happened. This monitor shows all the different cameras Jack has installed throughout the floor."

"What makes ya'll think he's gonna slip up now?"

"Jack spent months feeding him false information all leading up to one very important final piece of equipment, a prototype of the company's latest technology—a game changer in the pharmaceutical field. Dirk believes it's worth billions, and it's arriving tonight via an armored vehicle. The armed security team—our team—will be personally delivering the prototype to the head of the company's security, also one of ours. She will secure it in the company safe. We believe Dirk will attempt to steal the prototype sometime after."

"And he's going to bypass all your security? How?"

"That's what we don't know yet. Jack's system will notify us the moment anything out of the ordinary happens, and believe me, Jack is prepared for everything."

"I don't know how I feel about leaving everything up to a computer."

"I wouldn't, but this isn't any computer. It's one of Jack's, but if it makes you feel any better, you can watch the monitors." Lucky removed one of the laptops from the locked cabinet beneath the console as well as two boxes, one of which he slid over to Mason. "Radio and earpiece." They removed the small radios from their boxes and clipped them to the waistband of their pants before putting in their earpiece. Once they were both online, Lucky logged into their system on the laptop and entered his credentials to get into the Kings dashboard.

"What's that?" Mason asked, leaning over to look at his screen.

"A list of my clients with invoices pending. Once a contract is signed, we open a new case or job on the system, and a special accounting program automatically creates an invoice, but we don't send them out automatically in case of changes, and there are always changes. During a job, notes are added. See here." He clicked on a tab that showed a page full of typed notes. "As we or our personnel work the job, we add notes relevant to the case, any additional equipment that may have been needed at the client's expense, any additional personnel added, and so on. I read the notes, check the invoice, and make sure everything adds up before sending it to the client."

"You fellas seem to rely an awful lot on technology," Mason grumbled, sitting back in his seat.

"Everything is backed up onto our cloud servers as well as external drives. We also keep hard copies. Many backups. It's all streamlined. King gets very twitchy otherwise. Not good for his blood pressure, or ours." Lucky went back to checking his invoices while Mason stared at the monitors. As soon as Lucky was finished, he logged out, then closed the laptop.

"That's pretty."

Lucky turned his attention to Mason. "What is?"

"The bracelet."

"Thank you. My mother gave it to me. She is very spiritual."

"What makes it spiritual?"

"The stones have many healing properties. This is tiger's-eye," he said, pointing to the gold-and-brown bead.

"And this is black agate. The black agate is for stabilizing and grounding while elevating awareness. It helps you focus and be courageous. It's also a protection stone."

"Makes sense. And the tiger's-eye?" Mason asked.

"It offers strength and protection but also helps you make decisions without being clouded by your emotions."

"Your mama knows you well, huh?"

Lucky peered at him. "Are you saying I'm emotional?"

Mason put his hands up in surrender. "Nope. I didn't say that."

"It's fine," Lucky said with a snort. "It's not as though I'm not told as much all the time by my family. If everyone says so, it must be true, no?"

"You're passionate," Mason corrected.

Lucky studied him. "You really think so, or you're just saying that so I won't argue with you?"

"I know so." Mason turned in his chair to face Lucky. "I have never seen you lose your shit over something you didn't care about."

It was true. Things affected him deeply. It was how he was made. If he didn't care about something, he didn't waste much time on it, but if he did care, he had a habit of getting worked up at times.

Not wanting to think about how well Mason seemed to know him, he stood. He needed to not be so close to Mason. It was only a few hours. "I need to stretch my legs."

Mason eyed him but didn't respond. He turned his attention to the monitors and sat back in his chair, his jaw muscles working.

Just a few hours, Lucky reminded himself. He could do this. As long as he didn't look at Mason for too long or talk about anything not related to work, or sports, or the weather, it'd be fine. He'd be fine.

A little while later, it was obvious he was *not* fine.

"Would you sit down, please? You're gonna wear a hole in the damn floor with all that pacing."

Lucky glared at Mason but took a seat. He checked his watch. Fuck, it had only been two hours.

"Are you telling me you Green Berets never had to be still for more than an hour?"

"That's different," Lucky muttered, playing with one of the beads hanging from the adjustable braided string on his bracelet.

"How is it different?"

"You train day after day, pushing yourself to the limit, preparing your mind and body for battle, for the missions that are to come. There is no failure because failing means...." Lucky swallowed hard, then shook his head. "It's very different."

"Is that what happened to your team?"

"*We* didn't fail. Someone failed *us*, and our brothers paid for that failure with their lives." Lucky stood and went to the espresso machine to make himself un cortadito.

"I'm sorry," Mason said, his voice quiet. "I didn't mean to pry."

"Ace never told you?"

Mason shook his head. "His time in the military is something he never really talked about. When he did, he didn't go into detail, so I didn't push."

"Even if you'd pushed, he wouldn't have told you. Most of what we did was classified. We don't talk about it, and we don't reveal secrets."

"Even after what happened with your unit? You said someone failed you and your brothers paid the price. Doesn't that make you angry?"

"Yes, of course, but we're still soldiers, always will be.

We no longer serve, but that doesn't change the man inside. No matter what happened, we won't betray our country. Our country is its people, not the politicians who place more value in their little party war than human lives." Lucky opened the black panel beneath the machine, and Mason laughed.

"Really? A refrigerator?"

"Of course. Where else would we keep the milk?"

Mason shook his head. "Right. How silly of me."

"You want one?"

"Sure."

Lucky removed the small sugar container from the cabinet, along with a stainless-steel pitcher. He added the sugar, then turned on the espresso machine, swapping the coffee pitcher for the one with sugar.

"I heard there's an art to making Cuban coffee," Mason said, studying him.

"In that, you are correct, my friend."

"What are you doing? Walk me through it."

"I'm making the espumita for the coffee."

"What's espumita?"

"The sugar foam." The coffee began to drip into the small pitcher, and when he had just enough, he swapped the pitchers. "Now you quickly stir a small amount of coffee and the sugar until you have this thick, creamy golden liquid. Once the coffee is finished, you poor the espumita into your coffee and serve." He removed two of the disposable espresso cups from the stack and filled them with the heavenly liquid. The truck smelled deliciously of freshly roasted Cuban coffee. Lucky placed Mason's espresso in front of him.

They sat together in silence, sipping their very hot, delicious coffee. At least until Mason let out a happy grunt, and Lucky smiled. "It's okay to admit you were wrong."

Mason's sigh was put out but cute. "I was wrong about the coffee."

Maybe this wouldn't be so bad after all, at least that's what Lucky thought before Mason decided to do everything in his power to annoy the ever-loving fuck out of Lucky. If he didn't know better, he would think Mason was trying to piss him off on purpose. Mason had gone from being still and observant to being obnoxious, whether it was tapping his fingers on the console desk or singing god-awful country songs. His singing voice was very pleasant, and Lucky enjoyed listening to it, but whatever the hell he was singing was painful. Three hours later, and Lucky was ready to murder him. If he'd been wearing chancletas, he would have smacked Mason over the head with one hours ago.

"Stop," Lucky warned the moment Mason started tapping a pen on the edge of the console.

"What?"

"Tapping the pen."

"This pen?" Mason held up the pen.

"Yes, that pen. The pen I'm going to stab you with. Is that what you want? Because I can do that."

"Oh yeah?" Mason leaned into him. "You gonna hurt me, Lucky?"

Lucky narrowed his eyes at him. "Is there a particular reason you're trying to get me to physically harm you?"

Mason snickered. "Please. Like you would lay a finger on me."

"I don't need to lay a finger on you to take you down, Cowboy."

"That." *Poke*. "So?" *Poke*.

Lucky stared at Mason. Cowboy had lost his fucking

mind. "Did you just poke me? *Twice?*"

Mason shrugged. "What are you going to do about it? Put me in a sleeper hold?" He leaned in, his grin wicked. "Can you do that? You can do that, right? Pressure points and all that shit?"

"You're an ass."

"Would you lighten up, darlin'?"

"Stop calling me your darling." Lucky stood and started pacing again. How the hell was he supposed to sit through— he checked his watch and groaned. Three more hours before the security team arrived with the supposed proto-type. *Fuck.*

"Fine. You don't want me to call you darlin'? How about I call you what you are? A goddamn pain in my ass."

"You wish I was in your ass," Lucky spat back.

Mason stood, his hands balled into fists at his sides. "That so, huh?"

"Please, why don't we just say what's going on here. You want me so bad you can barely stand it."

Mason thrust a finger in Lucky's face. "You're a cocky little shit, you know that?"

"Yes, that's true, but tell me I'm wrong."

Mason's skin flushed from his neck up to his ears, his nostrils flared, and his jaw clenched tight. He looked like a bull ready to charge. "Sure, if you tell me you don't want me just as bad. And, *darlin'*, if anyone's gonna be in anyone's ass, it'll be me in yours."

Lucky let out a snort. "Now who's being cocky?"

"I got your cocky right here," Mason growled motioning to his crotch.

"Oh fuck," Lucky said with a laugh. He shook his head, then wiggled his fingers at Mason. "Las palabras se las lleva el viento."

"What the fuck does that mean?"

"Actions speak louder than words, my friend."

Mason got up in Lucky's face. "You're asking for trouble."

"You're all talk, Cowboy. Now move."

"Or what?"

"Or I will move you."

"Yeah? Big bad Green Beret gonna show me what's what?"

Lucky narrowed his gaze. "Back the fuck up."

Mason dropped his eyes to Lucky's mouth. "You gonna put your hands on me, *darlin'*?"

"Just remember, you asked for it." Lucky's smile was evil as he wrapped his fingers around Mason's wrist. The big man's breath hitched, and Lucky moved fast. He was out and behind Mason before Mason even knew what the hell was going on. In seconds, Mason was on his knees with his arm twisted up behind his back and Lucky's free hand around his neck, forcing him to look up. "You look good on your knees, Cowboy."

Mason narrowed his eyes, but remained still. His bright blue eyes had darkened, and his chest rose and fell with heavy breaths. Lucky slid his hand up from Mason's neck to his chin, his thumb caressing Mason's lips. Their eyes met, and Lucky released him before he did anything stupid. He turned away to get ahold of himself, but he was grabbed and shoved up against the counter. Mason's body pressed against Lucky's, his muscular thigh pushing against Lucky's hard dick and Mason's hard length stabbing Lucky's leg. Lucky could have moved him, easily, but his treacherous body wasn't cooperating.

"I am *done* playing games," Mason growled. He reached for Lucky's face, but Lucky snatched his wrists before

Mason touched him. "Do I scare you, darlin'? That why you keep running from me?"

"Fuck you. I'm not scared of shit."

"Have the soldier stand down, and then tell me that."

Lucky hated that Mason saw through him. He released Mason's wrists, his heart pounding in his ears. Mason shook his head and started to turn away. *Fuck it.* Lucky snagged a fistful of Mason's shirt and jerked him down, bringing their mouths together in a crushing kiss and throwing fuel on the fire already burning inside them. A raging inferno had been ignited, and it was all-consuming.

Mason wrapped his arms around Lucky, crushing Lucky to him as their tongues dueled for dominance. Lucky had never tasted anything so good, and he let out a low moan as he dug his fingers into Mason's back, kissing him with a need that bordered on desperation. His senses were on overload from Mason's scent, taste, and feel. All that hard muscle pressed against him, the way Mason was leaning his heavier weight into Lucky, drove him insane.

With a growl, he raked his fingers into Mason's hair, gripping fistfuls of it. He was so damned hard, it was painful. His body thrummed with desire, and all he thought about was having that big, thick, gorgeous cock inside him.

"Fuck," Mason said through a gasp. He spun Lucky around and bent him over the counter, his large hand on Lucky's shoulder holding him in place.

Lucky groaned, widening his stance and pushing his ass out in invitation, a shiver racking his body when Mason growled and reached around to unfasten Lucky's belt. They shouldn't be doing this, not here, not now. *Fuck.*

"Tell me to stop." Mason's voice was low and gravelly. "Or I'm gonna fuck you right here."

Lucky rubbing his ass against Mason's rock-hard cock

should have been answer enough, but in case Mason needed it spelled out for him, Lucky snatched the radio off Mason's belt. He lifted it to his mouth and hit the PTT button. "Taking a break. Call if you need something."

"Copy that, boss."

Tossing the radio to one side, Lucky gazed at Mason over his shoulder. "Let's go for a ride, Cowboy."

Mason cursed under his breath, his pupils blown, his hair a sexy mess as it fell over his brow, and his lips swollen from their kissing. Fuck, he was hot. Mason captured Lucky's mouth again, his kiss hard and quick before he jerked Lucky's pants and underwear down below his ass.

"Goddamn. I've been dreamin' about this ass for months." Mason smacked Lucky's right asscheek, and Lucky gasped at the delicious sting. It was almost enough to have him coming right then. He released a moan, his grip on the edge of the counter so hard his fingers hurt. The sound of Mason's belt clinking and the rustling of clothes had Lucky shivering with anticipation. Mason wasn't the only one who'd been dreaming of certain things. "You got a condom and lube?" Mason felt around Lucky's pockets. "'Course you do."

"Fuck you. You complaining?" Lucky was always prepared. He never knew when a sexy-as-sin cowboy's manhandling would turn into something more. Not that he was going to admit as much to Mason.

"No complaints here." Mason took hold of Lucky's chin and kissed him as if he were afraid Lucky would change his mind. Leaving him breathless, Mason moved his hungry mouth to Lucky's ear and took his earlobe between his teeth, sucking and nibbling. With a lick to Lucky's jawline, Mason pressed a lubed finger to Lucky's hole. Lucky sucked in a sharp breath and pushed back onto Mason's finger, their loud groans and curses filling the truck. "Fuck. Look at that. Greedy pucker, ain't it?"

"Are you going to fuck me or talk to me about it?"

"Jesus, the mouth on you."

"Like my mouth doesn't make you hard."

"There's nothing about you that don't make me hard, darlin'." Mason added a second finger, and Lucky moaned.

¡Ay, Dios mío! That was so damned good. "I really need you to fuck me," Lucky growled. "Like, right now."

"Suit yourself." Mason pulled his fingers from Lucky's ass and replaced them with the head of his cock.

Lucky's hiss turned into a low groan as he was breached, the burn from Mason's thick shaft stretching his hole oh so good. His breath came out labored as Mason sank into him, and Lucky just couldn't wait anymore. He impaled himself on Mason's dick, making them both cry out.

"Fuck! Jesus Christ, Lucky!" Mason doubled over, his chest pressed to Lucky's back. "You trying to kill me?"

Lucky grinned wickedly. "The thought has crossed my mind on occasion."

Mason laughed. "You little shit." He gripped Lucky's hips, pulled almost all the way out, then plunged back in, and this time it was Lucky's turn to curse. Mason repeated the move, and Lucky was grateful to have Mason holding him or he might drop to his knees from how good it felt to have Mason driving into him.

"Fuck! *Oh fuck.* Yes! Come on, Cowboy." Lucky's pulse soared, and his body trembled with need as Mason plunged into him deep and hard. He was stretched impossibly wide, and his ass was going to be sore for hours, but *santo cielos*, it was divine!

Mason pounded into him, and Lucky threw his

head back, prompting Mason to wrap a hand around his neck, keeping him in place so Mason could turn his head and kiss him. They tore at each other's mouths, their kisses sloppy and wet. Their tongues tangled, their breaths mingling as their bodies became one. There was nothing sweet or gentle about what they were doing. It was raw and desperate and animalistic. The truck filled with the sound of their curses, grunts, panting breaths, and bodies smacking together. Lucky mumbled nonsense in Spanish, but it seemed to drive Mason wild, so he urged Mason on in his native language. Mason might not understand what he was saying, but Lucky's tone left no doubt that what he was saying was filthy.

"This what you want, darlin'?"

"Yes, oh God, yes. Harder." Lucky welcomed Mason's bruising grip on his hips. He wanted to feel Mason for days. If this was the last time they'd be doing this, Lucky didn't want to forget it. "Your cock feels so good inside me, Cowboy."

Mason moved an arm around Lucky's chest, straightening with him and holding him in place, his chin coming to rest on Lucky's shoulder as he continued to plow into him. "Milk that pretty dick of yours, darlin'. I want to see you come."

If Mason wanted a show, Lucky would give him one. He cupped the back of Mason's head and with his free hand used his precome to get himself nice and slick. He smiled at Mason's curse as Lucky matched his strokes to Mason's erratic thrusts.

"Goddamn, you're beautiful."

Lucky gasped and a shiver traveled up his spine. He shut his eyes, not wanting Mason to see how much his words meant, even if what he'd said was in the heat of the moment. "Wreck me, Cowboy."

Mason let out a roar as he shoved Lucky back down over the counter and pumped himself into Lucky like a madman. He shouted out his release, filling the condom. Lucky followed with a cry a heartbeat later. Jack was going to kick his ass if he found out what they'd done in his precious truck. He'd warn Mason later. Right now, he could hardly catch his breath much less use his brain.

Mason's head rested against the back of Lucky's, his arm still around Lucky's chest as he kept him close, the only sound their panting breaths. A soft moan escaped Mason, and he nuzzled Lucky's temple before delivering a feathery kiss, his fingers softly caressing Lucky's chest. The tender gesture was far too intimate, and Lucky cleared his throat.

"I need to clean up so we can get back to work."

Mason let out a resigned sigh. "Right." He gently pulled out, and Lucky winced. He didn't turn to look at Mason. He simply straightened like nothing had happened, opened one of the drawers, and pulled out a packet of wet wipes. After cleaning himself up, he pulled up his pants, then cleaned the bottom cabinet he'd come on. After throwing away the evidence, he opened the fridge and grabbed a bottle of water for himself and one for Mason, who was already seated at the console, his gaze focused on nothing in particular. Lucky held the bottle out to him.

"Thanks."

Taking a seat, Lucky twisted the cap off and took a long gulp, pretending he didn't know Mason was watching him. The air in the van was thick, both from sex and the tension between them. Lucky couldn't afford to let his guard down around Mason. It would be far too easy for him to fall, and that would only lead to heartbreak. Lucky had lived a lifetime of disappointments, and he wasn't going to add Mason Cooper to that list.

One of the monitors beeped, and a map with a red blinking dot appeared. It slowly moved through the streets of downtown Jacksonville. "There's the armored truck." Lucky tapped his earpiece. "Okay. Everyone remain vigilant. Truck's twenty minutes out." They had no idea what to expect. They were talking about a fake prototype worth billions of fake dollars. Lucky had known men who'd killed for far less. It was a little after eight in the evening, and few employees were left on the floor other than security personnel. "Keep an eye on that dot," Lucky told Mason as he stood and walked to the slim black locker at the end of the truck. He entered his security pin, unlocked the door, and pulled out one of the black tactical vests. "Put this on."

Mason turned to him, and Lucky handed him the vest before he strapped himself into one.

"Shit, are we expecting gunfire?"

"We don't know what this man is planning, and I'm not going to let you die on my watch, Cowboy."

"Thanks," Mason muttered. "I think."

Lucky chuckled. He tapped his code into the large biometric lock box on the shelf below and when prompted, placed his finger to the scanner. The box unlocked, and he removed a Glock in its tactical holster. "Here. Secure this to your vest."

Mason did as asked without question, and Lucky smiled to himself. A part of him had thought Mason wouldn't be happy about taking orders from him, but Mason didn't hesitate when Lucky asked him to do something. He just did it. Lucky secured his own holster to his vest, then closed the lock box, checked it was secure, and locked the cabinet before he joined Mason at the console.

The armored truck was approaching their street. When the truck was down the road, the screen with the map switched to footage of the truck. They watched as it pulled up in front of the building and the back doors opened. A team of six armed security agents hopped out, and one of them was handed a medium-sized armored box. The team secured the agent carrying the box, and they swiftly made their way into the building.

Lucky tapped his earpiece. "The package is in the building."

They watched the screen, the footage now of the team inside the lobby making their way toward the elevators. One of the security agents swiped a key card. Lucky leaned his elbows on the console, his gaze fixed on the screen. He didn't move a muscle, barely breathed, his eyes locked on the movement in front of him. The team took the elevator up to the executive suites, and soon they were inside the CEO's office.

"So how much security are we talking about here?" Mason asked, motioning to the monitor.

"That's Johnson in front, the team leader. He has to swipe through the security system six times to get to the safe room. Once to get into the building, the elevators, the executive lobby, the executive floor, the CEO's office, and then the safe room. The safe contains a biometric lock, which requires an authorized user key card, security pin, fingerprint scan, and retina scan. If just one of those doesn't match what's in the system, the safe and the safe room go into lockdown mode, which alerts Jack and his team. The only way to get it reset is with Jack's credentials."

"What if Jack's not available?"

"Then there is a failsafe and one of the Kings can reset it."

The team successfully bypassed all the security measures as expected. They secured the box inside the safe, locked the safe, and headed out. Johnson's voice came through their earpieces.

"Package is secure. We're heading out."

"Okay. Remain vigilant."

The team made it to the truck, climbed in, waited a few minutes, then left.

Nothing.

Mason sighed. "You really think he's gonna make a move so soon after?"

"It depends how desperate he is, and from what we've seen of his bank account, I think he's pretty desperate."

AN HOUR PASSED with no movement. More employees went home for the day, leaving only the security team in the lobby, security office, and the five guards making their rounds.

"Wait. What's that?" Lucky peered at the screen and the black BMW with tinted windows that pulled up in front of the building. The driver climbed out, closed his door, and opened the back door for a tall man with salt-and-pepper hair.

"Who is that?"

Lucky tapped away at the closest screen and brought up the profiles of the company's executive personnel. He pointed to the photo of the man currently entering the building. "That's Angelo Ruiz, the CEO."

"Why is that weird?"

"Mr. Ruiz called in sick today."

"Maybe he's feeling better and decided to check on things? That's not unusual."

"No, it's not, but something doesn't feel right." Lucky always listened to his gut. After years of special ops missions, he learned to trust his intuition. Something was wrong. They kept their eyes on the screen while Angelo swiped his key card in all the same places the team had. When he'd swiped to get into his office, Lucky called Jack.

"Lucky, what's wrong?"

"I need to see all the footage we have of Angelo Ruiz swiping his key card at the office."

"On it. One second."

"Thanks. I'll call you back." The screen on the left suddenly switched to several rows of smaller screens, all filled with footage of Angelo swiping his key card. "Shit, that's not Angelo."

"How do you know?"

Lucky pointed to the screen. "Every single time he swipes his card it's with his left hand. He's left-handed." Lucky pointed to the screen of the impostor. "That man has swiped with his right every time."

"Are you kidding me? How—"

Lucky tapped his earpiece. "Everyone, move in. Proceed with caution. The man who just entered the building may not be Angelo Ruiz." He had no idea how the thief planned on getting past the retina scan, but Lucky wasn't about to wait around to find out. He snatched the tablet off the console and shoved it into one of the deep pockets of his black combat pants. "Stay close."

"Yeah, I've done this before, hotshot."

"Good. Then you know not to take stupid risks." Lucky hurried to the door of the truck, threw it open, and jumped over the stairs. He hit the ground running, Mason on his heels. They joined the armed security team, and Lucky nodded to Johnson, who motioned for some of his agents to cover the exits of the building. He swiped his key card to get them into the lobby. With Glock in hand, Lucky waited for the team to go in first. Johnson motioned for half the team to take the stairs while the others took the elevator with him. Lucky signaled that he and Mason would take the emergency stairwell.

Reaching the door to the emergency exit, Lucky removed his tablet, entered his credentials, and turned off the alarm just to the lobby door. He didn't want to turn off all the alarms and alert Dirk—or whoever the hell it was—to their presence. With that done, he returned the tablet to his pockets, and gun at the ready, they hurried up the stairs. Lucky had a sneaking suspicion their thief wasn't going to walk out the front door with the box.

They'd reached the ninth floor when Lucky heard a *click*. He put his fist up, motioning for Mason to stop. Gingerly, Lucky approached the railing. Safety off, he leaned over to look up. A bullet pinged against the steel rail, and he darted back. Mason grabbed his arm.

"You okay?"

"Yeah." Lucky tapped his earpiece as a door slammed somewhere above them. "He's on the tenth floor. Be careful. He's armed." He took off, Mason right behind him. Lucky took the left side of the door and motioned for Mason to take the right. When he nodded, Mason grabbed hold of the door handle and opened it. No bullets flew through, so Lucky peeked inside. The floor appeared deserted, but he knew better than that. He motioned for Mason to follow, and they both took cover behind one of the desks. A door opened, and Lucky sneaked a glance, relieved to see it was the security team. They fanned out, concealing themselves behind office furniture and equipment. Johnson's voice came through Lucky's earpiece.

"The authorities are en route."

With a quick thanks, Lucky removed his tablet from his pocket and brought up the building's security feeds, logging into the tenth floor. "Well, hello, Mr. Not-Ruiz," Lucky whispered at the video of their thief. "He's in the men's room." Lucky frowned. "He's trying to get to the window."

"That's crazy. We're on the tenth floor. What the hell's he planning to do? Jump?"

The hairs on the back of Lucky's neck stood on end, and he tapped away at his tablet, his eyes going wide when he saw the open dumpster conveniently located beneath the bathroom window. It looked like it was filled with some kind of foam or padding. "Shit. He's tossing it out the window!" Lucky took off toward the men's room, slammed through the door, and launched himself at the thief, who'd been balancing on the garbage can, giving Lucky enough time to tackle him, but not before the man tossed the box out the window.

They hit the tiled floor hard, and the thief kneed Lucky in his ribs. Thankfully, his vest cushioned the blow, leaving him free to block a right hook aimed at his head. He slammed the man's hand into the floor, making him cry out, his gun toppling out of his grip. Lucky punched the guy in the face, cringing when part of his face melted.

"What the fuck?"

Mason joined them, his gun aimed at their thief. "Don't move!" Tilting his head, Mason scrunched up his nose. "What did you do to his face? That's not... that ain't right."

As the security team flooded into the bathroom, Lucky poked the guy's cheek. "Wait, this is...." He tugged on the guy's shirt collar, his eyes going wide. Taking hold of the

seam, he pulled at the latex and peeled off the man's face—
or rather an exceptionally detailed mask.

"Well, damn." Mason let out a whistle as he helped
Lucky roll the guy onto his stomach. "That is some *Mission
Impossible* shit right there."

Once the zip ties were secure around the guy's wrists,
Lucky rolled him onto his back and smiled down at him.
"Hello, Mr. Grant. That was very clever, you know? But
now you will be going to jail." He grabbed Dirk's arm and
stood, hauling the man up with him.

Dirk's grin was smug. "You're too late. The box has
been delivered."

"Oh, good. Then the employer you stole for will also be
joining you in prison. Hey, maybe you'll be cell buddies."

"What?" Dirk's face went ashen. "What are you talking
about?"

"The only thing in that box worth any money is the
tracking device hidden inside." Lucky's grin was all teeth.
"Surprise!"

Dirk shook his head in horror. "No. That's not
possible."

"I'm afraid it is. The prototype never existed." Lucky
booped the tip of Dirk's nose. "Much like the chances of you
getting away with your thieving." He handed Dirk over to
the police officers who swarmed the bathroom. Clapping a
hand on Mason's shoulder, Lucky motioned toward the
door.

"Let's go, Cowboy. Now the real fun starts."

"Oh?"

"Yes. I'm sure you're very familiar with this particular
procedure. It's called filling out a shit ton of paperwork."

Mason groaned. "And here I thought it was all fun and
games with you Kings."

Lucky's laughter echoed through the empty office floor as they headed for the elevator. "You're adorable."

"That's what I keep telling you," Mason teased. "But you didn't want to listen."

"Ass." Lucky chuckled. He thanked the team waiting outside and told them to have a good night. He was very pleased with how this whole evening had gone.

"What about the box?" Mason asked. "Who's tracking it?"

"A second team." Lucky removed his tablet from his pocket, logged in, and accessed the secure feed with the tracking information for the device inside the prototype box. He showed it to Mason. "The red dot is the box. The green dot is our team, who is in communication with the police. The moment the team gives the word, the police will move in, and from the direction they're heading, my guess is they're going straight to the rival company. Someone is in for a very bad night."

A couple of police officers approached, along with the real Angelo Ruiz, who was looking a little beat-up. Apparently, Dirk thought the best way to get the prototype was to kidnap Angelo, which would explain how Dirk had managed to get past the retina scan. He and his accomplice used high-tech software to scan Angelo's retina on Dirk's phone, which could then be displayed for scanning at the safe room. Angelo had no idea who'd kidnapped him, but once Dirk had the box, he'd given the all-clear to his partner, and Angelo had been released. The plan was to walk out with the box, drop it off in the bin, drive off, and show up to work the next day as if nothing had happened.

Angelo held out his hand to Lucky, who took it. "Thank you so much, Mr. Morales. You and your team have helped save my company."

"We're very glad we could help," Lucky replied.

Angelo shook Mason's hand and thanked him before moving on to thank the rest of the team.

Checking traffic, Lucky crossed the street. The sound of tires burning rubber caught his attention, and he turned in time to see an SUV with pitch-black tinted windows speeding down the street. Mason was almost to the sidewalk when the SUV made straight for him.

"Mason!" Lucky launched himself at Mason, grabbing hold of his vest and throwing his weight into the maneuver, sending them soaring through the air. They hit the asphalt hard, Mason's full weight landing on Lucky and knocking the wind out of him. The SUV careened around the corner and disappeared, followed by one of the police cars that had been parked outside the office building. Mason scrambled up, getting off Lucky, and gently cupping his face.

"Fuck. Are you okay? Darlin', talk to me."

"I'm okay," Lucky wheezed, letting Mason help him sit up. He touched his temple and winced.

"You're hurt."

"It's just a scrape," Lucky promised. "I'm good."

Mason didn't look convinced. He checked Lucky over to make sure before standing and helping him to his feet. The team came running, and Lucky held up a hand.

"I'm okay. Johnson, I want to know if the police catch up with that asshole, and I want to know who they are."

"It was probably some drunk idiot," Mason offered.

"They could have killed you," Lucky growled before turning his attention back to Johnson. "Keep me informed."

Johnson nodded and ran off.

If the cops didn't find the guy, their team would. The last thing Lucky wanted was to hear about that bastard running down some poor innocent person. Jesus, what if Lucky hadn't gotten to Mason in time?

"Everyone, go home." Lucky headed to the truck with Mason at his side, his hand on Lucky's shoulder, as if he was afraid of letting him out of his sight. As soon as they were in the truck, Mason pointed to one of the seats at the console.

"Sit. I assume there's a first aid kit or portable hospital in this rig?"

Lucky snorted. "Do you really think Red would let us go anywhere without a kit he's personally put together?" He pointed to one of the cabinets, and Mason shook his head in amusement when he saw what was inside.

"You fellas really don't do anything by halves. It's like a mini ER in here." He removed the duffel bag and unzipped it, then pulled out one of the small compact first aid kits. "What's this?" He lifted a vintage-style tin of bandages. "Bravery Bandages?"

Lucky snickered. "Yes. Red loves those things." They were bandages that looked like military medals, each one with a cute saying like "I've Had Worse" or "Suffered Valiantly."

"It's just a scratch," Lucky repeated. "I've had much worse, believe me."

"I'm sure you have, soldier, but how about you let me fuss over you for a sec, huh?"

Lucky held back a smile and nodded. If Mason wanted to fuss over him, so be it. It's not like Lucky wasn't used to being fussed over. He came from a Cuban family, after all. He sat very still, observing Mason's every move as he pulled on gloves and brought over one of the disinfectant wipes. Standing over Lucky, Mason dabbed at Lucky's temple.

"Wow, didn't even flinch at the sting. Bet you laugh in the face of paper cuts."

Lucky chuckled and did his best to ignore how close Mason was, how tender his touch. "Oh no, Cowboy. Paper cuts are serious business. You should see Joker when he gets one. You'd think he was about to lose a limb."

Mason's laugh was soft and squeezed at Lucky's heart. What would it be like to be with a man like Mason? To be important to him?

"Hey."

The soft-spoken word made the butterflies in Lucky's stomach flap wildly, but not as much as when Mason placed a sweet kiss on his lips. Their eyes met, and Mason's smile stole Lucky's breath away.

"Thank you for saving my life, darlin'."

"You're welcome." Lucky's words were no more than a whisper, but Mason heard him. He dropped his gaze to Lucky's lips before leaning in for another kiss. Like a sucker, Lucky allowed it. Who was he kidding? He *needed* it. Parting his lips in invitation, Lucky welcomed Mason's tongue inside his mouth. His lips were warm, soft, and tasted heavenly. Mason cupped Lucky's jaw, deepening the kiss, but keeping it gentle, like he was determined to kill Lucky with tenderness. When Mason pulled back, Lucky's heart was in his throat. Fuck, he was so beautiful. "We should go," Lucky murmured, relieved when Mason smiled warmly at him.

"Okay, darlin'. Vamos a casa."

Casa.

Home.

If Lucky wasn't careful, he might just give into his temptation and ask Mason to come home with him, especially after the day they'd had. He needed to go home. *Alone.*

Tomorrow everything would be different.

FIVE

FUCK, he was exhausted.

Mason tossed his keys onto the small table by the door and headed for the kitchen but stopped halfway there when he got this odd feeling in the pit of his stomach. Something was... off, but he couldn't put his finger on it. Following his gut, he quickly but carefully checked his apartment. He went to his bedroom first, paused in the doorway and scanned the room. Checking his nightstand, he was relieved to find his personal Glock still secured in its locked box. Nothing looked out of place or missing. With the bedroom clear, he moved on to his bathroom, the hall closet, and from there headed back into the small dining area, living room, and kitchen. The whole process took only a few minutes. As a cop, he trusted his gut, but he could find nothing. No strange noises, no movements—everything exactly as he'd left it.

It was most likely his head messing with him after the incident with the SUV. Holy shit, if Lucky hadn't moved as fast as he had.... Shit. He couldn't think about that. It was probably what had him on edge now. That and how tired he was. Why the hell was he so damned tired?

That's one hell of a dumb question.

Other than spending most of the day sitting on his ass, there was the tiny matter of him fucking Lucky. As Mason walked into the middle of his tiny kitchen, it struck him— holy shit, he'd fucked Lucky. He rubbed his hands over his face. Not only had he had sex with Ace's cousin, but Lucky was like a brother to King. King, who'd have his balls if he got so much as a hint of what Mason had done with Lucky while on the job. Technically they'd been on a break, but Mason had a feeling that wasn't going to fly with King.

"I'm a fucking dead man," Mason groaned. He needed to eat something, shower, get into bed, and forget this whole mess even happened. *Yeah, good luck with that, asshole.*

Never in his life had he been this damned turned around over a guy. Most of the time, he didn't know whether he wanted to strangle Lucky or fuck him. Lately the urge to do the latter had been winning out, but he'd thought he had a handle on it. How wrong he'd been. It didn't help that Lucky had a habit of ending up in his space, or that Mason loved it when he did. Bastard drove him up the fucking wall.

Maybe he was overthinking things. For all he knew, he'd taken the first step in getting Eduardo Morales out of his system. Maybe now he could move on. This was good, right? For months they'd been flirting, the heat and sexual tension building between them, and they finally did something about it. It was explosive and hot as hell. This was it. Now things would go back to normal, or who knew? Maybe they were on their way to an actual friendship.

Mason felt lighter at the thought. Lucky was probably feeling the same way. It had stung when Lucky brushed him off after they had sex, but Mason should be thanking him. Things were less complicated now. Of course, the second the thought entered his mind, he recalled their kiss at the end of the night. It had been sweet, tender, and the way Lucky had responded to him, opened up to him, had been incredible, not to mention surprising. He hadn't known what to expect when he'd kissed Lucky. Best-case scenario, a rejection. Worst-case, a punch in the balls. He never knew with Lucky. Damn, but the man was beautiful with his fuckable pouting lips, long lashes, and those rich brown eyes that turned the color of whiskey when the light hit them right. He was all long legs with a spectacular ass and a toned athletic body Mason wanted to run his hands all over. Lucky was also complicated, and Mason tended to avoid complicated.

His stomach growled, reminding him he hadn't eaten all day. Things had moved so quickly after the armored truck showed up that Mason had forgotten all about food. He removed a TV dinner from the freezer, smiling to himself at the thought of what Lucky would say about his dinner. His phone rang, and he pulled it out of his pocket. It was like he'd conjured Lucky up.

"Hey, Lucky."

"Hi. I wanted to apologize."

"For what?" Mason tore open the frozen dinner box and poked holes in the film.

"For not feeding you."

"It's okay. I'm a big boy." He popped his dinner into the microwave and set the timer.

"Are you eating now?"

"Yep. Heating dinner as we speak."

"What are you making?"

"Um, I don't think I want to tell you."

There was a pause before Lucky spoke up, his tone suspicious. "Why don't you want to tell me?"

Mason cringed. "Because I know you. You're gonna get all indignant."

"I will if you don't tell me."

"Frozen TV dinner."

Rustling noises were followed by muffled curses in both English and Spanish.

"You okay?" Mason asked, holding back a laugh.

Lucky let out a strangled noise that was probably supposed to be some kind of acknowledgment. He breathed heavily into the phone. "It's okay. I'm okay. No judgment."

"Glad to hear that. I mean, I'm not entirely sure what the Salisbury steak is made of, but I'm sure the gravy will cover up any odd textures. The mash potatoes are looking a little translucent, but some butter should help with that."

"¡Madrecita mía, ayúdame con este hombre!"

"It's fine. There are also peas and carrots. No, wait, it's mostly peas. Are carrots supposed to be black?"

"Do *not* eat that!"

"Well, it's kinda late, and I'm really too tired to whip something up."

"Mason, do *not* eat whatever horror is in your microwave right now. Food is coming."

Mason blinked. "I'm sorry, can you repeat that? For a moment there, I thought you said food was coming."

"Yes. It's very good food. You'll like it. Do *not* tip the delivery guy, no matter what he says to you. Tell him I said to kiss my ass."

"Um... okay."

"Talk to you later."

Mason stared at his cell phone screen. "Yep, he hung up." What the hell just happened? He had no idea, but if

Lucky said food was on the way, then food was on the way. Whatever it was had to be a hell of a lot better than what he'd been about to consume. In the time it took him to throw away the TV dinner, the doorbell rang. "Damn, that was fast." He opened the front door, shaking his head in disbelief at the sight of Ace standing there holding a huge insulated bag, a fool grin on his face from ear to ear.

"Special delivery."

"You feeding an army?"

Ace let out a snort. "Cuban, remember? You never know who might need feeding. It just so happens we had dinner at Lucky's last night and he cooked. You get to have his famous Puerco Asado."

Mason's mouth watered. "Did he make that rice with the red beans in it?"

"Yep, moro, plus yucca with mojo, and plantains."

"Christ. I need to marry that man." Realizing what he'd said, he cleared his throat. "I mean, you know what I mean."

Ace gave him a knowing look. "Yeah, I know what you mean. Speaking of my wayward cousin...." Ace let himself in, and Mason sighed. There was no getting rid of him until he wanted to go. He might as well heat himself up some dinner.

"I'm going to make myself a plate. You hungry?" Mason walked into his kitchen and placed the bag on the counter.

"I'm good." Ace crossed his arms over his chest and leaned against the doorway. "Heat up your food. Also, you owe me a tip."

Mason grinned at him. "I have instructions not to tip you and to tell you to kiss his ass."

Ace laughed. Much to Mason's relief, Ace decided to go easy on him while he ate dinner. There was at least a week's worth of food in the various sealed containers, and that's with Mason eating as much as he did. He sat at his tiny dining room table on one of the two folding chairs, and Ace took a seat opposite him.

"God, this is damn good. Now I know why you and Lucky work out every day." When Mason had eaten his weight in pork, rice and beans, and everything else, he sat back in his chair with a groan. "I think I'm gonna explode. Where is your cousin anyway?" If the food was in Lucky's house, why didn't Lucky bring it himself? Why send Ace? "Wait, you and Colton are in Ponte Vedra. That's almost an hour away. How'd you get here so damned fast?"

"We were at Lucky's house. He sent me to bring the food because he's elbows deeps in reports right now. Then he's gotta head to the office to sort out a last-minute case with King and check the inventory on some equipment in the armory."

"There's an armory at Four Kings headquarters?"

"Well, yeah. Where else are we going to keep all the weapons? Can't just lock the grenade launcher up in the broom closet."

"You have a grenade launcher? What the hell would you need a—nope, you know what? I don't want to know. Deniability."

Ace snickered. "Heard tonight's job went without a hitch."

"You heard that, did you?" Mason took his glass and plate and walked them to the kitchen sink, Ace right behind him.

"Anything else happen? Besides you almost getting hit by a car? By the way, the car was a rental, paid for by a stolen card, and the guy who rented it used a fake ID. There's no footage of him with a clear view of his face, so all we know is that he was under six feet tall, wore a black hoodie and black baseball cap. Cops are trying to identify him, and they're going to keep us posted. Excluding that, anything interesting happen?"

"Ace, I care about you, so I say this with the utmost respect. It's none of your damn business."

"Lucky's my family."

"He's also a grown-ass man."

"Doesn't mean I'm not going to look out for him."

"Fair enough." Mason washed up his plate and cutlery. He dried his hands before turning to face Ace. He leaned against the sink, arms crossed. "I don't know what else I can say other than it's complicated as fuck."

"Complicated as fuck is our family motto. It's on our crest and everything. In Spanish of course. Complicado como carajo. Has a nice ring to it, don't you think? You should see it on a T-shirt."

Mason shook his head with a chuckle. "You're an ass."

Ace was a very attractive man, with sharp green eyes and a warm smile. His smile was what had attracted Mason when they'd first met. The cousins shared many similarities, like their sense of humor, fierce sense of justice, and unshakable loyalty, but the two were different in so many ways. Just a few months ago, Mason tried to get Ace to give him a second chance, and now, the only man he wanted a chance with didn't want him. Okay, so maybe that wasn't entirely true. Lucky wanted Mason, but he wasn't interested in *keeping* Mason.

A heavy sigh left Ace, as did his smile. His eyes filled with concern. "What are you doing, Coop?"

"I don't know," Mason said, running a hand through his hair. "I just... I care about him, I really do, and it's different with him, even if at times, sweet Lord, he can drive a man to drink, but I think that's part of why I can't seem to walk away. He pushes back."

"Yeah, well, you keep pushing his buttons and he's going to do more than push back, Cowboy."

Mason cringed.

"Oh God, what did you do?"

"I was being annoying, *really* annoying, trying to get a rise out of him. He told me to stop, and I kept going. I poked him a couple of times."

Ace held a hand up. "Let me stop you right there before you go on. Don't *ever* pinch him."

"What?"

"I'm fucking serious about this," Ace said solemnly. "Don't pinch him. It's this thing he has from when he was a kid and his mom used to leave him with a neighbor to babysit. The neighbor had an older son who used to pinch him *all* the time. He will fucking lose his shit and kick your ass, believe me. I found out the hard way."

"Thanks for the warning."

"You're welcome. Now continue. You poked him, and he took you down."

Mason opened his mouth to ask, then thought better of it. "That's pretty much what happened."

"Of course it did. Have you forgotten that when it comes to my cousin, no shits are given? If you do something stupid, he's gonna make sure you know it."

"Yeah, I'm kinda figuring that out the hard way too."

Ace stepped in front of him, a hand to Mason's shoulder. "Coop, just be careful, okay? I love you both, and I don't want to see either of you getting hurt. I know you, and I know Lucky. You two have a lot of shit from your pasts to work through, but if you both want this to happen, you'll find a way to make it work." He patted Mason's arm, then headed for the door. "Nice job on your first day, Cowboy. Talk to you later."

"Thanks, Ace."

Mason locked up after Ace, then went to take a shower. Unless Lucky called him in for a specific job, he'd be heading back to Four Kings Security headquarters in the morning. After throwing his clothes in the hamper, he grabbed a clean pair of boxer-briefs, a pair of pajama bottoms, and one of his comfortable T-shirts, then walked into the bathroom. It took forever for the damn water to heat, and he began seriously thinking about moving out. Funny, he hadn't really cared before. He was only ever here to sleep, and he never brought anyone home, so what did it matter? Now for some reason, he thought about Lucky here, and he couldn't picture it. Not because he was ashamed of his place, but because he wanted Lucky to be comfortable. Man, he was an idiot.

Mason stepped beneath the showerhead, the hot water pelting against his skin relaxing his muscles. He leaned a hand against the tiles, and let the water sluice over his body. He washed his hair, wiping it back out of his face. All he could think about was Lucky's naked body, that gorgeous ass spread in front of him. What Mason wouldn't give to taste him, to shove his tongue inside that greedy hole, eat him out good. No, he wanted more than that. He wanted to taste every inch of Lucky, wanted to run his hands over all that tanned skin, feel Lucky's stubble rub against his own bare skin.

Mason slid his hand down his abs toward the heavy cock jutting up against his belly. He was so fucking hard at the thought of Lucky, of running his tongue over his sleek muscles. Shit, his tattoo. Mason had been so damned hot and horny when he'd fucked Lucky, he hadn't gotten a good look at Lucky's tattoo. All he knew was it ran down the right side of his body. He'd seen a small piece of it from when Mason had pushed up Lucky's shirt to where it disappeared inside Lucky's pants. God, he'd love to run his tongue over that tattoo. Mason palmed his cock, hissing at how hard he was. Closing his eyes, he replayed their time in the truck, stroking himself off. He thought about Lucky on his knees sucking his cock, and fuck, Mason almost came.

"Fuck, darlin'. I bet those lips would look just sinful wrapped around my cock." He pictured Lucky on his knees, those long lashes resting on his cheeks as he guided the head of Mason's cock into his mouth, his tongue flicking out to lap up the pearls of precome on the tip of Mason's dick. Would he swallow Mason to the root? "Yeah, I bet you're real good at taking it down deep." Mason's hand moved faster as Lucky swallowed him whole, his hands on his own beautiful cock as he drove Mason wild with his mouth, the little black clover tattoo on his right hand between his thumb and forefinger so fucking sexy. "Oh fuck!" Mason came hard, his body trembling as his orgasm rolled through him. *I am so screwed.*

Washing himself up again, he finished quickly, then rinsed and dried himself before he got dressed. He walked into his bedroom, turned on his bedside lamp, then turned off the overhead lights, the only other light in the room coming from the sliver of moonlight peeking through the broken blinds of his window. Climbing into bed beneath his blanket, he grabbed his e-reader off the nightstand, then settled back against his pillow to do some reading. That lasted about as long as it took him to open his e-book. He couldn't get Lucky out of his thoughts, so why bother? He held his right hand up in front of him.

"It's you and me, buddy."

He'd just gotten a good rhythm at the thought of Lucky riding him when his phone went off. He cursed and considered ignoring it until he saw Lucky's name and grumpy face fill the screen. His fool heart did a flip, and he answered, smiling into the phone like the dope he was.

"Hey, darlin'. Thanks for the food. Best roast pork I've ever had."

"You're very welcome. I'm happy you did not eat the frozen cardboard mulch. No offense."

Mason chuckled. "None taken. That's pretty much what it would have tasted like."

"Are you okay? You sound a little out of breath."

"Um, yeah, I'm good." He placed his e-reader to one side, followed by his blanket now that his body was boiling over, thanks to Lucky reminding him of his little fantasy in the shower.

Silence. "Shit. I'm sorry. I didn't mean to interrupt. You could have just let the phone go to voicemail."

"What?"

"You're with someone."

"No. I'm not." Mason couldn't help feeling a little smug at Lucky's put-out tone, despite his acting like he was okay with whatever he thought Mason had been getting up to before he called.

Another pause. "Oh."

Mason smiled to himself, knowing Lucky was dying to know why he was out of breath. He purposefully let his voice go low and gravelly when he next spoke. "Did you need something?"

"¿Que?"

"You called me."

"I did?"

Mason held back a laugh. The guy was so goddamn adorable sometimes. "Yeah, you did."

"Oh, yes. Pack a bag for the weekend. Tomorrow we leave for Orlando. A young actress is doing a conference, and two of her bodyguards got very bad food poisoning. Are you up for a protection job? It's nothing you won't be able to handle. I'll come by in the morning around seven to pick you up. We can grab some breakfast on the way."

"Sounds good." After their little takedown job, he was looking forward to working another case with Lucky.

"Okay."

The line went quiet again, and Mason wondered if Lucky had hung up. "Lucky?"

"Hm?"

"Ask."

"Why are you out of breath?"

"Because after I came in the shower to the thought of you sucking my dick, I got into bed and was masturbating to the thought of you riding my dick."

"Jesus Christ."

"No, I was definitely picturing you." Mason chuckled at Lucky's Spanish curses. "You asked."

"I did."

"Lucky?" The silence didn't bode well. The longer Mason spent around Lucky, the better he knew his quirks. Generally, silence meant two things. Either Lucky was thinking hard on something or he was about to lose his shit. Mason hadn't done anything to make him lose his shit. Not in the last couple of hours anyway, so he figured it wasn't the former.

"It can't happen again."

Mason sighed. He'd been expecting it, but that didn't mean it didn't hurt his foolish heart. "I know."

"Do you?"

"I'm not going to ask you for something you're not prepared to give."

Lucky was quiet again.

"That's what you want right?" Was he holding his breath?

"Sí. Yes. It's what I want."

"Okay." Mason closed his eyes, his arm bent over his face.

"Maybe we start tomorrow."

Mason dropped his arm. "Oh?"

Lucky let out an annoyed huff. "Well, now all I can picture is you in bed with your hand on your dick, and that's not a very nice thing to do, to give me that image and then expect me to go to sleep like nothing."

"Hm, that's not nice at all, is it?"

"No, it's not. You can't just hang up and leave me with this image of you, and now I'm all flustered and uncomfortable. It will not be good for my sleep."

"Well, I wouldn't want to be responsible for you not getting a restful night's sleep."

"That's very good of you. What do you propose?"

"How about you turn the lights off, get into bed, and wrap your hand around your dick."

Lucky sucked in a sharp breath, and Mason grinned. He heard rustling, and then Lucky released a low moan. "Okay." His voice was breathy, and just like that, Mason was hard again. He closed his eyes and palmed his cock, gingerly stroking himself as he pictured Lucky in his bed.

"Now close your eyes, bend your knees, and spread them. I want you to picture me laying between your legs, my hands moving up your inner thighs, my face in your crotch. I'm taking a deep breath, inhaling your scent. You smell so fucking good."

"Mason." His name was barely a whisper, making Mason groan.

"That's it, darlin'. Can you see me?"

"Yes."

"Good. I'm licking a trail from your balls up to the base of your cock. Fuck, you're so hard for me, aren't you?"

"Yes. So hard."

"Do you want my hands on you? Touching you? Fondling your heavy sack?"

"Sí. Por favor, Mason."

"Move your hand slowly, just like how I'm moving my mouth on your dick after I swallow it down to the root."

"Fuck."

"Mm, yeah, that feels good, doesn't it? Slip your fingers in my hair and hold on tight. I love it when your hands are in my hair. I'm going to move my mouth faster now, but before I do, I'm going to wet a finger, and press it to your tight little hole. Do that for me now. Put the phone on the mattress next to you on speaker, and slick your finger up." Rustling met his ear, and then Lucky moaned. It went straight to Mason's cock. Fuck, he was so damn hard right now. His body was thrumming with need, the precome helping ease the glide of his hand. "Is your finger inside you?"

"Yes."

"Good, now I'm fucking your hole with my finger and sucking you off, working my tongue over that pretty pink head and sucking the pearly drops of come out of your slit."

"Oh fuck. *Fuck.*"

"That's it, Cariño."

Lucky's breath came out in pants. "I love when you speak Spanish to me."

"Yeah?"

"Tell me you do it for me, even if it's not true."

"Baby, I *am* doing it for you."

"Fuck!"

"That's it. Come in my mouth, Lucky. I want to taste your come on my tongue," Mason said through panting breaths. He saw Lucky so clearly in his mind, his gorgeous body naked and on offer, one finger inside himself as he jerked off to the image of Mason, his beautiful face a vision of pure pleasure as he pumped his cock.

"Fuck, yes!"

"Oh God. I'm so close, baby." Mason tweaked a nipple, thinking of Lucky's mouth on him.

"I want you to come all over me. Make a mess of me, Cowboy." Lucky gasped. "¡Ay, Dios mío! Mi amor, no puedo...."

"Yes, you can, darlin'. That's it," Mason purred, his heart soaring at Lucky calling him his love, even if he didn't mean it the way Mason wished he did. "You're so fucking beautiful. Come on, baby. Come for me. Come in my mouth." The image had Mason roaring his release, followed by Lucky seconds later. His bedroom filled with the sound of their gasps, panting, and curses as they came to the thought of each other. Soon it was only the sound of their breath steadying until Lucky spoke up.

"Holy shit."

"Yeah."

"That was.... I don't even know."

"Fucking amazing," Mason offered, his hand on his chest, as if by doing so he could steady his heartbeat.

Lucky laughed softly, making Mason smile. "Is it true?"

"What?" What he wouldn't give to have Lucky here in his bed with him, curled up beside him. Mason rolled over, his phone held close to his ear. God, he was such a sucker.

"About the Spanish. Why you're learning."

"If it was?"

"Why?"

"Do you really want me to answer that?"

"Maybe no," Lucky said softly. "You're a good man, Mason."

"But?"

"I will hurt you, or you will hurt me, and I don't want any of those things."

"Neither do I. Who says those things have to happen?"

"Why did my cousin leave you?"

Mason sighed heavily. "Because despite what you think, I'm not a good man, darlin', but I'm trying to be."

"And whatever it is that makes you think you're not a good man, did Ace know this?"

"No."

"Ah, that's why he left."

"Yes. You know your cousin. The truth is everything to him."

"And to me."

"Yeah. Which is why you're right, about us hurting each other." They were too combustible as it was, and that didn't bode well for any kind of long-term relationship. Once the explosions were over and the smoke evaporated, what then? What would happen to them after the fire fizzled?

"I am not my cousin."

"I know, baby."

Lucky let out a little huff at the pet name, making Mason smile again. The man had no idea how endearing he could be, or how Mason smiled more around him than he did with anyone else in his life. Despite their heated arguments, Mason felt safe around Lucky, like maybe he wasn't as terrible a person as he believed himself to be.

"How long will you be punishing yourself for whatever it is you did?"

Mason opened his eyes. "What are you talking about?"

"I've seen many terrible things in my life. In Cuba and as a soldier. I know a man haunted by his past deeds when I see one. It's in your eyes. You have very sad eyes."

Well, shit. What the hell was he supposed to say to that? Lucky was certainly more observant than Mason gave him credit for, but then it made sense. Lucky had said it himself. Once a soldier, always a soldier.

"You lose yourself in your job. It's what drives you. When was the last time you took time off? I bet the answer is never. That's why you went to King for work, no? To not be alone with your thoughts?"

"I knew you were more than just a pretty face."

Lucky chuckled. "Cabrón."

"I like you, Lucky, I really do." *Too much.*

A quiet pause before Lucky spoke, his voice soft, resigned. "I like you too, Cowboy. Most days."

Mason laughed at that. "Little shit."

"Goodnight, Mason."

"Goodnight." Mason hung up, knowing if he didn't do it now, he wouldn't do it at all. He loved listening to Lucky talk and could easily just lay there listening to him breathe until he fell asleep. He returned the phone to his nightstand, grabbed a couple of wet wipes from the drawer, and cleaned himself off. He tossed the little towelettes in the small trashcan beneath the nightstand, then put away his e-reader and turned off the lights. Rolling onto his side, he closed his eyes, and despite the finality to Lucky's words,

Mason didn't feel them in his heart. He needed to give them some serious thought. If he wanted any kind of future with Lucky, he'd have to come clean. It wouldn't guarantee Lucky would want to keep him—in fact it was likely he'd never want to speak to Mason again—but at least he'd stop wondering *what if*.

SIX

TODAY WAS A SUIT-AND-TIE DAY.

It was odd having to change his wardrobe based on the job he was doing. As a detective, his job was always the same—investigate. Working for the Kings, he'd learned he needed to adapt to each job. One day he was working surveillance, the next protection. It certainly left no room for predictable routine.

The next morning, Mason dressed in the black suit, white shirt, and black tie, as per Lucky's instructions. It had been a while since he'd worn his suit. Thank God it still fit. Lucky arrived to pick him up, dressed the same, though he looked far sharper in what was clearly a slim-fitting designer suit. It was tailored for his athletic frame. Mason smiled as he clicked his seat belt into place, his eyes landing on Lucky's black clover cufflink, the center of which housed a small black jewel.

"Looking fine, Mr. King of Clubs."

"You too, Cowboy."

Fine was an understatement. Lucky was breathtaking. Yet, all Mason could think of was unwrapping him like a

Christmas present. Maybe he should turn the AC up in the SUV before he melted from his sinful thoughts. Mason was pleasantly surprised when they stopped at Colton's house for breakfast on the way to Orlando. He reminded himself it was Ace's house too, but it was hard associating Ace with the multimillion-dollar mansion. They got out of the SUV, and Mason groaned as he was met with a waft of hot air.

"Fucking Florida. It's October and still ninety degrees." Combined with the humidity, he was sweating in his suit by the time they got from the driveway to the front door.

"Don't worry. In a month or two, it will drop down to, like, maybe seventy," Lucky teased. "Who knows. This could be the year you get to wear a Christmas sweater."

The thought horrified Mason. "Sweater? You think I own a sweater living in this ostentatious overheated swampland you call a state?"

"You are so precious in the morning before coffee."

Was he?

"You know, for someone who is from Texas, you bitch about the heat a lot. Like, *a lot*."

Mason shook his head. "Not the same. Yeah, in the summer Texas is hot as all get-out, but it's the goddamn Florida humidity that'll kill ya, and the bugs. And stupid people. I have a list."

Lucky laughed at him. "I bet you do, Cowboy."

The door opened, and Colton greeted them with a big smile. "Mason, so good to see you. Look at you. You clean up nice, Mr. Cooper."

"What about me?" Lucky asked, holding his arms out. "I'm chopped liver?"

Colton rolled his eyes. "I see you every day, but yes, you look very handsome as always."

"Thank you."

At the end of the hallway, Ace popped his head out from around the corner, his eyes narrowed. He motioned between Colton and Mason. "Have I mentioned how deeply I disapprove of this?"

"Yes, love. Many times." Colton chuckled and stepped aside so they could come in.

"You better not have eaten all the bacon already," Lucky warned his cousin.

"Bacon? What bacon? I'm making oatmeal. Healthy, mushy oatmeal."

"Don't mess with me, Ace." Lucky stormed off and disappeared around the corner.

Mason shook his head in amusement. Never a dull moment around those two. He started to follow, but Colton caught hold of his elbow, his big gray eyes filled with worry. Mason was glad Ace had found a good man like Colton, someone who made him happy and gave him what he needed.

"How are things between you two?"

Mason patted Colton's hand where it rested on his elbow. It was good to have friends who cared. As much of a pain in the ass as the Kings and their significant others could be, they were good people, and Mason considered himself blessed to have them in his life. "We're working through it. Neither of us is very good at the whole relationship thing."

"Do you want to be?"

"I think so." He was shocked at how true that was. And Jesus, wasn't that just so fucking typical of him? The guy who *had* wanted commitment, who'd wanted a life with him, Mason hadn't been able to hold on to, but the guy who'd clearly stated he wanted nothing more was the one Mason wanted to keep. *Fuck my life.*

"Then work at it. I know it doesn't seem like it at times, but I really do think you're good for each other."

"Thanks, Colton."

They walked into the kitchen, and Mason smiled at Red and Laz, who sat at the kitchen counter, heads close together, talking quietly. Red stood when he saw Mason and hugged him, giving him a hearty pat on the back.

"Hey, Cowboy."

"Hey, Red." Mason turned to Laz. "Hey, Laz. Nice to see you both." There was a commotion at the door, followed by a bark. "That the neighbor's golden retriever come to fetch some more of Lucky's shoes?"

Lucky glared at Mason over his shoulder from where he stood by the stove with Ace. "Very funny, Cowboy. We'll see how funny you think it is when she turns *your* shoe into a chew toy."

"Hey, if she can haul one of my steel-toed boots off, she deserves it. Things weigh a fuckton."

Joker and Jack rounded the corner, something furry and black whizzing by them to get to Mason.

"Well, who's this now?" Mason asked, crouching down in front of the gorgeous black dog wagging its tail at him.

"That's Chip. He's an attention whore," Joker replied with a crooked grin.

"Like his human," Ace pitched in from beside Lucky.

Joker flipped him off.

"It's true, though," Lucky said, laughing when Joker rushed over, threw an arm around him, and playfully punched him in the ribs. He planted a sloppy kiss on Lucky's cheek.

"Pot, kettle, Morales."

Mason ruffled Chip's fur, giving him some good

scratches behind the ears. Speaking of which.... "You've got some epic ears there, buddy. What breed is he?"

Joker walked over, giving the tip of one a little rub. "He's a Belgian Malinois. His hearing is so good, sometimes he howls when we're at the park and I swear it's because he can hear Ace's bad singing from all the way over here."

"Keep it up," Ace grumbled, thrusting a fork in Joker's direction, "and Chip's going to get all your bacon."

At the word *bacon*, Chip barked and darted over to Ace, pawing at him and wagging his tail.

Joker threw up his arms. "What did I tell you guys about using the *B* word around him?"

Mason stood with a chuckle. "Won't stop bugging you until you give him some, huh?"

"If only." Joker planted his hands on his hips, his expression firm as he narrowed his eyes at Chip. "No bacon."

Chip studied Joker's face before letting out a little whine.

"No."

With a huff, Chip sat, flopped onto his side, and just lay there in the middle of the kitchen giving Joker the side-eye.

"You see. This is what happens. He will literally lay there until you give him what he wants." He shook his head at Chip. "Get up. You're embarrassing yourself."

Chip made some doggy noises that sounded like he was arguing, making everyone laugh.

"Don't encourage him. He's being an asshole."

Chip barked, and Joker crossed his arms over his chest. "Don't you take that tone with me, pal. I'm the boss around here, not you."

Chip continued to argue his case for bacon while Joker argued in return. The more Joker refused, the louder Chip got.

"What if you're on the job?" Mason asked, curious.

"That's different. Despite his diva attitude, if he's focused on the job, you can slap him with a steak and he won't budge. My boy's a soldier like his daddy."

"Smarter than his daddy too," Ace teased.

Joker flipped him off again. "Chip's better trained than most people." He cast Ace a pointed look before turning his attention back to Chip. "Watch." Joker's demeanor changed from one heartbeat to the next. His body tensed, and he turned deadly serious. "Chip, steh."

Lunging to his paws, Chip's body went rigid, his complete focus on Joker.

"Setzen."

Chip sat, his gaze never leaving Joker's.

"Wait, that's German, isn't it?" Mason had come across a few K-9 units whose dogs were trained to follow German commands. In some cases, the dogs were actually from Germany and had been trained there.

"Yep. On the job, he follows German commands, but he only takes orders from me anyway. It helps with security and keeps him from getting confused. Braver hund!"

Chip immediately relaxed, tail wagging, mouth open, and tongue out in a happy smile. Joker took the bacon Ace handed him and put a finger up. "Don't scarf it." He held out the bacon, and Chip took it gently between his front teeth, then trotted off with it.

"Okay, breakfast is ready," Ace announced. "Sit your asses down."

Lucky stole a piece of bacon, ignoring his cousin's curses. He stopped in front of Mason, snapped the crunchy piece in half, and held one end up to Mason. "Here. Try it. It's really good."

Mason wrapped his hand around Lucky's wrist, leaned

in, and took the piece of bacon into his mouth, his eyes never leaving Lucky's. The way Lucky's whiskey-colored eyes filled with scalding heat was a thing of beauty.

"Mm, that is good, darlin'. Thank you."

"This is weird," Ace muttered, staring at them. "My boyfriend is friends with my ex, who's got the hots for my cousin. This is my life. It's like one of my mom's telenovelas but with less slapping and flaring nostrils."

Colton chuckled and kissed Ace's cheek. "You're so cute when you're scandalized. Now come on, the horde is getting restless." He helped Ace carry plates of bacon and scrambled eggs into the dining room.

Mason leaned into Lucky, murmuring in his ear. "Ace isn't wrong, you know."

"That his life is like a telenovela? Yes, I know this."

"No, that I have the hots for his cousin."

Lucky gasped. "You have the hots for Checho?"

Mason blinked at him. "Your cousin's name is Checho?"

"Well, his name is Sergei, but everyone calls him Checho." Lucky headed for the table with Mason at his side.

"Oh, right. The whole nickname thing." Mason sat at the table, smiling to himself when Lucky took a seat next to him instead of near Ace. "Wait, what's *your* nickname."

Lucky shook his head, his gaze everywhere but on Mason. "I don't have one."

Ace let out a bark of laughter. "Oh my God, you are so full of shit!"

The table burst into laughter at Lucky's scowl. If looks could kill, Ace would be in a whole heap of trouble right now.

"His nickname is Candi," Joker offered, earning him a daggered look from Lucky.

Mason put a hand to his heart. "Aw, your family calls you candy?"

"No," Jack corrected. "Candi. It's short for candela. Fire."

"Is that right?" Mason laughed. "That is just perfect." He knew Ace's nickname because he'd heard his family call him Chulo—meaning cute—rather than his real name, though his mother tended to use a different term of endearment every time she spoke to him. Mason had learned real quick that everyone in Ace and Lucky's family had a nickname, either a shorter version of their name or one relating to their personality. It still confused the fuck out of him, and he had no idea how the family kept track of everyone, but they did.

"What's all the ruckus about?"

"There he is!" Ace grinned wide at King as he rounded the corner, shaking his head at them.

"Looks like they just let anyone in here," Jack teased, getting a flick to the ear from King.

Mason snickered. "Well, I'll be damned. Ward Kingston eats?"

"Didn't know you were a comedian in your spare time, Cowboy." King took a seat in the empty chair across from Ace.

The room filled with the sound of ribbing, talking, and laughter. It struck Mason that this was the first time he'd been invited to a meal with the Kings in one of their homes. When he'd been dating Ace, he'd eaten with Ace in his apartment, and although they'd joined Ace's brothers-in-arms for plenty of meals, it was usually at Bibi's or a local bar, never in their home where they all gathered.

The Kings shared meals together, often at Colton's house since it was the biggest, had a game room, and access to a private section of the beach. These meals were reserved for family, and although Mason had been informed he *was* family, this was the first time he'd truly felt it, and it was because of Lucky.

Lucky leaned into Mason, his tone concerned. "You okay?"

"Yeah, I am. Thanks." And it was the truth. He beamed brightly at Lucky, nudging his shoulder playfully to reassure him. The meal was amazing, a combination of Cuban and American dishes, everything from bacon and scrambled eggs to chicken croquettes, café con leche, and Cuban bread. Lucky frowned as he scanned the table.

"¿Oye, Ace, y las empanadas?"

"Shit. They're in the oven. I didn't want them to get cold."

Jack scoffed. "Yeah, right. You just wanted to keep them for yourself."

Ace gasped. "How dare you insinuate I would try to keep such deliciousness from my beloved brothers. I am offended."

"Wow." Joker shook his head. He turned to look at Jack. "He actually said that."

Jack snickered. "You're talking about the guy who told his last boyfriend he had food poisoning so he could wait in line for the new iPhone."

Mason sat up. "Wait a second. *I* was your last boyfriend! You shit. I was worried about you puking your guts out, and you were standing me up for a phone?"

Ace blinked at him. "My usual contact got the flu, so I had to wait in line like normal people. It sucked."

"Ace," Colton said sweetly, and the whole table went silent. *Uh-oh.* "Remember last month when we were going to visit my mother and you got food poisoning?"

Ace cringed. "In my defense, I *was* actually sick."

Joker and Jack exchanged glances before bursting into laughter. Joker wiped a tear from his eye. "Oh my God, I can't believe you did it."

Colton narrowed his eyes at Ace. "What did you do?"

"Um...." Ace shot to his feet. "I should get those empanadas."

"Anston Sharpe! Did you make yourself sick to get out of visiting my mother?"

"Only a little bit," Ace admitted. "Come on, babe. Your mom's real nice and all, but she keeps trying to dress me."

Colton stood and threw his napkin on the table. "She's trying to connect with you."

"By making me wear a wool suit? It's *Florida*! You know how itchy wool makes me?"

"I hope the couch doesn't make you itch because that's where you're going to be sleeping for the foreseeable future!" Colton stormed off and a door slammed somewhere in the distance not long after.

Ace glared at Joker and Jack. "You guys are assholes."

"Hey," Joker scolded, shaking his head at Ace. "Who's the one who gave himself food poisoning to get out of spending time with his boyfriend's mother? I mean, come on, Ace. That was a dick move."

King tilted his head, his mouth full of Cuban bread. "He has a point."

Ace growled in frustration, most likely realizing that—heaven forbid—he was actually wrong, before he went after Colton.

"I hope they'll be okay." Laz looked toward the hallway where Ace disappeared to, his eyes filled with concern.

"They'll be fine," Lucky assured him. "Ace isn't stupid, even though he sometimes does stupid things. He's crazy about Colton, so now he gets to make it up to him. I'll be right back. I'm going to get the empanadas." He was back in no time, presenting the plate to Mason. He pointed to one side. "This side is guayaba, that side picadillo."

"What's picadillo again?" He knew guayaba was guava, but he always forgot the other one.

"Ground beef."

"That's right. I'll have one of those." He took a ground beef pastry because it was breakfast and he wasn't really a sweets-for-breakfast kind of guy.

A cell phone rang, and Laz pulled out his phone, his expression lighting up. "It's Gio. Excuse me, guys. I need to take this." Laz jogged out of the dining room and slipped outside through the glass doors to the patio.

"Ah, Saint Gio." Joker grunted. "Does that guy even fucking exist?"

Red scowled at him. "Yes, asshole, he exists."

"Why haven't I ever seen him, then? I mean, come on. A billionaire who travels the world saving people? Who is this guy? Batman? All we hear is how amazing he is. No one is that good."

Red rolled his eyes. "First of all, he's not a billionaire. Second, believe it or not, Gio has better things to do than worry about whether you believe he exists."

Joker waved a hand in dismissal. "Yeah, yeah. Being a saint is tough. Whatever."

Jack frowned at his friend. "What is the deal with you and this guy? You've never even met him, and you've got a hard-on for him."

"I do not have a hard-on for him. I just think he's hiding something."

"J," King warned. "Ease up."

"Come on, King. There's no way this guy is as perfect as

everyone thinks he is. He might have all of you fooled, but until he's in front of me and I can look him in the eye, I'm not buying it."

Red stood and narrowed his gaze at Joker. "Fine, but you keep your opinion to yourself. Gio means the world to Laz, and I don't want you upsetting him. He's also Colton's best friend. It's hard enough for them with Gio being gone all the time."

"I won't say a word." Joker held his hand up in promise.

The room erupted into cheers when Colton and Ace returned. Colton's cheeks were flushed, his suit a little rumpled, and his tie crooked. He was smiling from ear to ear at something Ace whispered. They made a very handsome pair.

"I hope you made him grovel," Joker told Colton, laughing at Ace's glare.

Colton took a seat at the table. "There was a sufficient amount of groveling." He kissed Ace's cheek. "He's making it up to me."

Ace nodded. "Yep." He turned to King. "By the way, I need next weekend off. I'm taking Colton's mother shopping in Paris."

"Must be nice to have a boyfriend with a private plane," Joker grumbled.

Ace stuck his tongue out before turning his attention back to King. "So, yes?"

"I'll need to do a little shuffling around with the schedule, but sure. Should be fine."

"And on that note, it's time for us to go." Lucky stood, patting Mason's shoulder. "Let's hit the road, Cowboy."

Mason stood, thanked Colton for his hospitality, and shook hands with the rest of the guys, leaving King for last. King was surprising him a lot lately.

"I just wanted to say good job yesterday. The client was exceptionally pleased. The security contract with their current company is ending next month, and they won't be renewing. The team we had in place was supposed to be temporary, but thanks to everyone who worked the case, we now have a new contract with Techu Technologies, so thank you."

"You're welcome. Not gonna lie, it felt good knowing I had whatever I needed at my disposal."

"Budget cutbacks are a bitch," King agreed.

Mason nodded. So much of his job involved a never-ending stream of red tape, budget cutbacks, not enough cars, equipment, personnel. He'd become a cop to help people, to make a difference, but at times it felt like he was fighting a losing battle. Sometimes justice wasn't served, and there was little he could do about it.

Thankfully the tension between Joker and Red had eased. The good thing about the Kings was that they couldn't seem to stay pissed at one another for long and preferred to talk things out. Joker acknowledged he was being kind of a jerk, and Red accepted that it was coming from a place of concern for both Laz and Red. From what Mason had learned about Joker, the guy was the least trustful of the group and the most cynical. He didn't know what Joker's deal was, since the guy never talked about himself, but he was glad to see things had quickly gone back to normal between everyone. Well, as normal as things could be with this group.

"That was nice, by the way." Mason fastened his seat belt as Lucky pulled out of the drive way. "Thank you for bringing me along."

"Of course. You're part of the family, Mason."

"Still. It was nice." He saw Lucky wanted to ask something, and he worried it was going to be about his family, or lack thereof, so he quickly changed the subject. "Who are we protecting?"

"Sienna Scott."

"Why's that name familiar?" They drove down Palm Valley Road, Nocatee Parkway, and Country Road 210 to get onto I-95 South. Traffic was pretty shit, but then it usually was at this time of day, despite having missed morning rush hour.

"She played a kick-ass comic book superhero in that summer blockbuster movie. It made her career explode, so this conference is going to be a little crazy. It's not a huge con like Comic Con or anything, but this is Sienna's first big event since the movie came out. From what her agent told me, she's very shy. There's an entire security team in place, but the two security agents with food poisoning were her personal bodyguards, one who was brought in at the last minute because of all the crazy. We'll be taking over for them. We keep her safe while the other security agents handle everything else."

"I'm guessing you got equipment for us?" Mason frowned at the black Jeep in their lane two cars back. Was it the same one that had been behind them when they'd left Colton's?

"I'll go through everything after we check in at the hotel." Lucky cleared his throat and shifted in his seat, drawing Mason's attention.

"What?"

"Hm?"

Mason was so not buying that innocent expression. "What aren't you telling me?"

"It's not a big deal. Thing is, the hotel has been booked solid for months because of the conference, especially after the movie came out, so there were no more rooms, which is fine, because the bodyguards we're filling in for were staying next door to Sienna."

"Okay." Mason peered at him. "What's the problem?"

Lucky cringed. "Well, no problem. Maybe. I don't know. There is only one bed."

"One bed? Were the bodyguards sharing?" Mason checked the passenger-side mirror for the Jeep, relieved to find it was gone. Working security must be making him paranoid. Having almost been run down by a speeding SUV the previous night probably didn't help either. He'd been a cop so long that it was second nature to question everything and look for connections that often weren't even there. In his book, coincidences were a rare occurrence. Lucky's voice snapped him out of his thoughts.

"Yes. Remember I said one bodyguard was brought in at the last minute? Originally there was only the one bodyguard scheduled to come, but with the craziness, things changed, so they added a second personal bodyguard. There were no more rooms, so they were going to share."

Mason waved a hand in dismissal. "It'll be fine. I'm sure there's a couch or something."

THERE WAS NO COUCH.

After checking in, they'd followed the bellman and luggage cart containing their bags—and a large trunk that looked like it belonged in an armored vehicle—to their room. Their one-bed, couchless room. Everything had been arranged before Sienna made it big, which meant no entire floor booked just for her and her entourage, no luxury penthouse suites, and no chance of cancellation due to the number of fans who'd come to see her.

Their room was nice as far as hotel rooms went. Mason had stayed in far worse places with questionable hygiene. The hotel being full to capacity meant no cots were available either.

They stood in front of the king-size bed, staring at it.

Fuck.

Shit, don't think fuck. You should not *be thinking of fuck.*

"It's fine," Lucky declared. "You take the bed, and I'll call for extra pillows and blankets, a duvet, and sleep on the floor."

"What? You're not sleeping on the goddamn floor," Mason growled.

Lucky waved a hand in dismissal. "*Pfft.* I've slept in much worse places for days on end, Cowboy. I can handle sleeping on a carpet for two nights."

"Who the hell knows what's in that carpet. I will not be responsible for you contracting some kind of hideous disease. You're not sleeping on the damn floor. It's a king-size bed. Plenty of room for both of us."

"I... don't think that's a good idea."

Was Lucky blushing? Probably just the lighting. "We're adults."

"Yes, we are. Adults who've had sex twice, even if once was over the phone."

"You saying we can't sleep in the same bed without having sex?"

Lucky shrugged. "I don't know. Can we?"

"That's not helping."

"I'm only speaking the truth."

"I can keep my hands to myself."

"Are you saying I can't?" Lucky crossed his arms over his chest, his eyes narrowed.

Mason shrugged.

"Fine." Lucky grabbed his black leather duffle bag and placed it on the bed.

Mason didn't know much about designer stuff. He'd been wearing the same brand of Wrangler jeans since he could remember. He'd heard of Coach, however, and knew they were expensive as hell.

"What is it with you and designer brands?"

Lucky cast him a sideways glance, and Mason quickly put his hands up. "I'm not having a dig. I'm genuinely curious."

"I would rather spend good money on something that is functional and fashionable that will last me for many years."

"And you can't get that with a less expensive brand?"

"You can," Lucky conceded. He let out a heavy sigh and dropped his gaze to his bag. "Growing up in Cuba, I had almost nothing. Whenever we got anything sent to us from overseas, it never lasted. It would be taken from us by members of the Comité."

"The what?"

"The Comités de Defensa de la Revolución. The CDR. A system formed by Castro back in the '60s. Sort of a fucked-up version of your neighborhood watch. It's a way for the government to spy on its people, often giving power to immoral and repulsive individuals. The president of our CDR wanted my mother, and because she refused him, he made our lives a living hell." Lucky took a seat on the bed and ran a hand through his short hair, staring off in the distance at nothing in particular. The pain in his eyes was clear as day, and all Mason wanted to do was reach out and bring him into his arms, but he didn't dare move.

"When money, food, or clothing was sent from our family, the president's men would either steal it the moment it entered the country or come to our house and take everything. My father struggled to find a job because no one would hire him. One bad referral from the president of your CDR and your family was marked. Had I stayed, I would not have been accepted into any college, my options most likely limited to joining the government. There were days when we had no food or had only scraps of bread. Our neighbors had been warned. Anyone who gave us food or help in any way would be marked as well.

"The president didn't care if we starved. One week, we had no food for two days, and I remember crying, telling my mamá I was very hungry. My father was in Havana, trying to find some work, and wouldn't return for another week. My mother held me, kissed my head, and told me she loved me very much. She tucked me into bed that night and said to stay, be good. I didn't understand why. She left and returned many hours later with a bag full of groceries. I was so excited. I had never seen so much food in the whole of my life."

Mason felt sick to his stomach. "Did she...?"

Lucky pursed his lips and blinked away his tears. "It was only when I was old enough that I understood what she had done, the sacrifice she had made. When my father returned from Havana, my mother burst into tears. I was sent outside to play. For a long time, my father felt like a failure, but it was not his fault. When I was fourteen, my tía sent for us. I don't know how she did it, but she found a way to bring us here." He removed a toiletry bag from his duffle bag and held it in his hands like it was something precious. It broke Mason's heart.

"When my family arrived in this country with only the

clothes on our backs, we worked hard. We were determined to make the most of the opportunities given to us. It wasn't easy. When you are 'fresh off the boat,' people are not always kind to you, not even some fellow Cubans. They believe you've come to live off them or take advantage of the American government. My parents worked in factories during the day and cleaned offices at night to save up for a home to call our own. I have worked since I was fourteen, doing whatever job I could that would pay money. It took many years, but we built lives for ourselves. I promised myself I would never be in the position my family was in ever again, that my mother would *never* want for anything. I know they are just things. Meaningless possessions."

"But they're not, are they?" Mason said softly, taking a seat beside Lucky. "They're a way for you to measure how far you've come, to physically see your success."

Lucky grimaced. "I think that sounded better in your head, no?"

"What I mean is, that everyone measures success differently. You've been through a hell of a lot in your lifetime, Lucky. You've seen and experienced terrible things. You're a successful adult who co-owns a business and works damn hard for what he earns. If you want to buy yourself a pair of Guiseppe Manicotti—"

Lucky burst into laughter. "Zanotti. Manicotti is a pasta."

"Close enough."

Lucky snickered. "Okay."

"What I mean is, you don't need to justify your actions to anyone. Not even me."

Lucky worried his bottom lip before speaking up. "That's not entirely true."

"Why?"

"Maybe I care what you think." He shrugged. "Maybe I worry you think I'm shallow and materialistic."

Mason put his fingers beneath Lucky's chin and turned his face so their eyes met. "I would never think that of you. You're an amazing man, Eduardo Morales."

"Thank you." Lucky popped a quick kiss on Mason's lips, then made to dart away, but Mason caught his arm.

"Whoa there, hotshot. Where's the fire?" He pulled Lucky back to him, spreading his knees for Lucky to step between them. He smiled wide at Lucky's flushed face. Emotional Lucky tended to go off like an explosion. Vulnerable Lucky, he tried to hide. *There's no hiding from me, darlin'.*

"What?" Lucky's grumble was sweet.

"You think you can just lay one on me like that and take off? What if I want to reciprocate?"

"Um, I'm not sure what that means."

"Return the favor, darlin'. I want to kiss you."

"Oh. We need to get to work."

"And we will. No funny business." Mason held a hand up and gave Lucky his most charming smile. "You have my word, Cariño."

Lucky eyed him suspiciously, making Mason laugh. "Okay." He leaned in and pressed his lips to Mason's, his eyes drifting shut as Mason tilted his head and parted his lips, welcoming Lucky's tongue. The kiss was slow, their tongues dancing, exploring, savoring. Lucky moaned against his lips, and Mason pulled back with a hum, smiling against Lucky's lips.

"Now we can get to work."

"You are impossible."

"I think you meant to say wonderful."

Lucky pretended to think about it. "No, I'm pretty sure I meant impossible."

"What's the game plan?"

Lucky tapped away at the tablet and brought up what looked like the layout of one of the hotel's floors, more specifically their floor. He went through the plan of action, pointing out the route they'd take, locations of the emergency exits, the elevators, and where the dressing room was in relation to the signing area. When he was done explaining the plan and backup plan in detail, he looked up at Mason. "Got it?"

"Yep." It all seemed very straightforward.

Lucky put down the tablet. "When we go into a room, I always go in first. You stay next to Sienna. When we get to an elevator, you go in first with Sienna, and I'll follow."

"Why is that?"

"If there is a threat, they have to go through me first to get to you and Sienna."

"You mean Sienna."

"That's what I said."

"You included me. I'm not your priority."

Lucky nodded, his jaw clenched tight before he answered. "You're right. Sienna is my priority, but I included you as well because I won't let anyone get to you either."

Mason's heart skipped a beat at the admission. Good God, the man's honesty was going to kill him. "Okay."

"You follow no one's orders but mine unless Sienna's life is in danger. Then you follow your instincts. I don't need to tell you what danger looks or feels like. You have plenty of experience with crowd control and spotting potential threats." Lucky walked over to the huge armored case and motioned him over. "You're the only other person in this hotel with access to this case. Enter your security pin on the keypad and press the hashtag key after, then press your index finger to the biometric scanner.

Mason followed Lucky's instructions, and the case unlocked. Inside was a small arsenal, including two conceal-able white vests in protective packaging. Lucky handed one to Mason.

"Put that on under your shirt."

"You planning on getting shot at?"

"Hope for the best, prepare for the worst. We never do a protection job without a vest. Unless you're Ace and think you don't need one, but then you get to be yelled at by King, so it's better to wear the vest."

"Got it." Mason stood and removed his jacket, then draped it over the armchair next to the case. His tie and shirt followed, leaving him in his white tank undershirt. He lifted his gaze and found Lucky staring at his arm. He flexed his bicep, and Lucky moved his eyes to Mason's, arching one eyebrow. "What? There's nothing wrong with admiring a fella. Come' ere. I'll give you a feel."

Lucky rolled his eyes and shoved the vest at him. "Put the vest on, Cowboy."

"Yes, sir." He strapped himself into the lightweight vest. "Hey, this is real nice." The Kings sure did have some nifty toys.

Once they were dressed, their vests beneath their shirts, Lucky handed him a Glock tucked securely into a holster that his belt slipped through. A small radio was clipped to his belt, and a discreet earpiece went into his ear.

Lucky headed for the door, and Mason followed. "We'll check in with the rest of the team to make sure everyone can be heard okay, but for now, we're meeting with Sienna and her agent, Ryan Mills. After, we can do a walkthrough." He checked his watch. "We have three hours until Sienna is due at the signing. Until she's secure, we don't leave her side for anything. Sienna will be signing for four and a half hours with a half hour break after two hours. Then she'll return to her room. When she's signing, I'll stand to her right, and you to her left. Tomorrow, fans who have purchased the photo package will be permitted to take pictures with her. We'll stand as close to her as possible without being in the picture. Fans have been given a list of what they can and cannot do." Lucky straightened and pulled his phone out of his pocket. He tapped away at it, and Mason's phone vibrated. "I've sent the list to you. It'll be up to us to enforce these rules."

Mason pulled his phone out of his pocket and read the list. It was straightforward. Nothing lewd, inappropriate, or offensive. There was a long list of examples which included no kissing. Sienna might be a celebrity in the public's eye, but she was still an eighteen-year-old who deserved to be treated respectfully.

Lucky greeted the two men standing guard outside Sienna's door. "Good day, gentleman. I am Eduardo Morales from Four Kings Security, and this is my associate Mason Cooper. I'm going to reach into my pocket to pull out my ID." They showed the guards their IDs and thanked them when they were let into the room.

A tall blond man in a tailored suit greeted them, his smile wide. "Gentlemen, I'm Ryan Mills. It's a pleasure to meet you. Thank you so much for helping us out. I know it was all very last minute. Please come in. Let me introduce you to—"

"Who is it?" a gruff male voice called out from the bathroom. Whoever it was, Ryan was *not* a fan, judging by his less-than-thrilled expression.

"It's the gentlemen from Four Kings Security, Wyatt."

The bathroom door opened, and a very large, red-faced man in a brown suit stepped out.

"Wyatt, we have one of the Kings here, as you requested, along with his associate. This is Eduardo Morales and Mason Cooper. Gentlemen, this is Sienna's father, Wyatt Smith."

Wyatt held his hand out to Mason. "Pleasure to meet you, Mr. Cooper. Thank you so much for being here."

"Happy to help, sir." Mason frowned when Wyatt turned to Lucky and instead of shaking his hand, looked him over, his smile gone.

"What experience do you have, Mr. Morales?"

Lucky looked from Wyatt to Mason as if perhaps Mason understood. When Mason frowned, Lucky turned his attention back to Wyatt. "I'm sorry?"

"Dad," Sienna said, looking mortified for some reason.

"No, I need to know you're in safe hands." Wyatt turned to Mason. "How long has he worked for you?"

Why the hell would the guy assume Lucky worked for—oh. "Mr. Smith, I'm not—"

"I know most people don't ask these types of questions, and your company has a stellar reputation, but this is my daughter's safety we're talking about. Since it's your company, I expect you know who your employees are. I just want your assurance that you've got the best with you."

"Sir, Mr. Morales is—"

"Listen, how you run your company is up to you, but I need to know everything is on the up and up. I know how things here in Florida work."

Jesus fuck. Was the guy even going to let him finish a damn sentence? Wyatt was really starting to piss him off, especially now that Mason knew why the man assumed Lucky worked for him.

"Is he *qualified*?" Wyatt asked.

Mason stared at him. Was this guy serious? That had to be the dumbest question he'd ever heard. He'd *just* said Four Kings had a stellar reputation. Why would he ask if an employee of said company would be qualified? Before Mason could respond, and no doubt stick his foot in it, Lucky spoke up.

"That's his way of asking if I am an illegal immigrant," Lucky offered, and a growl rose up from Mason's chest as he balled his hands into fists at his sides. Lucky put a hand to Mason's bicep. "Easy, Cowboy."

Wyatt put his hands up. "It's a perfectly valid question."

Ryan took Lucky's hand in his, his face doing a great impression of a tomato. "Oh my God, I am so sorry, Mr. Morales."

"Why are you apologizing?" Wyatt asked. Realization seemed to dawn on him, and his eyes went huge. He moved his gaze to Mason.

"Yeah, I'm not a King," Mason drawled. He pointed at Lucky. "He is. *I* work for *him*."

Wyatt fidgeted with his tie. "I, uh, I apologize, Mr. Morales. I'm just looking out for my daughter."

Mason had to give Lucky credit. He was a much bigger man than Mason would have been. His smile was friendly, and he tipped his head in acceptance of Wyatt's apology.

"Of course. Maybe next time, you are not so quick to judge a man, you know?"

"Right. Again, my apologies," Wyatt said, his skin flushed from his neck to his ears.

"Please, call me Lucky." He held his hand out to Wyatt, who shook it.

Wyatt cleared his throat and showed them over to the couch—because of course *they* had a couch. "I admit, I didn't pay much attention to the photos, but the packet I received from your office says you fellas were in the military."

"Yes, sir. Special Forces."

"Thank you for your service."

Lucky nodded before turning to Sienna with a bright smile. "Hello, Ms. Scott. It's a pleasure to meet you." They each shook her hand, greeting her warmly. She was a beautiful young lady with bright red hair and a shy smile. When Wyatt turned to speak with Ryan, Sienna leaned in to them, her voice quiet so the others wouldn't hear.

"I am so sorry about my dad. He's really protective, and not at all good with people."

"Don't worry about your father," Lucky replied gently. "We're here for you, okay?"

Sienna nodded.

"Now, it's very important that you communicate with us. If you're uncomfortable at any point. If you don't feel well, are scared, or someone gives you a bad feeling, you need to tell us, okay? We're here to help in any way we can."

"Thank you." She toyed with the hem of her stylish tunic. Poor girl was all nerves.

"Now, you're going to pick a code word," Lucky said. "Something easy for you to remember but that you wouldn't normally say. This will be your signal to us that you feel uncomfortable or unsafe. If you say this word, Mason and I will escort you to somewhere private, yes?"

"Okay." Sienna worried her bottom lip with her teeth in

thought. Her eyes went to Mason, and her cheeks turned pink. "Rodeo."

Lucky snickered.

"Is that okay?" Sienna asked, uncertain.

"It's perfect," Lucky replied, he tipped his head at Mason. "He's a real cowboy, you know."

Sienna's eyes went wide. "Oh my gosh, for reals? Like, an actual cowboy who rides horses on a ranch?"

Mason chuckled. "Yeah, just like that." He didn't mention how he'd walked away from that life a long time ago and never looked back, or how he'd spent most of his adult life trying to atone for what he'd done. She didn't need to know what he thought of himself every time he looked in the mirror or how he had to change his phone number every few months so his family wouldn't try to contact him. How he used a UPS mailbox for everything instead of his actual address so his father wouldn't show up on his doorstep. Sienna deserved to keep her storybook fantasy of what she believed him to be.

"See," Lucky said, interrupting Mason's bleak thoughts. "You have a big, strong cowboy protecting you. You got this."

Sienna's smile was dazzling as she nodded enthusiastically, but then Lucky seemed to have that effect on people.

They confirmed the time they'd be back, then left to do their walkthrough. Before Mason knew it, they were in the elevator heading to Sienna's room to pick her up. Lucky put his fist out to Mason.

"Show time, Cowboy. We got this."

With a chuckle, Mason fist-bumped him. "We got this."

The elevator doors opened on their floor, and everything went to shit.

SEVEN

"WHAT THE FUCK?"

Mason stared at the throng of people squished into the hallway ahead of them. Lucky's phone rang, and he quickly picked up, his expression grim as he listened to the panicked voice on the other end.

"Ryan, you need to calm down because I can't—*what*?" Lucky stilled, his body rigid as if he were standing at attention. There were few times Mason had seen Lucky's demeanor change in that manner, and it tended to involve the acknowledgment of a threat. His body suddenly relaxed, and he pinched the bridge of his nose. After a deep breath, which he released slowly, he was once again centered and calm. "Okay. I'm going to clear a path. When I knock on the door, both of you be ready. If I see Wyatt, we're going to have a problem. He is to stay away from Sienna until the signing is over. Understand? Now get ready. We're going to be making a quick exit." Lucky hung up and turned to Mason.

"What the hell happened?"

The dozens of fans crowding the hallway were getting

rowdy, especially with the ones in front trying to push past the two security guys guarding Sienna's room. What a clusterfuck.

"Wyatt decided he wasn't in the mood for room service and went downstairs to eat in one of the very public, very full restaurants. Someone recognized him, followed him up without him knowing, then called their friends, who called *their* friends, and now this. Hold the elevator. I'm going to get Sienna." Lucky stepped out and shouted, "Holy shit, it's the hot dude from *Aquaman*!"

It was like something out of a horror movie. Dozens of heads whirled around at the same time before a cacophony of shrieks and screams exploded in the hall. A stampede en masse promptly followed.

Lucky thrust a finger to his left. "He ran around the corner. I think he's heading for the stairs!"

The horde charged, a mixture of teenagers and adults. Mason had never seen anything like it. He'd worked plenty of crowd control jobs over the years as law enforcement, but most of the time, folks had been secured behind barriers or lines of security. Here, they were running wild with no one to corral them.

"Works every time." Lucky grinned before his smile slipped away. "Let me know if anyone starts heading back this way."

"Where the hell is the rest of Sienna's security?"

"Downstairs trying to stop the rest of Sienna's fans from coming up, which means we're getting off on the first floor and taking the stairs down to conference level. Ryan's making arrangements to get Sienna's hotel room and ours swapped with rooms on a different floor. It's going to cost them a hell of a lot of money to make it work, but they have no choice. I'll be right back." Lucky took off for Sienna's room while Mason held the elevator door open. A heartbeat later, Lucky emerged with his arm around Sienna as they hurried toward the elevator, Ryan and the two guards in tow.

"Sienna!"

The war cry had been sounded, and soon several fans were running for the elevator, but Lucky got everyone inside and the door closed before anyone reached them.

"That was intense." Sienna looked unsettled, and Mason couldn't blame her. Large crowds were unpredictable, and no matter how innocent the reason for the gathering, all it took was one asshole and the whole thing could turn ugly.

They reached the first floor, and when the elevator opened, Lucky stuck his head out. With the coast clear, he motioned for them to follow. As per Lucky's instructions, he walked ahead of them and Mason stuck close to Sienna, with Ryan close to her other side and Sienna's two guards behind them. The floor was silent, and thankfully they made it to the stairwell without incident. Lucky went first, opening the door and checking things out before he signaled for Mason to follow with Sienna. They quickly made their way down the stairs, past the lobby level, and down to the conference level below.

"Stay here." Lucky disappeared through the exit door and returned not long after. "Everyone is still crowded outside the elevator. We'll need to make a run for the doors to the staff entrance. From there we can take the back way into the dressing room behind the conference hall." He turned his attention to the two guards. "Mason will walk on Sienna's right, one of you walk in front of him, the other behind. We want to block their view of her as much as possible." The guards nodded, and Lucky smiled at Sienna. "We got this, yes?"

Sienna nodded somewhat hesitantly.

"No, no, no." Lucky placed his hands on her shoulders and bent down so they were eye to eye. "You are a confident, independent, powerful woman. Those people are here to see you because your talent speaks to them. You're an artist. You've worked very hard, and now everyone sees how amazing you are. Repeat after me. I am a confident, independent, powerful woman."

Sienna took in a deep breath and released it slowly. "I am a confident, independent, powerful woman."

"Yes, good. You keep repeating that in your head, okay?"

"Okay."

"Now. Do you got this?"

"Yes," Sienna said firmly, her expression determined. "I am a confident, independent, powerful woman. Let's do this."

"That's it!" Lucky turned and glanced at Mason over his shoulder. "Ready, Cowboy?"

"You bet."

Lucky opened the door, and they moved together as quickly as possible without drawing attention to themselves, the guards staying close to Mason. Thankfully, the elevators were at an angle, meaning as soon as they cleared the exit and made it to the hallway, their view was obstructed. With everyone else in line outside the main conference hall, it meant they made it to the back doors without anyone seeing them. As soon as Sienna was in her dressing room, she and Ryan let out a sigh of relief. Lucky informed the rest of the security team, who were now on their way to the signing area, while the two guards with them remained outside the dressing room door.

The dressing room was cozy but nice. Sienna took a seat on the black velvet couch on one end while Ryan grabbed a bottle of water from the large bucket of ice on the black coffee table. He handed one to her before taking one for himself, then took a seat beside her. The room was what one would expect a backstage dressing room to look like, though maybe not as fancy as in some places. It had the essentials, though—a big plush couch, a clothing rack against the far wall next to a tall three-panel divider that served as a changing room if needed, a large framed mirror, and a few vases with flowers. The decor had a white, purple, black, and silver color scheme. Mason stood to one side of the dressing room door when they received word the event manager was outside. After clearing her credentials with Ryan, they let her in. She took a seat on the couch with Ryan and Sienna, and while they talked, Lucky came over to stand by the door with Mason.

"You're doing great, Cowboy."

Mason felt a little tickle of pleasure at Lucky's approval. He hadn't been seeking it, but now that he had it, he'd hold on to it. "Thanks."

"When it's time, we'll accompany her out to the booth. You'll stand to her right, and I'll stand to her left. They may take pictures with her while she sits at the table, but they may not come around the table. Either way, we'll have guys on each end of the table to ensure that."

"Got it."

"Lucky?" Sienna called over, and Lucky placed a palm to Mason's back, giving it a rub, then a sweet pat before he left, leaving Mason wanting more of his touch. When King said they'd be working together, Mason had expected to find himself in King's office within the first few hours. A small part of him felt guilty for believing Lucky would find a way to get Mason off his back. That Lucky wouldn't be able to look past whatever was going on between them to work with Mason, but he'd been very wrong. Lucky was a professional. It was obvious now that when he was on the job, he was focused on the task at hand and everything else came second.

Their time together in the surveillance truck popped into his head, but he quickly brushed it aside. The pressure between them had been building. It was bound to explode, and it had, but it was out of their system now. They could move on. *Like you moved on that night when you had phone sex?* Okay, that was... *hot, so fucking hot.* No. That was a one-off. The whole truck incident had thrown them off their game. It wouldn't happen again.

"Time to go," Lucky announced.

Everyone took their positions, and Lucky gave Sienna another pep talk before the doors opened and they headed out to the sound of cheers. The hall was huge, divided up into sections with numerous booths and tables housing various celebrities, artists, and vendors. Mason and the rest of the security team did exactly as Lucky instructed, escorting Sienna to the movie studio's booth. She smiled and waved to her fans as she stepped behind the wide table. The line was akin to those in theme parks, wrapping around to make room for as many people as possible. Mason folded his arms in front of him as he stood to Sienna's side. She seemed nervous at first, but when Lucky placed his hand on her shoulder, she visibly relaxed. After the first few encounters, she was off, and by the second hour, she was working the crowd like a seasoned pro. She smiled, chatted with her fans, joked, and posed for the camera from her seat. The crowd loved her. She also seemed to be enjoying herself.

The first two hours went by in a blur, and thankfully

everyone behaved themselves. A couple of rowdy teenage boys stepped forward, their expressions less than whole-some as they whispered conspiratorially to each other. One of them approached Sienna and opened his mouth to say something when he glanced up at Lucky and promptly decided against whatever he'd been planning on saying. Mason sneaked a peek over at Lucky and had to cough into his hand to keep from laughing. If looks could kill, the teen would have been eviscerated on the spot. Lucky's narrowed gaze was a warning and a dare all in one.

The kid promptly handed a T-shirt over to Sienna, and while she signed it, he kept sneaking glances at Lucky. If Lucky made any sudden movements, Mason was pretty sure the kid would shit himself. Lucky wasn't as tall or big as Mason or the rest of the bodyguards, but one look and you knew the guy was trained in a way that meant pain for anyone stupid enough to force him into action. The kid was so freaked-out, he thanked Sienna, bowed awkwardly, turned, grabbed his very confused friend, and hauled ass.

Things went smoothly after that, and next thing they knew, it was time for Sienna to take a break. They escorted her back into the dressing room, where food had been brought in. Sienna moaned at the sight of the huge burger with the side of fries.

"Oh my God, that smells so good." She ran over to the couch and dropped down onto it. "Don't tell my dad. He thinks because I'm famous now, I'm going to start eating like a freaking rabbit. It's not like they don't make me work out all the time. Besides, they're so mistaken if they think I'm going to give up fries." She popped one into her mouth and did a little happy dance. It was cute.

Lucky stole one of her fries, and she gasped in mock offense. Watching Lucky with Sienna was fascinating. As she ate, she chatted with him like they were best friends. With Sienna, Lucky was charming, warm, kind, and soft-spoken. He teased her, made her laugh, and provided a distraction when she needed it. With the rest of the security team, he was firm, professional, but polite, giving them a smile to assure them he was helping.

The second half of the signing went even quicker than the first half, and by the end, Sienna was exhausted. "I can't wait to get back to my room and have a bubble bath."

"The front desk called," Ryan informed them. "They're ready to have us move upstairs to the new rooms." He turned to Sienna. "Also you have that interview tonight, remember?"

Sienna groaned. "Darn. I'd totally forgotten about that."

Lucky turned to Ryan with a frown. "Wait a second. What interview?"

"It's a last-minute thing. One magazine reporter, and it'll be in Sienna's room. We don't need to change anything."

"What time?" Lucky asked.

Ryan looked at his watch. "Um, in half an hour?"

"Okay, we change rooms. Then Mason and I will come to the room."

"It's not necessary. It was a last minute promo op and—"

Lucky arched an eyebrow at Ryan, and Ryan held up a hand.

"Right. Sorry. You're right."

With that settled, they headed for the elevator. Unfortunately that meant passing the conference hall and the many people outside it. This time they had the rest of the security team, and they formed a wall between Sienna and the crowd that made a rush for her the moment someone spotted her. Mason and Lucky gently but quickly hurried Sienna toward the elevator.

"It's loud," Sienna said, her voice barely audible. "I didn't know there'd be so many people out here."

"We're right here with you," Lucky assured her. "Are those Gucci?"

Sienna looked down at her shoes. "Yeah, my stylist insisted on them."

"They're beautiful. They go perfect with that dress."

"You think so?"

"Honey, trust me. I know my Gucci."

Sienna giggled.

"You should tell her about the time the dog ate your Gucci sandal," Mason prompted, knowing what Lucky was trying to do.

Lucky crossed himself. "My poor Gucci. You are in a better place."

The crowd was huge, everyone trying to get past the wall of muscle to get to Sienna, but she quickly forgot all about the noise and people as Lucky regaled her with the tragic demise of his Gucci sandal at the paws and jaws of a fluffy golden retriever.

They reached the elevator and pressed the button, and the doors immediately opened. As they stepped inside, a large group of men and women with bags and equipment rushed forward, intent on joining them in the elevator. Sienna's entourage. Mason moved in close to Sienna anyway, aware of how she sucked in a sharp breath and gripped Lucky's arm tight.

"Lucky… I don't think…. It's too many people."

Lucky stepped into the doorway, his shoulders back, body rigid like he was standing at attention. He held an arm out to the group, and they came to an abrupt halt in front of him. "Whoa, whoa, whoa. I'm afraid you have to take the next one."

A woman in front wearing a bun so tight it had to be cutting off her circulation turned her nose up at Lucky. "We're with Ms. Scott. We're her hair, makeup, and wardrobe team."

"Yes, I understand, but you need to wait and get the next elevator or take a different one."

"What? That's ridiculous. There's plenty of room. Just squeeze in."

"Please," Lucky stated pleasantly but firmly.

"There's. Plenty. Of. Room," she repeated like he didn't understand her.

Lucky's eyes narrowed. "I heard you the first time. You're still not getting in this elevator."

"I don't think I like your attitude, Mr...?"

"Eduardo Morales. Four Kings Security. My job is to ensure Ms. Scott's safety and comfort. No one else is getting in this elevator. You can meet her upstairs, and make sure *no one* follows you. Can you do that?"

"Excuse me?" the woman asked indignantly.

"Can you or can you not get to the room without being followed? If not, I'll send security up with you. In fact...." Lucky craned his neck and pressed his PTT button. "Francis!"

One of the guards turned, and when he saw Lucky, he came running over. "What can I do for you, Mr. Morales?"

"Escort Sienna's people upstairs to her new room, please. I don't want anyone following and finding out where it is."

"Sure thing."

"Fine," the woman replied through her teeth before she

spun around, the rest of the entourage following her as she stomped away after Francis.

Lucky stepped back and hit the button to close the door. He immediately turned to Sienna. "Okay?"

Sienna nodded, her eyes filled with stars as she gazed up at him. "Yes. Thank you, Lucky."

"You're very welcome."

Mason was a little starstruck himself. He'd never really seen Lucky in bodyguard mode. He hadn't known what to expect from him while on the job. Lucky often came across as sort of a hothead. If he was unhappy about something, the whole world was going to know about it, but as it turned out, the guy was far more complex than Mason gave him credit for.

THE REST of the day flew by, with them moving their stuff to their new room six floors up as well as helping Ryan and Wyatt move Sienna's belongings to the new room next to theirs. The magazine reporter arrived for the interview, and they stood guard inside the room.

Thankfully the interview was pleasant, with no inappropriate or sexist questions. Mason had seen his fair share of celebrity interviews, and it never failed to shock him how inappropriate the questions became when female celebrities were being interviewed. Male celebrities were asked about their acting process, how they did their own stunts, or what inspired them to create that particular piece of music, while female celebrities were asked about what they wore under their costumes or about their diet. What the hell happened to manners? To respect? Fuck, he sounded like his grand-dad, but his granddad had been right on that front, so he'd take it. The interview lasted about an hour, and by the end, Sienna was pretty much asleep standing up, poor girl.

"Goodnight," Lucky said. "If you need anything, just call."

Outside in the hall, Lucky loosened his tie. "I'm starving. Want to grab some food?"

"Sure. What did you have in mind?" Mason followed Lucky's lead and loosened his tie. Man, he was beat.

"We never leave the hotel during a job unless our team is in charge, so it looks like it's hotel food, but one of the restaurants here is actually pretty good."

"Lead the way."

Turned out the restaurants were packed to the brim with a wait time of over an hour. Way too tired for that nonsense, they decided to order in pizza. The moment they walked into the room, Mason got that feeling again. Like something was off. It was starting to annoy the hell out of him because nothing looked out of place. If someone had been in their room, Sienna's guards would have noticed and said something. Hell, if someone had been in their room and taken something, or moved something, Lucky would have been the first to notice.

"You okay?" Lucky asked, concern written all over his handsome face.

"Yeah, just feeling outta sorts. Probably from being on high alert all day." Not that he wasn't used to being on alert as a cop, but working a security job for hours on end meant not letting his guard down for even a moment and being prepared to spring into action from one heartbeat to the next.

Lucky nodded. "You'll get used to it."

While they waited for pizza, they took turns in the shower, and it wasn't until after they'd eaten and it was time to turn in that Mason remembered the whole one-bed situation. With views of the night sky and city lights from the large window, along with the glow of the beside lamps, the room looked a little too intimate for Mason's liking.

"So, um, which side do you want?" Mason asked, doing his best not to stare at Lucky's ass or the way the thin soft-looking material of his pajama bottoms accentuated his plump cheeks. His feet were bare and his graphic T-shirt fit snug against his sleek torso and tapered waist. He probably smelled amazing too. Fuck, this was going to be a very, *very* long night.

"The right. I always sleep on whichever side is closest to the door."

Mason didn't ask why that was, and Lucky didn't offer an explanation, which told Mason it was either something from his childhood or his time in the military. Both were very plausible. Mason closed the curtains while Lucky climbed into bed beneath the duvet and turned off his bedside lamp. Joining him, Mason turned off his lamp, then lay on his back, same as Lucky. He stared at the ceiling, feeling like an idiot. They were both so aware of each other. Their arms barely touched, but Mason felt Lucky's heat as if he were pressed against him. Thank God, Lucky liked the room cool, because Mason was burning up.

"Goodnight." Lucky rolled onto his side, most likely away from Mason.

"Goodnight."

They were both clearly very awake. Mason could feel it. He rolled onto his side, facing the center of the bed and found Lucky facing him. "Hey."

Lucky's smile was sweet. "Hey."

"Some day, huh?"

"Yes. We make a pretty good team, you know?"

"We do, don't we?"

"When we're not trying to kill each other or—" Lucky cleared his throat, and Mason was pretty sure if there'd been more light in the room, Lucky's cheeks would be pink. Mason knew exactly what he'd been about to say. He smiled wickedly.

"Fuck each other?"

Lucky huffed out a laugh and rolled onto his back. "You are taking this honesty thing to heart."

"You asked me to."

Silence filled the room, broken only by the sound of the air conditioner turning on.

"It's weird, huh?" Mason asked wanting nothing more than to reach out and touch him.

"What is?"

"Us sharing a bed after... everything. Then I guess this whole whatever you want to call it between us kind of came out of nowhere."

"I don't know about that."

"No?"

Lucky rolled onto his side again to face Mason. He searched Mason's eyes, for what Mason had no idea. "You can't tell Ace, though. He'd never let me live it down."

"You have my word."

"I was jealous of him when he was dating you."

"You were?" Mason had no idea. Lucky had never given the slightest indication.

"I was jealous he'd found this gorgeous man to be his. Ace is a one-man kind of a guy. He wants the fairy tale. The husband, house, dog, and happy ever after."

"And you don't want that?"

"I do."

Mason was floored. "But I thought—"

Lucky put a finger to his lips to quiet him. "But I'm not willing to risk the heartache that comes with trying to make that fantasy come true. In the end, you broke Ace's heart. I was jealous, but I never wanted that for him. I wanted him to have his fairy tale." He traced the line of Mason's lips with his finger, his eyes on Mason's mouth.

"So, what you're saying is this is all on me?" Mason wasn't angry or upset. He was just trying to understand where he stood with Lucky. How did he fit into Lucky's life, if he fit in at all?

Lucky closed his eyes and sighed. "No, Cowboy. This is on me too. That is why I have sex and nothing more."

"And do I fall into that category? Sex and nothing more? I'm trying to work out what I am to you. Friend with benefits? Lover? Occasional fuck buddy?" Mason caught Lucky's hand when he started to pull it away from him. He placed a kiss to his palm. "You don't have to answer that, darlin'. Go to sleep, okay? Get some rest. Tomorrow's gonna be another long day."

Lucky nodded. He gently pulled his hand out of Mason's before rolling over onto his other side, curling up on himself, the gesture squeezing Mason's heart. He reached out but stopped. If he started something now, he'd end up feeling like shit for it later because Lucky clearly needed time to figure this out. Hell, they both did. The bed felt too big, too cold, the space between them a chasm rather than the few inches it was.

This was ridiculous. How could Mason offer forever when there was no such thing? He couldn't promise Lucky he wouldn't break his heart. Lucky was right. Look at what happened between him and Ace. He hadn't *planned* on hurting Ace, but he had, and now what? He was going to do it all over again with his cousin? Because if he didn't tell

Lucky the truth about what he'd done, he'd be living a lie, and Lucky would end up walking out, like Ace had. And if he told Lucky everything, Lucky would leave anyway.

Rolling away from Lucky, Mason closed his eyes in the hopes he'd get at least a few hours of sleep, but as he suspected, he was plagued by nightmares, but they were the least he deserved.

EIGHT

WARMTH.

Lucky snuggled closer to whatever was radiating the incredible warmth. There was nothing like sleeping in a cool room under a warm blanket. It was heavenly, and he was so comfortable he didn't want to move. He sighed in pleasure and rubbed his cheek against the soft cotton. Something heavy tightened around him, and he snapped his eyes open. Wait a second....

Shit. Mason.

The warmth was coming from Mason, who had his beefy arm wrapped around Lucky. It wasn't the only limb wrapped around Lucky. They lay on their sides, facing each other, their legs intertwined, Lucky's arm around Mason's waist, holding him close, and his cheek pressed to Mason's chest. There was also the not-so-little matter of Mason's very hard morning wood poking Lucky in the stomach, and Lucky's own dick, which was eager to play with Mason's. Judging by Mason's breathing, he was still asleep.

Well, if Mason was still sleeping....

Lucky inhaled deeply, loving Mason's scent—a mixture

of fabric softener, shower gel, and his male musk. Gingerly he rubbed his cheek, like a cat leaving his scent. He splayed his fingers against Mason's lower back just above the curve of his ass. God, how he loved this. He never stayed long enough in anyone's bed after sex, and if he did, it still wouldn't make him feel the way Mason did. After sex, Lucky was usually up and out as fast as could be. There was no time for cuddling—and Lucky *loved* to cuddle. No time for getting to know every inch of the person next to him, to become familiar with every dip and curve. He wasn't interested in listening to their heartbeat or the way they breathed.

Mason let out a soft sigh in his sleep, making Lucky smile. Such a big man yet so tender. Mason stirred, and Lucky remained very still. He closed his eyes, his heart melting when Mason placed a kiss to Lucky's head, his words whispered in a sexy, sleep-filled drawl.

"Good morning, beautiful."

Did Mason realize they were tangled together, or was he still half-asleep?

It was wrong for him to pretend to be asleep, but he told himself one more minute. One minute of Mason's strong arms around him, holding him close, like nothing could touch them while they were like this. For that one moment, everything was perfect. Opening his eyes, he placed a feathery kiss against Mason's chest.

"You awake, Cowboy?"

Mason's grunt was cute.

"We should get up."

"No. I don't think we should. I think we should stay right here, like this."

Lucky chuckled. "Nice try, Cowboy. ¡Vamos, levántate! Necesito café." He smacked Mason's butt and made to roll away when Mason caught him around the waist. He rolled onto his back, taking Lucky with him. "Mason," Lucky scolded, his reprimand not sounding much like one, considering he was laughing. "Suéltame."

Mason pretended to give it some thought. "Nope. I don't think I will let you go. I reckon I'll keep you." He popped a kiss on Lucky's cheek. "I like you." He wrapped his arms tightly around Lucky, keeping him from going anywhere, not that Lucky couldn't get loose if he wanted to.

"You're maybe a little bit crazy, you know?"

"Maybe." Mason shrugged. "Doesn't change what I said."

Lucky stopped struggling, and with a resigned sigh lay sprawled over Mason's larger frame, his face tucked against Mason's neck. "I guess this is nice." He felt Mason's rumble of a chuckle all over.

"I'm glad you think so."

"Can you free my arms please?"

"I *can*. The question is, should I? Are you going to try and escape?"

"I need coffee, Mason. It's essential to my well-being."

"And you'll get your coffee. I promise."

Lucky sighed. "Fine."

Mason released him, but not completely. He slid his arms under Lucky's to hug Lucky to him. "See. I can compromise."

It was Lucky's turn to chuckle. *Dios, ayúdame.* This man was going to kill him. It struck him then that they were in bed together with Lucky on top of Mason and they weren't having sex. They weren't even moving or kissing. They were simply enjoying the closeness. It was incredibly intimate. His lips were so close to Mason's skin, his stubble wonderfully thick. He was one of those guys who had to shave every day or he'd have a full beard by the next morning. Mm, he smelled good.

¡Ni lo pienses! Don't even think about doing what you're thinking of doing. Lucky ignored the little voice of reason in his head and flicked his tongue out, loving Mason's sharp intake of breath as he licked a trail up to Mason's jawline before nipping at the stubble there. Mason groaned.

"Okay, you need to get up. Fast. Or I'm going to have you flat on your back waking up the guests."

Lucky rolled off him, landing on his feet beside the bed. He chuckled at Mason's pout.

"You're an ass," Mason growled.

"You mean this ass?" Lucky turned, lifted his arms, and shook his ass.

"You little shit." Mason jumped out of bed, and Lucky made a dash for the bathroom and shut the door before Mason reached him.

"You can't stay in there forever, Morales. That's going to cost you!"

Lucky leaned against the door. "Oh yeah? How?"

"A kiss at the very least."

"I don't know. That's a pretty steep price."

"You shoulda thought about that before you went wavin' that red flag in front of this bull."

Lucky snickered. "Okay, Cowboy. One kiss. But I choose when."

"You have twenty-four hours."

"Fine. I'm going to shower now."

"Unlock the door. I gotta take a piss."

"Such a gentleman." Lucky opened the door, shaking his head in amusement only to have Mason cup his face and take his lips in a kiss that made his toes curl. Lucky's brain shorted out and his body took over, opening his mouth so his tongue tangled with Mason's. When he pulled back, he was floating.

"Did I say twenty-four hours? I meant twenty-four seconds." Mason smacked Lucky's ass playfully before turning and heading back into the room.

"I thought you had to piss?" Lucky called out, shaking himself out of it.

"Nope. Just needed you to open the door."

"Cabrón." Lucky closed the door but didn't lock it. He turned on the little shower radio he traveled with and stepped into the shower, all the while wondering if Mason was going to try and join him. He wasn't sure how he felt about that. On the one hand, he would certainly not be opposed to having Mason naked and wet in front of him. On the other hand, having Mason naked and wet in front of him would lead to other things, and he was trying to keep things nonsexual between them, though he wasn't really doing a very good job. If he wanted to keep his distance from Mason, this was *not* the way to go about doing that. He needed to do better. If they kept this up, one or both of them would end up hurt.

After a quick shower, Lucky dried off and wrapped a towel around his waist. He trimmed his stubble and put on some deodorant and cologne, all the while singing to Madonna's "Like a Virgin." It was the one thing they hadn't been able to take from him in Cuba, his love for music. Growing up, there were days where they had no food, but they had music from the old radio his abuelo had gifted his father when he was a boy. His father would play it low enough so no one outside could hear and know they still had the little radio, and when the president or his men came, his father would hide it in an old beat-up coffee can.

Music was a part of him, a part of his soul. From his

parents' old favorites like Celia Cruz, Beny Moré, and Tito Puente, to artists like P!nk and Adele, music had always been in his life, and always would be.

"Are you singing Madonna?"

"Yes. She is my queen. Next to Celia Cruz, Lady Gaga, and Beyoncé."

"Really? Makes sense."

"Oh?" Lucky arched an eyebrow at him. "What are you trying to say?"

"That it takes a diva to know a diva."

Lucky opened his mouth to argue, then shrugged. "You're right. Also, I'm fabulous." He tossed his nonexistent hair back.

"No denying that, darlin'." Mason leaned against the doorframe, arms crossed over his chest, his biceps stretching the fabric of his white V-neck T-shirt. Lucky was onto him.

"Stop doing that."

"Doing what?" Mason blinked at him innocently, but Lucky knew better. Mason's bright blue eyes were filled with mischief. He smiled, causing little lines to form at the corners of his eyes. "Not fooling ya, am I?"

"Nope. You're flexing to tempt me." Lucky stopped on his way past, jutting a finger at him. "I will not be tempted."

As he walked by, Mason yanked his towel away.

"¡Ay, cabrón!" Lucky cupped himself and spun around to glare at Mason, who threw the towel over his shoulder with a laugh. The laugh quickly died down as he blatantly raked his gaze over Lucky from head to toe. He pulled his bottom lip in between his teeth and groaned.

"Shit, my little prank backfired."

"That so?"

Mason nodded. "Oh yeah. Baby, you are fuckin' beautiful."

Lucky lifted his chin arrogantly. "This is a fact I know."

"And that's what makes you dangerous," Mason said with a huff. "Can I see your tattoo?"

"Some other time. Go shower. That is your punishment for that little stunt."

"Goddammit." Mason turned, grumbling as he walked into the bathroom and shut the door.

"Don't use the Lord's name in vain. I will tell my mother on you."

Mason poked his head out of the door. "Wait, does your momma know about what's going on with us?"

Lucky rolled his eyes. "Mason, I talk to Ace about everything, and Ace talks to his mother almost every day. His mother is my mother's sister. The whole of Miami *and* Cuba know about you."

"*Fuuuuck.*"

"Yes, very much so. Everyone in my family refers to you as 'ese vaquero que le rompió el corazón a Chulo, y ahora está detrás de Candi.' The cowboy who broke Chulo's heart and is now after Candi. But my mother still thinks you're very handsome, even if she wants to throw her chancleta at you. Fair warning, if you see her, she may do so."

Mason's eyes were huge. He quickly closed the door, as if doing so meant he was protected from Lucky's family.

Once they were both ready in their suits, they headed downstairs for some breakfast. Lucky always ate breakfast. It was a Cuban thing. Meals were never skipped unless absolutely unavoidable. Lucky said a little prayer of thanks that the restaurant had espresso.

"I never understood that," Mason said, pointing at Lucky's café con leche. "The whole tiny cup of espresso before you have a latte that also has espresso."

Lucky shrugged. "I don't know. My parents have always

done it. El buchito de café is something you have first thing in the morning before anything else."

"Let me get this straight, you make a coffee in order to be able to start your morning and then you make another coffee for breakfast?"

"Something like that. Except el buchito is straight up espresso. Café con leche is less café and more milk. I don't know. Don't question tradition, man. It just is."

Mason laughed. "Okay, okay."

They finished breakfast and used the restroom before heading up to Sienna's room. The guards greeted them pleasantly, and Ryan opened the door for them when they knocked and announced themselves.

"Good morning!" Sienna was bright and cheerful, looking beautiful yet casual in her designer jeans, comic book T-shirt, and leather jacket that matched her leather boots. Her red hair cascaded around her shoulders, and her bright pink lipstick gave her a playful look.

"Ready?" Lucky asked. Today was going to be longer than yesterday since it was several hours of posing and taking pictures with fans.

"Let's do this." She held her fist out to Lucky, and he bumped his fist to hers.

"Where's your dad?"

Sienna rolled her eyes. "I sent him out. He's the reason people found out about where our room was."

"Yes, but it was a simple mistake," Lucky soothed.

"No, it wasn't," Sienna replied, her frown deep. "He did it on purpose. For publicity. He thought 'the excitement' would make me more popular."

Lucky gritted his teeth. If he opened his mouth, unpleasant words would come out, and he didn't want to ruin Sienna's good mood. There was a time and a place, and this was neither. Sienna was geared up and ready to greet her fans. He wouldn't take that away. Pasting on a smile, he motioned to the door. "Time to shine."

The trip to the conference hall was thankfully uneventful.

After the photo session, Sienna had a couple of panels along with some fellow actors, but she would be done by dinner. She'd be taking photos with fans for several hours with breaks in between sessions. Her hope was to get everyone in to see her, but with a line that was several people wide and reached halfway down the room, it was doubtful.

Lucky and Mason stood side by side to her left, just outside the camera's view, while two other guards stood to her right. The rest of the team was divided up, some close by while others made rounds, walking down the line of people and keeping vigilant. Every few minutes they checked in with Lucky. Fans of all ages from all parts of the world had come to see Sienna and take their picture with her. She took pictures hugging people, making funny faces, doing silly poses, pretending to be her character in the movie. Some people came dressed up, others wore T-shirts with her character on them. A few teens had to be warned and reined in, but for the most part, people were respectful.

A man in his early fifties waved a greeting at Sienna as he stepped up for a picture. She smiled sweetly, and he leaned in to murmur something in her ear. The color drained from her face, and her eyes widened. She darted her gaze to Lucky, her eyes filled with fear, so much so it was clear she'd forgotten the safe word. Lucky sprang forward, snatching the guy's arm as he pulled his hand out of his pocket, aware of Mason grabbing Sienna and hauling her away from the guy. Knowing she was safe, Lucky twisted the man's arm, knocked the scissors out of his hand, and kicked at the back of his leg, ignoring the man's yelp when Lucky slammed him into the carpet face-first, his arm twisted up behind his back.

"I just wanted a piece of her hair for eBay!"

"She's only a kid, you piece of shit," Lucky spat in the man's ear. "You should be ashamed of yourself." He pulled a zip tie from his pocket, and bound the guy's wrists together before hauling him to his feet as event security ran over. Lucky talked to security, waiting with them until the police arrived to take the guy off their hands.

Lucky joined Mason and Sienna in the dressing room. She was on the couch, her face buried in Mason's chest as he held her, offering comfort.

"Are you okay?"

"Oh my God, oh my God, oh my God." Sienna threw herself into Lucky's arms and burst into fresh tears. Judging by the black streaks running down her cheeks, she'd already had a good cry.

"It's okay, love," Lucky soothed, hugging her tight as she cried into his chest. He ran a hand over her hair, speaking softly. Mason brought over a box of tissues, and Lucky thanked him as he took one. He handed it to Sienna, who blew her nose.

"Thank you. I'm sorry. I know it's stupid."

"It's not stupid," Lucky assured her. "No one has the right to make you feel how you felt out there with that man."

Sienna nodded. "I know. I just... nothing like that's ever happened to me before."

Lucky's heart went out to her. From here on out, her encounters with fucked-up people was only going to get more frequent. Her career was taking off, and that brought out all the nut jobs.

Ryan was on the phone chewing someone's ear off. He was so pissed, he was practically vibrating. Whoever was on the other end was in big trouble and rightfully so, because no one should have gotten into the conference hall with a weapon. Ryan tried to get Sienna to cancel the rest of the event, but she shook her head.

"Those people have waited hours to see me. I'm not going to disappoint them because of one asshole." She stood, her hands balled into fists, her expression one of determination. "Get me makeup."

Ryan hopped to it, and the makeup crew was in the dressing room within minutes. They redid Sienna's makeup, and she was raring to go. Lucky was so very proud of her. She wasn't about to be deterred. In fact, she seemed more determined than ever. As soon as she stepped outside, the crowd roared with cheers. She waved at them as she walked back in front of the camera, opening her arms to a little girl dressed in her superhero costume.

The rest of the event went off without a hitch, and Sienna stayed to take photos with everyone in line, finishing far later than was required, but she'd insisted. They escorted her up to her room, and she hugged them both.

"Thank you, guys. I don't know how I would have done this without you."

"You would have been equally amazing," Lucky said. "We were just backup."

"If you're ever in Cali, look me up." She winked at them, then disappeared into her room.

"I hope Hollywood is good to her," Mason said as Lucky let them into their room.

Lucky hoped so too, but it wouldn't be an easy road by

any means. He had a couple of friends trying to make it into show business out there, and it was hard for young stars not to lose their luster.

Man, he was beat. He turned to ask Mason if he wanted to use the shower first when Mason exploded.

"What the hell is wrong with people? I mean seriously? Attacking a young woman to cut off her hair so you can sell it online? How does that make any fucking sense? Like, who thinks that's a good idea?"

Lucky took a seat on the edge of the bed as Mason paced in front of him. "More people than you think."

"Fucked-up people. I mean, if he'd, I don't know, gone to her hairdresser or something after she'd cut her hair or whatever. I mean it's still fucking weird, but okay. How the fuck did the guy even get that past security?"

Wow. That was a lot of "fucks" in the span of a few breaths. "I don't know, but I have a feeling someone is about to lose their job."

"Christ."

"Are *you* okay?"

Mason stopped and blinked at him. "What?"

"You're worked up about this."

"Of course I am, I mean…. Shit. I know I shouldn't be because it's the job, but…."

"You care, and that's okay. This is good," Lucky said, patting his shoulder when Mason joined him on the bed. "Out there, you did what you had to, and you were professional. Here, now, you can lose your shit. It's what you do as a cop, no?"

Mason sighed. "Yeah."

"On this job, you won't see the kinds of things you see as a homicide detective, but you'll still meet monsters. It's our job to protect others from those monsters."

"You know, I hadn't thought of that."

"What?"

"My cases involve people who didn't have anyone to stop the monsters from getting to them. You stand between the monsters and the people they're looking to turn into my cases."

"We do our best," Lucky said quietly.

"What you do matters. A lot. Jesus, Lucky. You get to save lives. What I do now.... Those people.... It's too late."

Lucky didn't know what to say. It wasn't as if Mason didn't know what his job entailed. Maybe he was seeing things differently? "Are you sure you're okay?"

"Yeah, I.... I guess I'm a little in awe of you right now. I can see why you fellas started this company after serving. You might not be doing whatever it is you did out there, but you're still helping people. I gotta admit to bein' a bit of an asshole. I mean corporate espionage? That's a bunch of rich white guys stealing from other rich white guys, but fuck, I was so wrong. Mr. Ruiz? Techu Technologies is his life's work. It's how he feeds his family, how his employees feed their families. It's a whole system of people, not just some corporate assholes. I know there are corporate assholes out there, but Mr. Ruiz wasn't one of them, and we saved his business. And now, we stopped some sick bastard from hurting an innocent girl. Granted, she's probably going to have nightmares about that fuckwit for who knows how long, but he didn't take a piece of her." He flew off the bed. "Shit, I'm rambling. I'm sorry. I.... Wow."

"Would you like a drink?"

"God, yes."

Lucky chuckled. He went to the phone and ordered a couple of beers. They were technically off duty, but until the job was contractually over, they wouldn't be letting down their defenses. While he was ordering them beer, he ordered some appetizers, along with hamburgers and fries. They showered and changed into their pajamas while they waited for the food to arrive. Half an hour later, they sat at the tiny table, eating, their legs touching beneath the table because there was nowhere else for them to go.

"Mm, Sienna was right." Mason let out a low moan after taking a huge bite of his burger. "These are damn good."

"The fries are even better," Lucky said, and it struck him how much he enjoyed spending time with Mason. For a long time, he'd worried the attraction was only physical, that they'd have nothing to talk about, especially with how closed off they both were about their pasts, but that wasn't the case at all. Instead, some strange kind of mutual respect had formed between them. Yes, Lucky wanted Mason to open up to him, trust him, but he was prepared to wait, because he had his own issues, ones he wouldn't like to be pushed on either.

They ate and talked about anything and everything, from the conference going on downstairs to their jobs. Even when they were quiet, it wasn't awkward. Lucky didn't feel the need to talk for the sake of talking.

"You know, it's strange," Mason said, sitting back when he'd finished his meal. He tilted his head as he studied Lucky. "I've learned more about you in the last few months than I have in the years I've known you."

"We've never spent this much time together just you and me." Lucky popped his last fry into his mouth. "It's always been with the guys."

"You're right."

"Feel better?" Lucky asked, motioning to the empty plate.

"Much. I'm sorry for, uh, unloading on you like that."

"I'm sure part of that is the adrenaline."

Mason frowned into his beer bottle. "It did make me think, though."

"About?"

"What I do."

"Oh?"

"I became a cop to help people."

"And you don't think you help people now as a detective?"

"I do, and I can't complain. I wanted this promotion, worked damn hard for it. It's what I wanted. At least I thought I wanted it. But my cases now mostly revolve around dead people, Lucky."

"Yes, but you get closure for their families. For their loved ones."

"I do my damned best to, but it doesn't change the fact there's no bringing them back. I couldn't stop whatever happened to them in the first place, and even when we catch the people responsible, justice isn't always served. I've got a few more years yet before I can retire, but I won't lie and hide the fact that I worry about what it's going to do to me."

"That's a very dangerous road to walk, my friend."

"I know." Mason sighed heavily. He took another sip of his beer, and Lucky almost suggested he come work for the Kings, but didn't. This was Mason's life. Whatever crisis he was going through, he needed to work it out for himself.

"If you need someone to listen, I can do that."

Mason's smile was sweet, despite the sadness in his eyes. There was more going on in his head than the job. *Fuck this.* Lucky stood and walked around to stand in front of Mason, who turned in his seat, his knees spread so Lucky could step between them.

"What is it that put that sadness in your eyes, Cowboy?" Lucky cupped his cheek, stroking a thumb over Mason's thick eyebrow. Mason leaned into the touch, closed his eyes, and covered Lucky's hand with his.

"A lifetime of regrets, darlin'." Mason wrapped his arms around Lucky's waist and lifted his chin. "You know what would make me feel better?"

Lucky held back a smile. Like he didn't know what Mason was going to say. "What?"

"A kiss from that pretty mouth of yours."

Lucky chuckled. "Well, I wouldn't want to deny you the chance to feel better."

"I sure do appreciate you looking out for my well-being."

"I'm very considerate that way."

"Yes, you are."

Lucky pressed his lips to Mason's, loving the sound of Mason's hum, and the way he opened up for Lucky. His lips were soft, warm, and he tasted slightly of beer. His tongue tangled languidly with Lucky's, and Lucky took his time, exploring every crevice. He slipped his fingers into Mason's hair, loving the soft, silky strands. With a sigh, he pulled back, his voice quiet when he spoke.

"Why is it every time I kiss you it's like this raging inferno ignites inside me? Like I will burn from the inside out if I don't have you?"

"I don't know. Maybe because that's what I feel when you kiss me."

"Yes?"

Mason nodded. "Oh, yes. I've never wanted anyone more. I don't understand what it is you do to me, darlin', but you're like an addiction. The more I taste you, the more I want, and the harder I try to stay away, to control the urges you bring out in me, the more I burn for you. If you only knew the things I want to do to you...." Masons thick, sexy drawl went straight to Lucky's dick.

"Like what?" *You're asking for trouble, Eduardo.*

"Remember our little sexcapades over the phone?"

"Oh." *Fuck.* Lucky groaned at the memory. He couldn't remember the last time he'd been so turned on or come so hard. Later that night he'd woken up and gotten himself off to the memory of what they'd done. Mason slid his hands over Lucky's ass, taking hold of his asscheeks.

"Yeah, *oh* is right. O, as in I want to rim that tight little hole of yours until you're coming apart for me. I want to fuck you with my tongue."

"Holy fuck, Cowboy." Lucky trembled, his hard cock tenting his pajama bottoms. He hissed when Mason wrapped a hand around his cock.

"You like when I talk dirty to you, huh?"

"Yes, very much," Lucky admitted. It was a combination of the sexy-as-sin man and that deep rumble of his voice with that accent. It hit all the right spots.

"You know what you're going to like even more?"

"Your mouth on my cock." Lucky shoved his pants and boxer briefs down, his cock bouncing back to his stomach, leave a smear across his stomach from the precome.

"Sweet Jesus." Mason wrapped his calloused fingers around Lucky's cock, and moved with Lucky so he had room to drop down onto his knees in front of him. He flicked his tongue over the slit, and Lucky sucked in a sharp breath. Unable to help himself, he slipped his fingers into Mason's hair, holding on tight as Mason sucked the tip of Lucky's cock into his mouth. He worked the head before swallowing Lucky down to the root, his nose buried in the curls of Lucky's groin.

"Shit." Lucky released his left hand from Mason's head to throw it on the table, needing to steady himself. He dropped his gaze to watch Mason sucking him off. With one hand he fondled Lucky's sac, with the other he got a digit nice and wet before placing it to Lucky's hole. Lucky closed his eyes, breathing in deep through his nose and letting it out slowly through his mouth. If he wasn't careful, he was going to come way too soon, and he didn't want this to be over yet.

Lucky tried his hardest to keep it together, but Mason was showing him no mercy. He took Lucky's cock deep down his throat, alternating between sucking hard, long, and slow, then fast and sloppy. If that wasn't enough to drive Lucky mad, he was working Lucky's hole, stretching him, teasing him. When he hit Lucky's prostate, Lucky cried out and doubled over. "Stop, stop, stop."

Mason popped off him, his grin wicked. "Get naked and on that bed, Eduardo."

With a groan, Lucky scrambled to get undressed, ignoring Mason's rumble of a chuckle. Why fight it? He wanted Mason more than he'd ever wanted anyone in his life, wanted his big, strong hands all over him, his mouth, lips, and tongue tasting, sucking, licking, biting.

By the time Lucky was on the bed, Mason had undressed and was holding a bottle of lube and a condom. He tossed them on the bed before he crawled over to Lucky, the sight hot enough to make Lucky writhe with need.

"Baby, you are the prettiest thing I've ever seen."

"Less talking, more of your mouth on me, Cowboy."

Mason saluted him. "Yes, sir." He kept his gaze fixed on Lucky's as he spread Lucky's bent legs, then got down on his stomach between them. "Don't you dare come until I tell you, you hear?"

Lucky nodded. What was it about Mason that had Lucky eager to follow orders? The man opened his mouth and it was like he put a spell on Lucky.

"Good." Mason nuzzled his nose against Lucky's groin and inhaled. "Mm, you smell so fucking good, sweetheart."

Lucky threw his head back against the pillow. This man was going to kill him, and they'd barely started. Mason's tongue flicked out to lick his sac, and Lucky shivered. He grabbed fistfuls of the duvet on either side of him, his breath already coming out heavy. Mason continued his torture, licking up the crease between Lucky's thigh and groin, sucking one of Lucky's balls into his mouth, his finger teasing Lucky's entrance.

"Fuck, Mason. Please!"

With a chuckle, Mason shifted, and Lucky's back arched up off the bed at the feel of Mason's tongue spearing his hole.

"Jesus, you taste good. Not that I expected you to taste any other way. Fuck, I want to taste every inch of you. Lick you, bite you, suck you, make you a part of me. I want you so bad, darlin'. It's bordering on the unhealthy."

Mason speared Lucky's hole again with his tongue. He didn't just rim Lucky, he dined on him like a starved man. When Lucky couldn't seem to take any more, Mason took hold of Lucky's cock, and swallowed him down to the root.

"Fuck!"

Mason popped off long enough to grin wickedly. "All in due time, darlin'."

"You're such a fucking tease," Lucky grumbled, making Mason laugh. He sat back on his heels, and Lucky moaned. "Why do you have to be so damn beautiful? Look at you.

It's obscene how perfect you are." The man was a wall of muscle—tanned, and thick all over, from his thighs and chest to his neck and biceps, his hands were big with long fingers. He was just big all over, and the thick, long, cock Mason slowly stroked had Lucky salivating. "If you don't put that monster cock inside me, Cowboy, I'm going to finish myself off." Lucky started to jerk off, grinning when Mason grabbed the lube and condom. He rolled the condom on, poured a generous amount of lube in his hand, then stroked himself. He'd already stretched Lucky out, which meant he went straight for lining his cock with Lucky's hole.

"Grab your knees and hold them to your chest."

Lucky did as he was asked, hissing at the sting from the initial breach. He closed his eyes and let his head fall back, relaxing his body and allowing Mason to slowly sink inside him. His heart told him maybe he should say something to Mason, let him know that before Mason, Lucky had never—

"Fuck, you're so tight."

"You need to move, Cowboy." With Mason buried deep inside, Lucky was full beyond measure, or so it felt. Something in his voice or expression must have given away his insecurities because Mason leaned in and kissed him sweetly, tenderly.

"I got you, darlin'," Mason murmured, brushing his lips over Lucky's. "You're really something, you know that? I've never met anyone like you."

The words were nothing new. Lucky had heard similar words before, but from Mason, he believed them. His heart swelled, and he was filled with ridiculous hope and happiness. The intimacy was almost too much, but instead of running from it, Lucky embraced it. He cupped Mason's face and returned his kiss, their tongues dancing together as

Mason began to move inside him. Lucky wrapped his arms around Mason's neck, loving Mason's weight on top of him as Mason lay on him, their chests pressed together, Mason's hands on either side of Lucky's face, his thumbs stroking Lucky's cheeks.

"Lucky, I—"

The raw emotion in Mason's eyes was too much. Lucky nipped at his chin. "Come on, Cowboy. Fuck me hard."

Mason's brows drew together, and he opened his mouth to speak, but Lucky reached between them and tweaked Mason's nipple.

"Fuck!" Heat filled Mason's gaze, and his lips curled into a sinful grin. "Okay, darlin'. Whatever you want." Mason snapped his hips, and Lucky cried out a curse. "This what you wanted, huh?" Mason pulled almost all the way out, then drove in deep and hard over and over.

"¡Santo cielos! Sí. Así es, my amor. Más duro. Por favor, Mason."

"You drive me so fucking crazy." Mason sat back on his heels, his arms wrapped around Lucky's legs as he pounded Lucky's ass. He changed his angle, and Lucky let out a string of curses. He pumped his cock, the bed creaking and moving beneath them with Mason's unyielding thrusts. Fuck, he was so damned sexy. Lucky wanted to lick him all over. He urged Mason on, begging him to fuck him senseless. The harder and faster Mason fucked him, the more Lucky begged. Sweat dripped down the side of Mason's face, and Lucky wanted to lap it up. Their bodies were slick with sweat despite the cool air coming from the AC. Mason changed his angle again and grinned wickedly as Lucky arched up off the bed with a cry.

"Liked that, huh?"

"Oh fuck yes!" My God, why had he waited this long to

have Mason in his bed? Mason undulated his hips once again at the same angle, and Lucky threw his head back. "Fuck, fuck, fuck, Mason!"

"I love hearing you scream my name. Love how your body responds to me. Like it was made for me. God, look at you."

"I want you to come in my mouth."

"Oh fuck yes." Mason carefully slid out, then pulled the condom off and tossed it to the floor. He knelt over Lucky and fed him his cock, groaning as Lucky's lips closed around his rock-hard length. Lucky's lips were swollen from their kisses, slick with saliva, and he looked like the fucking sexiest thing Mason had ever seen. "That's it, darlin'. You look so damned good with my dick in your mouth. Fuck that feels good."

Lucky sucked him hard, his fingers digging into Mason's muscular thighs. He stopped moving his head, and met Mason's gaze, inviting him to fuck his mouth.

"Darlin', you are going to be the death of me one way or another." Mason fucked Lucky's mouth, the room filled with the sounds of their panting breaths and Mason's moans. "Oh God, I'm gonna come." Mason's thrusts grew erratic as he pumped himself inside Lucky's mouth until he came with a roar. He doubled over as he filled Lucky's mouth, his body trembling from his release. As soon as he was done, Lucky slid him down his body to rut against his ass. "That's it, baby, come all over my crease."

Lucky cried out, his release thundering through him as he unloaded all over Mason's ass. He shivered from head to toe, his body convulsing with the force of his release. Mason got up and disappeared into the bathroom, then returned with a damp washcloth. He cleaned them both off and disposed of the condom and the washcloth before gently nudging Lucky to get under the duvet.

Not overthinking it, Lucky climbed beneath the duvet and let Mason pull him into his arms, holding him close against his warm, firm body. Mason placed a tender kiss to Lucky's brow, and after a long, languid kiss that seemed to go on forever, Lucky snuggled close. He knew he shouldn't get used to this, but he would be stupid not to enjoy it while he could.

"This is more than just sex," Mason said hesitantly, his words echoing Lucky's thoughts. "I know we don't have a name for it yet, but it's not just sex, right?"

Lucky considered lying or not responding, but he couldn't do that to Mason. Or himself. Mason's body went rigid, his breath caught before Lucky spoke up, his voice quiet. "Right." The tension seemed to melt away, and Mason relaxed. He sighed deeply and kissed Lucky's temple.

"Okay."

Lucky remained awake long after Mason had fallen asleep. He had no idea what the hell he was going to do. What would happen when the investigation was over and Mason went back to work? Would they go back to the way things were? Maybe whatever was between them was more than sex, but that didn't mean it translated into a relationship. Becoming exclusive didn't guarantee a happy ever after. It seemed like minutes after Lucky fell asleep, he was waking up, though looking at his phone it had been several hours. The name flashing on his phone had him sitting up. He carefully but quickly got out of bed and hurried into the bathroom to answer.

"You okay?"

"I'm so sorry. I know it's late, but I need you."

"Okay. Text me your location. I'm on my way."

As soon as he had the information on his phone, he hurried back into the room. He used the moonlight coming from the window, since they'd forgotten to close the blinds, and the flashlight on his phone to grab his clothes. Pulling on his boxer-briefs, he straightened, almost jumping out of his skin when he saw Mason sitting up in bed watching him.

"You scared the shit out of me."

"Did I now." Mason's voice was gruff, part sleep, part something else.

"I need to go. A friend needs my help."

Mason ran a hand through his hair, his sigh heavy. "Sure."

Lucky froze. "You don't believe me?"

"No, it's fine."

"That was you not answering my question." Did Mason not trust him?

"Go help your friend, Lucky." Mason lay down, pulled the duvet over his shoulder, and rolled away, turning his back to Lucky.

"Wow, okay." It was like Mason had plunged a knife into his heart. Had he given Mason any indication he was going to run off to be with someone else? Maybe they hadn't settled on anything official, maybe Lucky was too afraid to label whatever was between them, but to have Mason think he was running off in the middle of the night to go meet a lover? That hurt. And pissed him off. "Get your ass up. You're coming with me."

"No thanks. I'm not into sharing."

"You are an asshole," Lucky spat, swiping up Mason's clothes to throw at his head, not caring where his belt buckle hit him. "Now get dressed."

"Ow, Jesus. It's two in the fucking morning. I'm not going anywhere, especially not to meet one of your—"

"One of my what? My booty calls? One-night stands? Because that's what you think of me, no? That's clearly what I do when I let a guy fuck me for the first time in my life. I run off to see another lover, yes?"

"Wait, what?" Mason turned and sat up, the duvet falling to around his waist. "What do you mean when you let a guy fuck you for the first time? And it's not the first time."

"Do you want me to say it in Spanish? I'm not sure how I can say it any clearer. You fucked me last night. Yes, you fucked me in the truck. The point is, you were the first guy to do it."

"You've never—"

"No," Lucky growled.

"I—shit, I'm—"

"Get dressed or I'm leaving without you, and if I leave without you, I suggest you not be here when I get back." Lucky hated threats, but he was so pissed off he could barely contain it. The pain eased a little at how fast Mason scrambled out of bed and pulled on his clothes. At least the fucker actually cared, and he knew Mason said what he did out of fear, but that was no excuse. Mason got dressed fast, nearly falling over while attempting to pull on his jeans.

Lucky placed the Do Not Disturb sign on the door and stormed out, Mason hurrying silently behind him. Neither of them said a word all the way down to valet. Mason made to take the keys from the valet guy, but Lucky swiped them.

"I'm driving." He tipped the man, then climbed in behind the wheel. It wasn't until Lucky was on I-4 that Mason spoke up.

"Where are we going?"

"Daytona." That was as much as Mason was going to get out of him. He'd have to wait until Lucky was good and ready to say more than a few words or he would *not* be happy with what came out of Lucky's mouth. His cowboy had good instincts, and considering he remained silent the whole ride up, Mason knew he'd fucked up. Shit. He'd just thought of Mason as *his* cowboy. He was so fucked.

NINE

IT TOOK LESS than an hour to get to Madeline Avenue. Lucky smiled when he spotted the bright flares plunged into the ground on the right side of the road near the small lake. Tommy had pulled off the road and gotten as far away from it as possible just like they'd taught him. The number of people in this state who were killed because they got out of their cars on the side of the road or got out to help someone who was stranded was obscene. Thankfully, Tommy lived at the end of Sunset Cove Drive in the cul-de-sac, so his car picked a good place to break down. Lucky pulled the SUV up behind Tommy's car. He left the car running, lights on, doors unlocked, and got out. Tommy's face when he saw Lucky was heartwarming.

"Thank you so much for coming, Uncle Lucky." Tommy threw his arms around Lucky and hugged him tight. He might be seventeen years old, but Lucky remembered the day he was born, a tiny little wrinkled bundle with a tuft of bright red hair. Spider had been such a proud daddy that day.

Lucky squeezed Tommy before pulling back and

cupping his face, his expression stern. "What are you doing out so late, hm?"

"I was studying at a friend's house."

Lucky arched an eyebrow, and Tommy laughed. "I really was. Don't worry, Mom knows. I'm staying with my friend while Mom's out of town for work, but I realized we needed a few things for our science project. I came back quick to get it. My friend lives just down the road. I can't believe I broke down so close to home. Stupid car."

Lucky turned to Mason. "Mason, this is Tommy, a family friend. Tommy, I'm sure you remember Ace mentioning Mason. He's doing some work for the Kings." *He is also in the dog house for being a dick.*

Mason cast Lucky a sideways glance at being introduced as nothing more than a coworker, but he didn't respond, instead he turned to Tommy and held out his hand with a friendly smile.

"Nice to meet you, Tommy."

Tommy shook Mason's hand. He looked from Mason to Lucky and back. "I'm sorry if I, um, interrupted something."

"You didn't interrupt," Mason assured him. "We were on a job close by."

"What's wrong with the car?" Lucky walked around to the popped hood.

"It made this funky noise, so I pulled over, and it died. I think it overheated."

"Okay, why don't you get inside and try to turn it on."

Tommy did as instructed, and Mason appeared next to Lucky. "Uncle? I thought you were an only child?"

"I'm like an uncle to him, like the rest of the Kings, Jack, and Joker. We've known him since he was born. His father, Spider, was part of our unit."

"Shit, I'm so sorry, Lucky."

Lucky shrugged. "We survived, they didn't, so it's our duty to take care of their families." He craned his neck around the hood and motioned for Tommy to stop trying to start the car. Lucky checked the usual suspects first. The thermostat was fine, no obstructions were blocking the grill, the fan and fan belt were fine. He checked for leaks, breaks, low fluids. Mason lay on the grass and looked under the car.

"We got a leak."

"What is it?" Lucky asked.

"Coolant."

"Shit." Lucky took a closer look at the water pump. "Yeah, water pump is fucked. Looks like the shaft seal is broken." Lucky straightened as Tommy walked over. "This isn't something we can fix right now. The water pump needs replacing."

Tommy cringed, and Lucky planted his hands on his hips, eyes narrowed.

"You knew it needed replacing?"

"Yeah, I got the replacement in the trunk. I was going to try and do it myself. The mechanic guy said it would cost, like, a thousand bucks to replace."

"First of all, you need a new mechanic. That man is a thief. This is a Honda not a Hummer. Let's get it towed to your house, and I'll get it changed for you." He turned to Mason. "Why don't you go back to the hotel. This will take a couple of hours at least. I can call someone to give me a lift back."

Mason's frown was deep. "I'm not leaving you two out here alone. There's probably gators in that lake."

Lucky blinked at him before letting out a bark of laughter. "Okay, Cowboy. You can help."

"Damn right."

"Okay, everyone in the SUV. I'll call someone to come

tow the car when we get to the house." Lucky closed the hood, took the keys from Tommy, and turned the lights off. He locked the doors, then climbed behind the wheel of the SUV. Tommy sat in the back and Mason in the passenger seat. He pulled out on the road, then made a left on Sunset Cove.

"You got some grease on your cheek." Mason leaned over and gently rubbed a thumb over the spot on his cheek.

Lucky chuckled. "I'm sure there's going to be plenty more when I get under the car."

"Why don't you let me do the dirty work, huh? You're gonna ruin your clothes."

"It's okay," Lucky replied warmly. "It's just clothes. They can be replaced."

Mason hummed, his smile making Lucky fidget in his seat. "That so, huh?"

"What?"

"Nothing. You never cease to amaze me."

Lucky felt his face flush. He didn't know what to say to that. Wait, he was supposed to be mad at Mason. Yes, mad. Very mad. He scowled, but it only lasted as long as Mason poking his side, making him jump and bark out a laugh.

"Are you crazy? I'm driving."

"Come on, Mr. Green Beret. Don't tell me you can't handle a little poke."

"Let's see how you like it when you get poked."

"That a threat or a promise?"

Tommy leaned forward in between the seats. "Are you two together? Wait." Tommy peered at Mason. "You dated Ace, and now you're dating his cousin? Is Ace cool with that?"

"Seat belt," Lucky and Mason said simultaneously.

Tommy sat back with a snicker. "Yes, Dads."

Lucky almost choked on his spit, and for some reason, Mason found that hilarious. When Lucky was done coughing up a lung, he pulled into Tommy's driveway, put the car in Park, then turned to punch Mason in the arm. "I was choking and instead of helping me, you're laughing? Asshole."

Mason's laughter turned into a snicker before he leaned in to cup Lucky's cheek. "I'm sorry, darlin'. You're so damned cute when you get in that horn-tossing mood, I can't help it." He placed a sweet kiss on Lucky's lips.

"I don't know what that means, but I will consider forgiving you. Maybe."

"I would really appreciate that."

"So... yes?" Tommy asked, looking from Lucky to Mason and back. "I'm guessing yes on Ace being cool with this since he's got Colton, who by the way, has *the* awesomest house ever. You should all hook up with billionaires. Just saying. No offense, Mason."

"Um, none taken."

"Is it a yes on the dating?"

Lucky and Mason exchanged glances before Mason replied somewhat hesitantly. "It's kinda complicated."

Tommy rolled his eyes as he unfastened his seat belt. "Not really, but whatever." He let out a snort. "And everyone says teenagers are dramatic."

"He's got a point." Mason shrugged, laughing when Lucky punched him in the arm again.

"Come on, Cowboy. Time to get to work." Lucky got out of the car and pulled out his cell phone to call one of the tow truck companies the Kings used. While they waited for the car to be towed, they followed Tommy into the house, turning on lights as they went. Lucky knew this house like the back of his hand. Same way he knew all the houses of his fallen brothers' families.

Tommy pointed at the kitchen. "You guys want some coffee or something? I make a mean cappuccino."

"Sure," Lucky replied. "Two teaspoons of brown sugar please."

"You're such a coffee diva."

"And don't you forget it." He turned to find Mason in the living room, and Lucky didn't have to be standing next to him to know what he was looking at. He joined Mason, his heart squeezing at the twelve smiling faces.

"King's actually smiling," Mason said, his voice quiet.

"He smiled a lot more back then. That was before we lost the guys, before his parents were killed."

"Ace told me. His parents were driving to help friends after Hurricane Charley when half the road washed out. I can't even begin to imagine how fucked up that was for King. To be deployed in the middle of God knows where, doing God knows what, all while leading a team of men, knowing he wouldn't be able to make their funeral."

"Yes. It was devastating for him, not only because he wasn't able to be there when they buried his parents, but because he wasn't there for his sister. Bibi of course never held it against him. She understood. But King...." Lucky let out a heavy sigh as he picked up the frame holding the eight-by-ten photo of their ODA. "He believes he failed her. Like he believes he failed us." It seemed like only yesterday they were all together, and then they weren't.

"From the little I know, none of what happened was his fault. I mean, the guy almost fucking died."

Lucky nodded. If it hadn't been for Red, they would have lost King as well. "I know, but you won't convince King of that." Lucky pointed to the big guy with his arm around a smiling Joker. "That's Spider, Tommy's father. He was our second engineer sergeant, and a good man. They all were."

"Coffee's ready," Tommy called out from the kitchen.

Lucky returned the frame to the shelf, the chill in his body chased away by Mason's arm wrapped around him as he walked with Lucky to the kitchen. They sat at the counter and thanked Tommy for the coffee. He excused himself to go open the garage for when the tow truck arrived.

Mason took a sip of his coffee. "He seems like a good kid, but then he's very lucky to have a bunch of uncles like you fellas to look after him."

"He is a good kid, but in some ways, I don't envy him."

"Why's that?"

"Because he can get away with nothing. At his age, the things Ace and I were doing?" Lucky crossed himself. "We did not have six Green Berets to keep us from getting into trouble."

Mason laughed. "Your poor mothers. Jesus. So what kind of trouble did you boys get into?"

Lucky shook his head. "Nope. My lips are sealed."

"Well, maybe I can unseal them." Mason leaned in to kiss him, chuckling against Lucky's lips when Tommy returned, his sigh very put out.

"Ugh, you guys are ridiculous."

A horn honked, and Mason got up. "Finish your coffee, darlin'. I'll go." He left without giving Lucky a chance to argue.

Lucky turned back to his coffee and found Tommy with his elbows on the counter and his chin in his hands. He had a silly sappy smile on his face. "So, tell us about the new boyfriend. Do you and Ace compare notes?"

"No, we don't compare notes. And no, he's not my boyfriend," Lucky muttered, taking a sip of his coffee.

"And whose fault is that?" Tommy arched an eyebrow at him, and Lucky groaned. Really? Was he about to be lectured on relationships by a teenager? "I don't know why things didn't work out between him and Ace. Ace never talked about it, but I know Mason's a great guy. Not to mention he's a cowboy, and fine. I would totally do him, and I'm not even into dudes."

"Hey!"

"*Pfft*. Don't act like you don't remember what it's like to be seventeen. You were probably having way more sex than I—"

Lucky narrowed his eyes.

"Am not having. As in you were having all the sex and I am not."

"You remember the talk, yes?"

Tommy's expression turned deadpan. "The talk? You mean the intervention? Where you Ace, King, Red, Jack, and Joker sat in my living room and scarred me for life by explaining sex? Is that what you're referring to?"

"It wasn't so bad."

Tommy threw his hands up, his voice going up in pitch. "King had a *PowerPoint* presentation, Lucky! How is that 'not so bad'?"

"Okay, that was maybe a little too much."

"You know what's too much?" Tommy asked, eyebrows near his hairline as he pointed to Lucky. "You all. You boys need Jesus. Though I admit, it was all worth it to see King's face when you did your little biology lesson on the vagina followed by your tips and tricks for getting a woman to orgasm using your tongue. I'm positive he was regretting his life choices at that moment."

Lucky burst out laughing, and Tommy snickered as Mason entered the kitchen. He smiled wide at them.

"What did I miss?"

Tommy patted Mason's arm as he walked by. "If King ever offers to show you one of his PowerPoint presentations, run away." He gave Lucky two thumbs up from behind Mason before he disappeared into the garage.

God, he loved that kid.

"What's he talking about?"

"You don't want to know, believe me."

Once the car was in the driveway, Lucky and Mason wheeled it into the center of the garage and got it onto jack stands. Everything they needed was in the garage. The Kings made sure to keep it stocked for emergencies and whatever car issues Tommy and his mom might have. The engine was cool by now, so while Mason loosened the radiator cap, Lucky got to draining the coolant.

Things moved much quicker with both of them working together, and Lucky was pleasantly surprised with how in sync they were. It took just under a couple of hours to get everything taken apart, put it back together, and refill the coolant.

"There we go. All done." Lucky washed his hands in the tiny sink at the end of the garage, and Mason did the same after.

Tommy threw himself into Lucky's arms and hugged him. "Thank you, Uncle Lucky. For everything."

"You're welcome." Lucky squeezed him tight. "You and your mom know that we will always be here for you, anything you need, yeah?"

Tommy pulled back, his eyes glassy. He sniffed and looked away. "Yeah, we know."

"Okay." Lucky hugged him again, kissing the top of his

head before letting him go. Tommy reminded him of how quickly time passed, of how short and unpredictable life could be.

Tommy surprised Mason by hugging him. "It was great seeing you." He whispered something in Mason's ear, and Mason nodded. What was he up to? They waited for Tommy to grab what he needed from the house, lock up, and get in his car, then they escorted him to his friend's house, despite his insistence that he'd be fine. It had turned four by the time Lucky merged onto I-4. Man, what a day. He let out a yawn, and Mason jerked next to him.

"Are you okay?" Lucky asked, worried.

"Yeah, sorry. Are you okay to drive? Maybe we should pull into a motel or something and get some sleep for a few hours, before we head back to the hotel."

"Why? It's less than an hour. I'm fine to drive."

"Are you sure? You were yawning and all."

"I yawned one time. I'm okay. Really. I'm not sleepy. Are you sure you're okay?"

"Yeah. No. I'm sorry. I was an asshole. You woke me up when you got outta bed, and when I saw you getting dressed, I thought the worst. I was pissed off at myself because you said you didn't want a relationship, and I'm trying to respect that, I am, but I won't lie and say it isn't getting harder by the minute with you. I don't judge you, at all, for not wanting more. I understand the appeal of keeping things simple, believe me, but there ain't nothing simple about us, darlin'. We said we'd be honest with each other, so that's what I'm doin'. You've never slept with anyone more than once. Why would I think I was different?"

"It is different." Lucky was trying his hardest not to get annoyed, but not at Mason, at himself, because Mason was absolutely right. About everything. Why wouldn't Mason think he'd decided to run away after they slept together? He did it in some form or another. He might not have run off to someone else, but he'd run.

"How is it different?"

"Because you matter," Lucky snapped. "None of those other people mattered, not the way you do, and you always have, Mason." He shifted uncomfortably in his seat. "If you didn't, I would have slept with you the moment I found out you were attracted to me, and then that would have been it. After the surveillance job? The truck? That would have been it. I lied."

Mason frowned. "About what?"

"About us having to share a bed. One of the other guards has a pullout couch in his room." Lucky's face burned with his confession, but since they were being honest....

"Wait, so you're telling me you *wanted* to share a bed?"

Lucky shrugged. "I didn't *not* want to share a bed."

"Nice try, darlin', but that dog won't hunt."

"You know, you have some very strange sayings in Texas."

"Is that right? This from the man who was talking about someone walking with his elbows?"

Lucky snickered. "When someone is stingy with money, you say that person 'camina con los codos.' The cousin Ace and I were talking about is very cheap."

"Don't go changing the subject, Eduardo. You wanted to share a bed with me."

Lucky sighed. "Yes, fine. I did."

"Why?"

Lucky turned off on their exit. "Why do I need to answer this?"

"Because I want to hear how much you wanted me."

Lucky stopped at a red light and turned to arch an eyebrow at a very smug-looking Mason. "Okay, after the night in the truck, and then again that night on the phone, I couldn't stop thinking about you and... wanting you. Happy?"

"If I felt any better, I'd think it was a setup. 'Course I am, darlin'. You're crazy about me. That makes me very happy."

Lucky rolled his eyes. "Ay, Dios mío." The light turned green. "Crazy? Most likely. Crazy about you? I need to think about this." He ignored Mason's chuckle.

By the time they arrived back in the hotel room, it was six o'clock in the morning. Lucky brushed his teeth, removed his boots, and fell back into bed with a sigh. Mason turned off the lights before joining him. Maybe they could get a nap in before check-out.

"You fellas make me feel like I should be doing more."

"What do you mean?"

"All the charity stuff, the people you help. How you help out the families of your fallen brethren? That's really something."

Lucky shrugged. "We're blessed, you know? We survived, were given another chance at life. If we can help others who are not so fortunate, we will."

"It's admirable."

"It's family," Lucky corrected. "That's what families do."

"Not all families."

At Mason's dark tone, Lucky rolled over, ending up face-to-face with Mason. He opened his mouth to speak but found no words as Mason reached up to caress his cheek.

"You're a better man than I am."

"What are you talking about? You're a good man, Mason. Sometimes a bit pigheaded—*Dios mío*, but you are pigheaded—*but* you're a good man."

"I'm not." Mason's eyes clouded over, and Lucky sat up, bringing his legs up and crossing them at the ankles.

"Mason? Talk to me. *Trust me.*"

With a sigh, Mason sat up. He turned, his legs over the side of the bed, and his back to Lucky. Needing to see his face, Lucky moved to sit next to him.

"Thing is, I do trust you, Lucky, and I care about you, which is why coming clean to you is both a relief and one of the scariest things I've had to do in a very long time." Mason took a steady breath. "A while back, I legally changed my name. Cooper's my grandma's maiden name. The name I was born with is Mason Chester Brooks Jr."

"Why did you change your name?"

Mason hesitated, and Lucky placed his hand to his shoulder, his tone gentle.

"Tell me."

"My family comes from money. Old money. Before I was born, my father decided to turn our ranch into a dude ranch. He wanted to capitalize on tourism. Our ranch was more of a resort. It was hard work, believe me, and while I was in college, my father expected me to go to school full-time and help out on the ranch." Mason took another breath, as if bracing himself.

"One summer, we got this huge tour group staying at the ranch, and my father called me up and said he needed me home to help. Every day after I finished with my classes, I'd rush over to the ranch and do whatever my daddy told me." His lips curled in disgust at the words. "One afternoon my father calls me into his office and tells me I need to fire Josiah Foster, one of our ranch hands. I was stunned. Josiah had been with us for years; one of the best ranch hands we had. I'd never fired anyone before, and I especially didn't want to fire Josiah, but I knew better than to refuse. When I asked my father what Josiah had done, he told me a child was in the hospital after being thrown off a horse that morning, and that was down to Josiah's negligence." Mason placed his fists on his thighs, his jaw clenched tight, and his gaze off in the distance. "That son of a bitch was lying through his teeth, and worst of all, he knew it."

"Who? Josiah?" Lucky asked, confused.

"No." Mason turned his tear-filled gaze to Lucky. "My father. Josiah tried to warn him about that horse, that it was acting up, but my father brushed it off as nonsense, convinced she was the kind of horse you could kick and she wouldn't run. My father insisted Josiah was overreacting. He wasn't about to spend money on another horse or lose money by cancelling the rides. I tried talking to my father about it after Josiah stormed off, but he didn't want to hear another word about it."

"So someone gets hurt, your father blames Josiah, and then wants *you* to fire him?"

Mason nodded.

"What did you do?" Lucky asked softly.

"I fired him." A tear rolled down Mason's cheek, and Lucky gently brushed it away with his thumb. It wasn't the end of Mason's story. Lucky could feel it down to his core. As much as he wanted to hear the rest, his heart was heavy for Mason and the guilt he carried for so long.

"What happened after?"

"Josiah was mad as hell, but not at me. With me, he was disappointed. He said, "I thought you were better than this, son." Here I was studying to be a lawyer, and I was condemning a man I *knew* was innocent. The next day, my father wakes me up in the middle of the night and yells at me to get to the ranch. Josiah was there and up in arms, stating he had proof against my father's accusations. My father said it was my mess and I had to fix it."

It took everything Lucky had in him to remain quiet and not curse Mason's father. Instead, he waited patiently as Mason continued.

"I was in the middle of finals and dead on my feet. I'd been working odd jobs under the table to earn money so I wouldn't have to rely on my father. Anyway, I tried to convince him to let me come down in the morning, but when Chester Brooks gives an order, you damn well hop to it if you know what's good for you. I set out to the ranch soon as I hung up the phone."

Lucky didn't like where this was going, but he remained silent, needing to hear the words from Mason.

"The road to the ranch is long and dark as fuck, with a few light poles scattered here and there. It's mostly dirt, lined with nothing but miles and miles of dead grass and shrubbery. I was doing everything in my power to stay awake. Next thing I knew I was jerked awake by the sound of skidding tires and an explosive crash. I slammed on the brakes, and jumped out of the car." A sob tried to escape Mason, but he quickly recovered, forcing it down inside so he could carry on with his story. "I ran over, stopping to be sick because my blood had turned to ice. I'd never seen a car so wrecked. It hit the light pole so hard it splintered the pole. Inside the car, the driver was...."

Mason shook his head. "It was Josiah, and his wife Sally. Thank God their son, Ryden, wasn't in the car that night. Ryden was only a few years younger than me, and all I could think about was what I'd done to his family. Anyway, I didn't know what to do. I told Sally I'd go get help, but she told me to go home and not tell anyone. That she'd take care of everything, how my life didn't have to be ruined. I didn't want to go, but she started screaming and crying, yelling at me to go, to not tell anyone what happened.

"When I got home, I was a right mess. I went straight to my parents, told them everything. I was a stupid kid. I didn't know what the fuck to do, so I turned to the people who I thought would help. The look my father gave me...." Mason shut his eyes tight, his bottom lip trembling. "Like I was his biggest failure. I mean, it was bad enough I was queer, but now this? He said he'd take care of it like he did everything and to not say a word. I told him maybe we should tell the truth, but all that got me was the back of my father's hand. The next day, Sally came to talk to my father, and the day after that, my parents shipped me off to my aunt and uncle's ranch in Montana.

Lucky ran his hand in soothing circles on Mason's back, not knowing what to say. He knew Mason wasn't finished unloading the heavy weight he'd carried for so long.

"I was sure news would hit the papers, the radio, something. I expected people to show up on my aunt's doorstep with pitchforks, or at the very least the police to come and take me away in handcuffs. I waited for Ryden to show up wanting retribution for what I'd done, but I never heard from him. For years, I looked over my shoulder, waiting for the other shoe to drop, but it never did. I changed careers and decided to do criminal justice instead. I changed my name, making it harder for my family to find me, because I know whatever happened, my parents had something to do with it. Then I became a cop. I wanted to help people, to maybe stop a kid like me from doing something stupid and ruining someone's life." Mason let out a shuddering breath.

"It wasn't bad enough I allowed an innocent man to take the blame for a crime he didn't commit, but I fired him for it, and then I killed him. I killed a man, Lucky, and then I ran like the coward I am. I've never stopped running."

"You're not a coward, Mason, and you're not running. Not anymore. You've spent your life trying to make up for what happened to Josiah. Was what happened to him wrong? Yes. Was it tragic? Absolutely. Could it have been avoided? That we will never know. Does what happened make you a killer? No, of course not." Lucky pushed off the bed and came to stand in front of Mason. "For as long as I have known you, you've been haunted by this." He put a hand to Mason's heart, smiling warmly when Mason covered Lucky's hand with his. "You have a very kind heart, one that has been filled with so much pain and guilt. That is not the heart of a bad man." With his free hand, he brushed Mason's hair from his face. "You cared for my cousin very much, and because you felt unworthy, you let him walk away."

"It just wasn't meant to be, but maybe that's a good thing." Mason pulled Lucky close, wrapped his arms around him, and lay his brow against Lucky's chest.

"You're a good man, Mason, and you deserve to be loved."

"There's so much I want to say to that, darlin', but it would probably terrify us both."

Lucky lifted Mason's face, their eyes meeting. "Then do not say anything. Show me."

TEN

SHOW ME.

How could two little words have the power to undo him so completely?

Mason pulled Lucky down to straddle his lap, his arms wrapped around Lucky's slender frame, pressing their bodies together. Lucky wasn't just beautiful; he was a whirlwind of passion and contradiction. The light in his soul burned bright, shining through the flecks of amber in his whiskey-colored eyes. It was all or nothing with Lucky, a roller coaster ride of emotions that sucked everyone around him into his orbit. Mason had never been pulled in so many directions by one person before, and he loved it, *craved* it.

Until now, Mason had been living half a life, fearful of finding happiness knowing he would lose it all too quickly because a man like him didn't deserve to be happy. Kissing Lucky, tasting his lips, feeling his warmth and affection, Mason was no longer willing to let happiness slip through his fingers. He wanted to hold on, to share his life with the gorgeous man who hadn't been content to merely poke and prod him until he woke from the fog he'd lost himself in, but who'd dragged him out of the darkness, ready to give as good as he got.

Mason stopped kissing Lucky long enough to pull his shirt over his head. He couldn't think of anything he loved more than kissing Lucky.

"I want to ride you, Cowboy."

Mason ran his hands up Lucky's smooth, soft skin. "I touch you, and I just want to drop to my knees and worship you."

Lucky's smile was radiant. It quickly turned sinful as he climbed off Mason's lap. He spread Mason's knees, and knelt between them, reaching for Mason's waistband. "I will let you worship me, if you let me take care of you. You need someone to take care of you."

"I do," Mason said hoarsely. "I never knew how much I wanted that until you." Mason cupped Lucky's cheek, loving the way Lucky leaned into the touch then kissed his palm. Lucky tugged at Mason's pajama bottoms and underwear, urging him to lift his hips. As soon as he did, Lucky pulled them down and off. Mason removed his shirt and tossed it to the floor, where it joined Lucky's. He kept his eyes on Lucky's, a shiver running through him as Lucky slid his hands up Mason's thighs, caressing his skin. Having Lucky kneeling between his legs, the want in his eyes as he wrapped a hand around Mason's hard cock was enough to have Mason grabbing fistfuls of the blanket.

Lucky took Mason deep into his throat, and Mason bucked his hips, a string of curses leaving his lips at the sudden wet heat. Instead of frenzied sucking, Lucky moved leisurely, making love to Mason's cock with his mouth. Mason wanted to close his eyes and throw his head back, but that would mean missing the glorious sight of Lucky's plump lips wrapped around him, or the way his hand moved on his own dick as he sucked Mason off. Soon it was too much, and Mason pulled Lucky off him and up into his lap, kissing him until they were forced to come up for air.

"Get the lube and condom," Mason said, breathless.

"Lube, yes. Condom, no."

Mason stared at him. "Are you sure?"

"You were tested recently, no?"

"Yeah, and you know all about the cough medicine. Everything else came back negative."

"And we get tested every quarter at work, the last one being a few weeks ago. The results were negative. I can show you." Lucky ran his fingers through Mason's hair. His voice soft. "I've never had sex without protection, I promise."

Mason brushed his fingers down Lucky's cheek. "I believe you, baby."

With a sweet kiss to Mason's lips, Lucky left him to get the lube, and Mason moved back onto the bed, his arm behind his head against the pillow, his eyes never leaving Lucky. The window provided enough moonlight for Mason to see Lucky's tattoo. It was stunning, running from his torso down over his hip to his thigh. The bottom of the tattoo was a mirror image of the top but flipped. The artwork was intricate and detailed, the profile of the lion's head majestic. A sword entwined with roses, vines, and thorns rested at an angle over the expanse of the lion's mane. A large cursive "L" was displayed prominently in the center, and much like a playing card, on the top left and flipped on the bottom right was a black clover. The whole thing must have taken hours upon hours with the amount of detail.

Lucky climbed onto the bed beside Mason, and Mason let out a low growl, unable to stop himself from reaching out and putting his hands on Lucky. Following his lead, Lucky straddled Mason and leaned in to kiss him, his lips soft against Mason's. He tasted so damn good, and Mason ran his hands up Lucky's toned arms to his back before caressing his way down Lucky's back to his firm, round ass. Mason slipped a finger between his cheeks, and Lucky moaned against his lips. He sat back and took hold of Mason's hand, then poured a generous amount of lube onto his fingers.

"Fuck me with your fingers, Cowboy. Get me ready." Lucky lay on Mason, his arms wrapped around Mason's head, and his knees drawn up as far as he could get them to give Mason easy access.

Mason cursed under his breath, and grabbed hold of Lucky's asscheek, pressing a finger to his hole. He loved the way Lucky shivered, how he closed his eyes while a deep groan rose up from his chest. Mason did as Lucky asked, fucking him with first one finger then two until he had Lucky writhing and panting.

"Please, Mason."

"I don't want to hurt you."

Lucky opened his eyes, those pools of whiskey mesmerizing. When he spoke, his words were all but whispered. "Then don't."

Something inside Mason broke loose at the quiet words, and a shiver racked his body. He released a shuddering breath, as if he were taking air into his lungs for the first time in decades. At that moment it struck him how fiercely he never wanted to hurt Lucky.

Lucky kissed Mason, and Mason swore he felt it down to his bones. Lucky's kiss was filled with more than affection. It was a desperate plea filled with an emotion Mason was too afraid to give a name to, because if he did and he was wrong, it would break him.

"Lucky," Mason breathed as Lucky moved his lips to Mason's jaw, trailing kisses down to his neck where he nipped and licked. Lucky moved Mason's hand to position himself, his eyes locked on Mason's as he guided the tip of Mason's cock to his entrance. With a wince, Lucky pushed Mason inside him, slowly, torturously.

Mason's eyes all but rolled into the back of his head as Lucky sank down onto him until his ass was sitting against Mason's groin. A small huff of breath and Lucky was slowly moving, undulating his hips, his hands on Mason's chest. He leaned forward, taking Mason's lips in a sweet but ardent kiss. Lucky's fingers entwined in his hair, and when they were forced to come up for air, Lucky nipped at Mason's bottom lip. With a sinful smile, he sat back, lifting his hips, then impaling himself on Mason's cock.

"Fuck!" Mason gripped Lucky's hips, his fingers digging in hard enough to leave bruises. "You're going to drive me out of my damned mind, you know that?"

Lucky's smile was wicked, but the vulnerability in his eyes betrayed him. "That's my plan, Cowboy. Drive you so crazy that you will never be able to walk away from me."

"I need you to understand that I won't walk away from you, Lucky. I want to stay. With you."

Lucky swallowed hard, his eyes glassy, but only for a moment before he blinked, and the vulnerability was replaced by heat. He started to move in earnest, bouncing on Mason, alternating between undulating his hips and fucking himself on Mason's cock. It felt fucking incredible, and Mason planted his feet on the bed so he could thrust up when Lucky came down.

"Oh fuck!" Lucky cried out, his mouth open in ecstasy,

and his brows furrowed as Mason grabbed hold of Lucky's asscheeks. He leaned forward, and Mason drove into him over and over, the sound of skin slapping against skin filling the room along with their panting breaths. The noises Lucky made as Mason fucked him, pumping up inside Lucky as far as he could, were driving Mason crazy.

"God, I love that I can do this to you. Make you look like you're about to fall apart in my arms," Mason said, breathless.

"Only you," Lucky replied. "I only want to feel you, no one else, and I don't want you to do this with anyone else. Fuck them. You're mine, Mason. Only mine."

"Fuck! Oh God, yes. That's all I want. Fuck. I'm gonna come, Lucky." Mason lost all rhythm in his thrusts, and he plowed inside Lucky, his orgasm raging through him. Sweat dripped down the side of his face, their bodies slick as they moved frantically together.

"Yes, please. Come inside me. I want you to leave a part of yourself inside me. I want to feel you with me wherever I go."

Mason roared out his release, his muscles strained as he came inside Lucky, his hoarse cry joined by Lucky's as he spurted across Mason's chest, his body shivering as he branded Mason, reminding him of his words. He'd called Mason *his*.

Lucky collapsed on top of Mason, and Mason wrapped his arms around Lucky as they steadied their breathing. He slipped his fingers between Lucky's cheeks, groaning at the feel of his come.

"You're very proud of yourself right now, hm?"

Mason's smile was ridiculous. "Yessir, I am."

Lucky's huff was sweet, and Mason kissed his temple, hugging him close. He loved holding Lucky to him, loved his weight on him, their bodies pressed together. As their bodies cooled, Mason rolled them over to unstick himself from Lucky, who grunted his disapproval at having Mason get up, but he needed to get them cleaned up. As soon as he did, he was back in bed, under the covers with Lucky in his arms. The fact Lucky hadn't needed prompting, that he pressed his body against Mason's the instant he was in bed, made Mason's heart skip a beat.

The room was so quiet, for a moment he thought Lucky was asleep when Lucky's soft-spoken words caught him off guard.

"I'm afraid."

"Of what?"

"I've lived my life waiting for things to be taken from me. It's the world I was raised in. If I had something good, it was only a matter of time before it was gone. Nothing is forever."

"You're right," Mason replied gently. "Nothing is forever. But you have people in your life who love you and would never leave you by choice, right? Ace, King, Red, the guys, your family."

"Yes, this is true."

"I want to try and be one of those people. I know maybe that's not what you want to hear, but I want you to give us a chance." Mason held his breath as the room went quiet again.

"Yes."

Lucky's reply was so low, Mason wasn't sure what he'd heard was an actual reply, or if he'd just heard what he wanted to hear. "Yes?"

"Okay." Lucky pushed himself onto his elbow to look down at Mason, their eyes meeting in the soft moonlight. "I want you in my bed, and in my heart. Don't hurt me, Mason."

Mason's heart soared at the words, and he couldn't keep the huge smile from coming onto his face. He laughed when Lucky rolled his eyes. "What? I'm happy."

"I'm happy too. Also, next time, maybe I get to fuck you?"

"Mmm, how long until next time?"

Lucky chuckled as he lay his head back against Mason's chest. "When we can both move without wincing, maybe?"

"Sounds like a date."

"No, a date sounds like you taking me out to dinner and maybe a movie, or dancing."

"Dancing, huh? I think I'd like that. See you moving this gorgeous body on the dance floor. 'Course that means other fellas are gonna be wanting a piece of this," Mason said, fondling Lucky's ass.

"They can want it as much as they like, but they won't be getting it. It's already taken."

"And if I have my say, it's going to be taken in the shower, on the couch, in my bed—"

"In *my* bed."

Mason wasn't going to argue with that. "Yeah, you got that big fancy house on the beach. Ooh, sex on the beach."

"No way, Cowboy. Sex on the beach is *not* sexy. Sand gets all up in places it shouldn't be. Not pleasant."

Mason chuckled. "I'll take your word for it."

"I have a pool. Sex in the pool."

"Now we're talking." Mason rubbed Lucky's asscheek. "Your ass is going to be in a permanent state of soreness."

"And what? You think you're going to walk away scot-free from all this sex?"

"Are you kidding? I expect fierce retaliation. No mercy."

"Just remember, you asked for it," Lucky mumbled, his voice laced with sleep.

"Can't wait." Mason closed his eyes, a smile plastered to his face. He'd never felt so... light, like the chains that he'd been dragging for so long had finally been removed. He was under no illusion that life with this amazing man would be easy, but Mason had every intention of doing right by Lucky. This was his chance to have something he never thought he'd have, so he wasn't about to give it up without one hell of a fight.

"YOU TWO ARE ON A ROLL."

King sat behind his desk, looking pleased as punch, and Mason had to admit he was a little pleased right now. When he and Lucky showed up for work first thing Monday morning—after a night of driving each other wild in Lucky's bed—King called them into his office. Mason had been uncertain, but Lucky had reassured him. They'd agreed to wait before announcing their change in relationship status to the rest of the Kings, seeing as how Mason might be returning to Major Crimes soon. He'd received a call that morning from his lawyer stating he should be receiving a response any day now. The thought didn't make Mason as happy as it should, but he brushed that sentiment aside for now.

"I got a call from Sienna Scott, her agent, *and* her father. All of them singing your praises. You make a pretty good team."

Mason smiled. "Thanks, King. 'Course, I have one hell of a boss." Mason winked at Lucky, who rolled his eyes.

"Yeah, yeah. Thanks, King."

King turned his attention to Mason. "You seem to be fitting right in."

"You fellas have a damn fine company," Mason said. "I'm honored to be a part of it, even if it is just temporary. It's been a real pleasure."

King nodded. His phone beeped, and he pressed a button to accept. "Yes, Jay?"

"Ace is here, sir."

"Send him in."

The door opened, and Ace walked in, huge smile on his face when he saw them. He tipped his imaginary hat before moseying over. "Well, if it ain't Wyatt Earp and Doc Holliday."

Lucky tipped his head as he studied Ace. "Have you been messing with Red's aromatherapy oils again?"

Ace narrowed his eyes. "No." At Lucky's arched eyebrow, Ace scrunched up his nose. "Maybe. Look, if he didn't want me messing with them, he shouldn't leave them lying around."

King let out a snort. "If you need a key to get to the oils, they are not lying around."

"How come everyone gets their own blend but me?" Ace planted his hands on his hips, looking affronted. "Even Lucky has a blend."

Lucky grinned at Mason. "I do. It's very pleasant. Bergamot, orange, spearmint, and ylang-ylang."

"See. Very pleasant. And me? No pleasant. Nothing. What the hell?"

"Are you bitching about the oils again?" Red asked, joining them. He shook his head at Ace, his frown deep.

"Damn it, Ace. Stop breaking into my drawers and touching my stuff."

"Those are definitely words no one wants to walk in on," Jack said with a shudder as he stopped beside Red. "Do I even want to know what's going on?"

Ace spun around and thrust his hand in Jack's face. "Jack, smell my fingers."

The sheer horror on Jack's face had Mason barking out a laugh. They were a bunch of loons, but Mason wouldn't change a thing.

"What the fuck, Ace! No. Get away from me."

"Smell my fingers, Jack! I need to know if this blend is me." Ace took off after Jack, who fled from the room like someone lit his ass on fire. Jack sped by, and Ace skidded to a halt, poking his head in the room. "Friday night, Sapphire Sands. Drinking and dancing. Ten o'clock. You too, King."

King opened his mouth, but Ace cut him off with a hand up.

"Nope. If I have to get Frank himself to haul your ass over there, I will. You keep promising him you'll come by, but you never do. You don't have to dance. God forbid you cut loose."

"Funny," King drawled.

"You're coming with us."

"Fine."

"Yes! Now if you'll excuse me, I have an Italian to rile up." Ace turned, shouting for Jack across the floor. "Don't hide from me, Jack! I'll get Chip if I have to."

Mason shook his head. "Poor, Jack."

Lucky snickered. "Don't feel too bad for him. Where Jack is, Joker is not far, and not even Ace will piss him off."

"Oh?"

"Short fuse," King offered. "But you didn't hear that from me."

Mason threw his head back and laughed. Holy shit, had King just made a joke? The twinkle in the guy's blue eyes confirmed it. Joker was the smallest and shortest of the bunch, and he *hated* being teased about his height. It was a one-way ticket to a kick in the balls.

Lucky turned in his seat to look at Red. "Why doesn't Ace have his own blend?"

"Because he wanted to pick his own scents," Red grumbled, crossing his arms over his expansive chest. "I warned him about putting certain ones together, but this is Ace we're talking about, so of course he ignored me. His blend sent everyone into a fit of sneezing."

"So, his blend caused chaos? Yes, that sounds like Ace. I would say it was successful."

Red chuckled. "Yeah, too successful. I told him to leave it to me, that I had something special planned, but that's like saying 'go ahead and do your own thing.' Anyway, I'll see you all later. Nice job on the Scott case, by the way."

The rest of the day went by in a blur. Even when Mason was at his desk doing paperwork, it was never dreary, as it tended to be broken up by one of the Kings chasing one of the others for thieving something from their office or eating something that didn't belong to them. Apparently it was a rare occurrence for all the Kings, Jack, and Joker to be in the office at the same time, but if they were, it was usually a Monday morning when everyone was catching up on paperwork. At one point, King bellowed from his office, and everyone's head shot up.

"Ace!"

"What?" came the shout from Ace's open office.

"Why in the hell are all the rubber bands neon pink!"

Ace poked his head out of his office. "Uh, they ran out of the regular ones?"

King narrowed his eyes. "Really? Are you really going to tell me our stationary supplier ran out of rubber bands and all they had was neon pink?"

Ace nodded slowly.

"If I call them up right now, they're going to tell me that's all they had?" King removed his cell phone from his pocket, and Ace's eyes went huge.

"It was Lucky!" Ace slammed the door to his office just as Lucky poked his head out.

"That's bullshit. I don't order stationary supplies."

Jay typed away at his computer, and his printer spit something out. He nonchalantly handed the piece of paper up to King, who took it.

"Thank you, Jay." King scanned the sheet, his scowl in full effect. He stormed over to Ace's office and pounded on the door. "Ace, open the damn door."

Ace's muffled voice came through the door. "Ace can't come to the door right now, but if you leave a message, he'll get back to you as soon as possible. *Beeeeep*."

"Don't make me use my key."

The door opened, and King shoved the printout in Ace's face. "You entered the wrong SKU number, jackass."

Ace took the printout. "Hmm, well, look at that. I did enter the wrong SKU number. My mistake."

"That's it?"

Ace shrugged. "Nothing we can do about it now. Your office needed a pop of color anyway."

"I'm gonna give you a pop of color in a minute," King growled.

Mason chuckled and returned to his reports as the two went back and forth. He spent most of the morning doing paperwork, and just before lunch, Lucky gave him a tour of the armory. Mason helped Lucky with an inventory check and listened with rapt fascination as Lucky went through each weapon, what it did, and how to use it. Several of the weapons Mason had heard of but never used during his career in law enforcement. After that they had lunch together.

Lucky ordered food, and they ate in the breakroom, fending off the guys as they dropped in to try and steal dumplings or eggrolls, but Lucky knew his brethren well, and he confessed to Mason that he ordered extra appetizers for them, despite his bitching. Mason had never felt this at ease at a place of work before. Maybe because he'd never worked somewhere so accepting. No one thought of him as a liability or harassment suit waiting to happen. His coworkers were friendly, greeting him cheerfully. They joked with him, teased him about being the new guy, and were genuinely happy he was there.

The pressure of having everyone's eyes on him, waiting for him to make one wrong move didn't exist here. The Kings expected him to give the job his all, and yes, they were friends, but they were also business men. As growly and gruff as King was, when it came to the employees, he was never anything other than patient. He was firm but fair.

As the week went on, Mason continued to learn about the company and how it ran. King went through the responsibilities of the different departments, the chain of command, what the different roles were, what they entailed, and how the teams were managed. He mentioned how he'd finally found someone to fill the position of team leader for Lucky's department, but how the guy would make a better fit in his, so the guys were swapping.

By the time Friday rolled around, Mason was ready for

a few drinks. He'd been run off his feet the second half of the week, joining one King or another on various jobs, everything from answering alarm callouts to smaller protection details and event security. The variety of cases kept Mason on his toes, and he enjoyed working with the different security teams. In the evening, he was put through his paces in a whole other way, a mind-blowing, toe-curling way that involved a gorgeous Cuban man with a sinful tongue and a *very* healthy sexual appetite.

MASON HADN'T BEEN to Sapphire Sands in months. Not since the night he'd run into Lucky after making the stupid mistake of hooking up with Oscar. He'd let his anger get the better of him, and because of that, he'd hurt Lucky. It had been an immature reaction he deeply regretted, and he wouldn't blame Lucky for changing his mind about going to the club with Mason, but Lucky surprised him by being excited about getting Mason on the dance floor.

Thanks to Ace, Mason held membership to Sapphire Sands, the exclusive, members-only gay nightclub and bar. It had been given to him as a present back when they'd been dating. Club membership was a perk the Kings received, thanks to their security contract with the club and its owner, Frank Ramirez. Frank also happened to be good friends with Colton. Mason liked Frank. He was the "salt of the earth" type. A former firefighter who'd worked hard to build his empire and prided himself on giving back to the community. As terrifying as he appeared in his signature all-black suit, towering height, powerful frame, and chiseled features, he was a genuinely good guy.

"Who let these troublemakers in?" Frank growled as he

approached the private booth they'd all been shown to, his deep scowl giving way to a grin when he reached their table.

With a big smile, Colton got to his feet and brought Frank into a tight embrace. "It's so good to see you."

"It's good to see you too, Colt." Frank tilted his head toward Ace. "You keeping him out of trouble?"

Colton let out a snort. "That's about as likely as you wearing those sparkly blue go-go shorts your dancers are so well-known for."

Frank grunted. "Point taken."

"Hey," Ace protested. "I resemble that remark."

Frank shook his head in amusement. He greeted each of them with a handshake and an additional pat to the arm for King. "Well, damn. And here I thought I'd offended you in some way."

King shook his head with a smile. "Nah, you know this isn't my scene, Frank."

"I know. But still. I'm glad you came. First round is on the house."

Everyone cheered and put in their order with the perky, cute waiter who sauntered over. The U-shaped booth was huge and fit them all comfortably, with enough room to get in and out easily. Lucky had slid in next to Mason as soon as he'd taken a seat and hadn't objected to Mason putting his arm around his shoulders. Ace gave Mason a knowing look from across the table but didn't say a word.

"To family," King said, lifting his pint glass.

They cheered and toasted, clinking glasses. The position of the booth off to one side of the expansive floor allowed them to have conversations. It was still loud, as nightclubs tended to be, but less so where they were. The club was impressive, with its sleek décor in all black with pops of its signature blue. Go-go boys in sparkly blue shorts danced seductively to the pulsing beat from atop raised platforms, and beyond the dance floor, the backrooms and curtained-off areas concealed men getting up to all kinds of naughty things, things he really shouldn't be thinking about with Lucky pressed up against him.

With their first round of drinks almost gone, Mason had been about to ask Lucky what he wanted from the bar when King pulled something out of his pocket and slammed it onto the table as he yelled, "Coin check!"

To his bemusement, the rest of the Kings, Jack, and Joker, hurried to shove their hands in their pockets. They each whipped something out, slamming their palms on the table, Ace being the last to do so.

"Damn it!" Ace threw his hands up as the rest of the guys cheered and teased him.

Mason leaned in to Lucky. "What's going on?" He motioned to the large coin Lucky had slammed on the table. The rest of the guys seemed to have something similar.

"It's an old tradition. When someone whips out their challenge coin and says what King did, everyone else has to quickly slam their coin down. Last one to get theirs down has to buy a round of drinks for everyone."

That would explain Ace's grumbling as he stood.

"What's a challenge coin?"

"They were given to us by our commander during our service for different challenges. Sometimes they're given out for morale or camaraderie. You'll find them everywhere in the military, and even certain branches of government. For some it's a symbol of solidarity, for others, bragging rights. It's also a good way to get yourself some free drinks," Lucky replied with a wink. He held his coin out to Mason, who took it.

"Wow, that's impressive, and heavy."

Lucky nodded, returning the coin to his pocket after Mason gave it back. Begrudgingly, Ace called over one of the waiters, and everyone put in their drink orders. Mason couldn't remember the last time he'd felt so relaxed, and having Lucky here with him, pressed to his side as if it was where he belonged, had Mason wishing for things he had no right wishing for.

"What's wrong?" Lucky asked, leaning into him.

"I feel like shit."

"Why?"

Mason moved his hand to the back of Lucky's neck, caressing his skin. The more he was around Lucky, the harder he found it to keep his hands off him. They were so close Mason felt Lucky's warm breath against his face. He loved how Lucky leaned into him.

"I don't want this to end," Mason murmured against Lucky's temple. It felt so damn good being here with him, like he'd finally found where he belonged.

"What do you mean?"

"For the first time in a long time, I'm looking forward to going to work on Monday at Four Kings, and that's real shit because *I* wanted to make detective. I worked fucking hard for it, and now the thought of going back to it makes me feel... I don't know. I'm being an ungrateful shit, aren't I?"

Lucky's smile was radiant, and Mason wondered if Lucky knew something he didn't. He leaned in and kissed Mason, the table erupting into whistles and catcalls, Ace's voice being the loudest as he shouted, "About fucking time!"

Mason laughed against Lucky's lips, both of them flipping Ace off at the same time, making everyone laugh.

"Come on." Lucky took hold of Mason's hand, pulling him to his feet. "Dance with me."

"Yeah?"

"Are you telling me you can't dance, Cowboy?"

"Oh, I can dance, but probably not as good as you." Mason ignored the cheers from the guys as Lucky led him out onto the packed dance floor. The music's pounding beat grew louder as they made their way through the crowd, Lucky's grip on Mason's hand tight. Finding a spot, Lucky turned to face Mason and wrapped his arms around his neck, his knee between Mason's legs as they started to move, their bodies pressed together as the beat of the music washed over them and swept them away. Mason gripped Lucky's hips, but he couldn't stop his hands from roaming over Lucky's body. Lucky's designer clothes molded to his body like they'd been made for him.

They writhed together, losing themselves to the pleasure of being in each other's arms. As far as Mason was concerned, there was only the beautiful man he held close. Lucky slipped his fingers into Mason's hair, pulling him down for a scorching kiss that set Mason's insides on fire. Mason returned the kiss, his desire for Lucky all consuming. Coming up for air, Lucky took a step back and with a sinful smile that went straight to Mason's cock, he started dancing for Mason.

The way he moved was wicked, and his hips? They gave Mason all kinds of naughty ideas. He danced with such fluidity, oozing sex and confidence as if he were one with the music, as if it flowed through his veins. Men around them undressed Lucky with their eyes, and Mason knew the moment he left Lucky on his own, they'd be all over him, which was why he wasn't going anywhere.

Listening to his most basic instincts, he wrapped his arms around Lucky from behind, brought their bodies together, and pressed his lips to the side of Lucky's neck. With a groan, Lucky tilted his head, giving Mason better access, inviting Mason to mark him, claim him. Mason had never felt anything like this. He'd never been possessive, and although he had no intention of starting now, he couldn't resist the opportunity Lucky presented him. To show all these men who Lucky belonged to.

Words Mason wasn't ready to put out into the world bubbled up from deep inside him, and he grabbed Lucky, spun him around, and crushed their lips together to keep the words from escaping. It was too soon, and Mason wasn't sure either of them were ready to hear such declarations.

"Hey, Mason!"

Shit. It couldn't be. Who was he kidding? They turned, and Mason wondered who the hell he'd pissed off upstairs to find himself in this mess.

"Oscar," Mason greeted pleasantly over the music. "Hi."

"I was hoping to run into you. I tried to get your number from Nash, but he's being all weird about it." Oscar turned to Lucky with a smile. "Hey, Lucky. Nice to see you. Mind if I cut in?"

Lucky smiled, but it didn't reach his eyes. "Sorry, but he's taken."

Oscar looked puzzled. Had Mason not been crazy about Lucky when he'd met Oscar, he might have pursued something with the petite, pretty man, who looked up at him with his bright gold-green eyes. He was a nice guy, but when he was pissed, the claws came out, and judging by the way Oscar was sizing up Lucky, he was clearly itching to sink said claws into Lucky. *Perfect.*

"I don't understand," Oscar said, looking between Lucky and Mason. "What do you mean *taken*?"

"Taken, as in not available to fuck anyone but me," Lucky replied, enunciating each word loud and clear.

Oscar's jaw dropped, and Mason stood dumbstruck. Oscar spun to face Mason, his hands planted on his hips and his nostrils flaring. "Wait, you're *dating* him? Since when?"

Before Mason could respond, Lucky spoke up, his eyes narrowed. "That is none of your business."

Oscar let out a humorless laugh. "Oh my God. Is that why you left so quick that night after he showed up?"

Oh fuck.

"You said you had no interest in a guy intent on fucking his way through the male and female population of St. Augustine. How he didn't give a shit about anyone but himself."

Mason opened his mouth, but Lucky cut him off, hurt in his eyes. "You said I didn't care about anyone but myself?"

Somehow it didn't surprise Mason that Lucky wasn't offended by the words against his sexual conquests, but about his selfishness. And he had every right to be hurt. Everything he did for his family, his brothers, the families of his fallen brethren, his company's charity? No one could accuse Lucky of being anything other than amazing.

Mason took hold of Lucky's shoulders, afraid he'd run off. "I did say that, but that was me letting my anger get the better of me. After what happened at the beach, I was so damn pissed off at you. It was immature, and I'm sorry. I didn't mean any of it, darlin'. You know when it comes to you, I'm a damn fool sometimes."

"Really." Lucky crossed his arms over his chest.

Mason wasn't sure what to expect. This whole situation was volatile, with the potential to escalate out of his control at any moment. He expected Lucky to curse him out and storm off, but neither happened. Lucky simply waited. That made Mason's heart skip a beat. At one point, Lucky wouldn't have even given him a chance to talk, much less wait around for an explanation.

"Darlin', we were both fit to be tied that day, remember?" He brushed his fingers down Lucky's jaw. "Do you think I'd have been that damn stupid if I weren't crazy about you? I was an asshole, and I hope you forgive me."

Lucky searched Mason's eyes, and whatever he found seemed to do the trick, because his expression softened, and he leaned into Mason's touch, covering Mason's hand with his own. "I forgive you. I was pissed off too and said some not-too-nice things."

"Oh, please." Oscar rolled his eyes and put his hand on Mason's arm. "Mason, he's the guy you fuck, not the guy you build your life around. He's a total slut, and hey, there's nothing wrong with that, but he's just going to break your heart."

This time it was Mason who cut Lucky off before he could speak. "What did you call him?"

Oscar threw up his arms in frustration. "Come on, Mason! Lucky doesn't date. Everyone knows that. As soon as the next hot piece of ass comes along, he'll drop you like a bad habit."

"I'm sorry if I gave you the impression I was interested in more, but I'm not, and I never was." Mason removed Oscar's hand from his arm, his tone icy. "I would also greatly appreciate you not speaking of the man I love in such a manner. We're together, so please respect that."

Oscar's eyes went huge, and Lucky choked on air. And holy shit had he just...? He had. Well, damn.

Excusing them, Mason took hold of Lucky's arm and led him off the dance floor, where he left Oscar standing there, stunned stupid. He walked Lucky to the back, found an empty room, and closed the door behind them. He pulled the curtain shut to let others know the room was occupied and no one was invited. It was small but comfortable, painted in all black with a lush black velvet couch, and in front of that, a fancy black coffee table with a bowl of condoms and lube in the center. Beside the couch sat a trash can and a small, high-black table with a silver tray of wet wipes. Frank seemed to think of everything.

"I'm sorry. I know this is not the appropriate time and place for this, but I meant what I said out there, Lucky. I love you."

Lucky slowly sank onto the couch, his eyes wide. He swallowed hard, and Mason took a seat beside him but didn't touch him, afraid he might spook Lucky.

"Darlin'?" Mason prodded softly. "Please say something."

Lucky let out a shuddering breath before turning to meet Mason's gaze. "Say it again."

Mason took Lucky's hands in his, his heart in his throat, and his smile so wide his face hurt. "I love you, Lucky. I don't know when it was that you stole my heart, but you did."

"Why?"

"Why do I love you?"

Lucky nodded.

"Because you're the most amazing man I've ever met, that's why. Because you set my soul on fire, along with everything else in me. When you came into my life, not only did I feel truly alive for the first time in years, but you made me realize how wrong I was, thinking I didn't deserve the love of a good man. You turned my whole fucking world upside down, and I secretly loved every minute of it." Mason put his hand to Lucky's cheek. "I love you, Eduardo

Morales. Love how damn ornery you are. Love how passionate and expressive you are. I love all your little quirks, like your obsession with good coffee, expensive shoes, and ability to drive your cousin batshit crazy. Baby, you are something else."

Mason brought Lucky's fingers to his lips for a kiss.

"Now you don't have to say nothing. I just needed you to know that no matter how pissed off I was with you that night, I *never* thought of you as anything other than the beautiful, generous, kind-hearted man you are. You steal my breath away, darlin', every time I look at you."

Lucky drew in a sharp breath, his eyes quickly filling. "Mason, I.... No one has ever said such things to me. I...." A tear rolled down his cheek, and Mason brushed it away.

Damn, but Lucky was perfect. Perfectly imperfect. And he was all Mason's. "It's okay, darlin'." Mason leaned in to press his lips to Lucky's ever so softly. "You don't need to say a word. When you're ready, I will be here, but, baby?"

"Yes?"

"The day you give me your heart—and I know you will —I promise I will cherish it."

"You seem very sure of this," Lucky teased softly, brushing his lips over Mason's.

"You sayin' it won't happen?"

Lucky nipped at Mason's bottom lip, his voice quiet when he spoke. "Who says it hasn't happened already?"

Mason sucked in a breath, and Lucky kissed him, once again showing Mason when words failed him. Lucky slipped his fingers into Mason's hair, grabbing fistfuls of it. He might not be ready to say the words, but with every breath he took, every kiss, every caress, Lucky told Mason how much of his heart belonged to him.

Whether old fears kept Lucky from saying those three

little words, Mason had no clue, but he would take whatever Lucky gave him, because he *knew* he had Lucky's heart, and he couldn't wait to see where this adventure took them, because life with Lucky would be nothing short of one hell of an adventure.

ELEVEN

EIGHT WEEKS.

That was how much time had gone by since Mason's suspension. For a very brief amount of time, he'd forgotten all about IA, the investigation, Major Crimes, and the fact that his time with the Kings would eventually come to an end. Had things not worked out like they had, Mason would have been up in arms, believing someone was drawing out the investigation on purpose, but as it was, he hadn't cared how damn long they took. Now, it was over.

Mason sat on the edge of his bed and stared down at the letter of Not Sustained. Next week, he'd be back on duty. He should be happy about it, so why wasn't he? With a sigh, he dropped the letter onto the mattress beside him, then ran his hands over his face and through his hair. He'd already told Lucky about it, hence their sleeping in their own beds. Not because Lucky was upset with him, but because he was feeling the same sense of loss Mason was. And wasn't that just ridiculous?

It wasn't like Mason was going far. True, they weren't going to be based out of the same office, and sometimes

Lucky would be off working in a different city, but when they were working cases for the Kings, it wasn't like they were attached at the hip. They'd been paired up often, but that was only because Mason had been learning the ropes. Lately he'd been working with one of the other Kings or their teams. Besides, he didn't work for Four Kings Security. It had all been temporary anyway.

That night after they'd come home from Sapphire Sands, Mason made love to Lucky, pouring his heart and soul into showing Lucky how much he meant. It had been hot, sweet, and achingly intimate. The following two days had seen them scrambling to take control of several events another security company had pulled out of at the last minute, which meant Mason and Lucky hadn't had any alone time together in forty-eight hours, but that was the job. They'd be compensated handsomely for the overtime, obviously, and Lucky informed him he'd put in a request for the following weekend off. 'Course that wasn't going to happen now because Mason would be back working Major Crimes.

This was their last case together.

With a grunt, Mason got up. He needed to pull his head out of his ass and stop acting like some lovesick teenager whose crush turned him down for the prom. This wasn't even about him and Lucky; this was about his career. Something had changed in the time he'd been working for the Kings, and Mason was struggling to figure out what the hell is was.

After a quick shower, he got dressed, had some coffee—not as good as Lucky's—some breakfast—also not as good as Lucky's—grabbed his overnight bag, and headed for the door. He was in big trouble. Lucky was spoiling him something fierce with his espresso lattes and delicious Cuban cooking. Lucky's house was also nothing to scoff at. It was a gorgeous four-bedroom house on the beach with a pool, and more importantly, a huge king-size bed, where Mason enjoyed making a mess out of Lucky.

Mason ended up at Lucky's more often than not, and he cautioned himself about getting too used to waking up with Lucky wrapped around him. Things were moving fast between them, and Lucky had yet to tell Mason how he felt, but Mason was okay with that. Good things were worth waiting for. He'd been about to step out of his apartment, when he spotted something on the floor. Picking it up, he wondered when Lucky had dropped it, and if he'd even noticed it was missing? Lucky would have certainly mentioned it.

Slipping the coin into his pocket, Mason locked up and headed outside into the cool fall air to his truck parked out on the curb. Today he was picking Lucky up at Bibi's, since Lucky had texted last night to say he was having a breakfast meeting with King. Dropping the coin into his cupholder so he wouldn't forget, Mason started up the truck and drove a whole seven minutes to get to Bibi's. The best part of living in St. Augustine Beach was that he was never more than a few minutes away from anything—good food, the beach, Lucky's house....

"Hey, Cowboy," Bibi greeted him when he walked in, the little bell above the door alerting everyone to his arrival. It was Friday morning after 10:00 a.m., so the café wasn't busy, what with the morning crowd having come and gone hours ago.

"Hey, sweetheart." Mason kissed her cheek, smiling when Nash came out to greet him with a hug and pat on the back. "Hey, Nash."

Nash's expression turned somber, his voice quiet so as

not to be overheard by Lucky, who was deep in conversation with King across the room. "I'm really sorry about that mess with Oscar. I'm not excusing his behavior, but he's not had a great run with guys lately, and I think he sort of set his heart on you, not realizing your heart was set on someone else. He feels awful about the night at the club and wants to make it up to you and Lucky."

"How's Lucky feel about that?"

Nash pulled Bibi to his side and kissed the top of her head. "He's being very magnanimous, which is good for all parties involved. Must be your influence, Cowboy."

Mason shook his head. "No, sir. If anyone's a good influence on anyone, it's him on me." He laughed when Nash squinted at him.

"Did you lose a bet? Is that what's got you spouting nonsense?"

"Speaking of bets," Bibi chimed in cheerfully, dramatically sweeping her arms toward the big blackboard behind the counter. "May I direct your attention to *the board*."

Mason let out a bark of laughter when Nash let his head hang in defeat. "Aw, I'm sorry, Nash," Mason said, patting his back. "Looks like you've been defeated."

Bibi scoffed. "Defeated? More like annihilated."

Poor Nash. Looked like his winning streak was finally over.

"Wow." Mason let out a whistle as he looked at the scores. "She's kicked your ass something fierce, huh?"

"That's what I get for betting on a freaking wedding," Nash grumbled.

"Wedding?" Mason asked, puzzled.

"My cousin's wedding," Lucky said, stepping up beside Mason, his smile wide. "Quinn and Spencer were supposed to be getting married this month, but they postponed it because Quinn was hurt on the job."

"Shit. He okay?" Mason asked. Lucky didn't look worried, so he was going to guess the answer to that was yes.

"He is. It was more of a close call. He was knocked out, but other than a few hours in the hospital, he was fine. Spencer, he was not so fine. He worries for Quinn. They decided to postpone the wedding until February. Quinn is giving Spencer a Valentine's Day wedding."

"Which was one of the bets I lost," Nash said with a huff. "I thought they were going to have a winter wedding."

"Nah." Bibi waved a hand in dismissal. "Quinn's too much of a romantic sap, especially when it comes to Spencer."

Lucky nodded. "It's true. They are very sweet together. I think maybe Quinn is thinking of retiring. The job down there is getting very dangerous. Oh, I was going to ask you if you would like to come to the wedding with me?"

Mason's smile couldn't get any bigger. "You bet."

"Okay." Lucky returned his grin as Bibi sighed dreamily.

"Aw, you two are so cute. Also, I won that bet."

Lucky rolled his eyes. "You two need to find another hobby that isn't betting on the Kings."

"But it's so much fun," Bibi whined.

Nash crossed his arms over his chest. "That's because you're winning."

"Okay, we need to go. You ready, Cowboy? We have a pretty long drive to Palm Beach. I had Bibi make us some sandwiches and café con leche to go." He narrowed his eyes as Bibi handed Mason a large brown paper bag. "Let me guess, you had toast for breakfast and your burnt-bean water."

Mason chuckled. "You know me too well, darlin'."

Lucky rolled his eyes and muttered something in Spanish under his breath before thanking Nash for the two large coffees. They said their goodbyes, Lucky told King they'd see him when they got to the hotel in Palm Beach, and they headed out to Mason's truck. Lucky climbed in, placed their coffees in the cupholders, then chucked his duffel bag in the back seat. He took the bag of sandwiches before Mason ran around to the driver's side and slid in behind the wheel. Good food, good coffee, and a good man at his side. What a great way to start the day.

Mason buckled up as Lucky picked up his coffee, his lips pulling down into a frown when he dropped his gaze to the cupholder.

"What's this?"

Mason clicked his seat belt into place. "Oh, I found that in my apartment."

"Um, okay." Lucky looked puzzled.

"What?"

"Didn't know you knew any Marines."

What the hell was Lucky on about? "I don't know any Marines."

Lucky held the coin up to Mason. "This is a Marines challenge coin."

"Wait, I thought it was yours."

"No." Lucky reached into his pocket and pulled out another coin. "This is mine." He showed it to Mason. "See? United States Army. Special Forces."

"Who the hell does this belong to, then? And how did it get in my apartment?"

Lucky's brows furrowed as he studied the coin. "This is not something someone would just leave lying around. You said you found it *inside* your apartment?"

"Yeah. By the door. You know, I've been getting this weird feeling lately."

Lucky's head shot up. "Weird? Weird how?"

"I don't know. Like something's been off. I've felt it a couple of times in my apartment, then our hotel room in Orlando, and a couple of other places, but there's nothing. I mean, I would've known if someone broke into my place. The first night I felt it, I checked the whole apartment, and nothing."

"You wouldn't know if I broke in. Or King, or Ace. We were trained to get into places undetected."

"What, then? You think a Marine broke into my apartment? That they've been following me around?"

"I don't know anything other than you found a challenge coin inside your apartment, and your instincts have been trying to tell you something. Fuck's sake, Mason, why didn't you say something? You're a detective. If your gut is telling you something is not right, you need to listen."

"I'm sorry, I just didn't think it was related. I mean my life's been pretty fucking off for weeks. When I checked my apartment, nothing was stolen or out of place. No one rifled through my drawers. I mean, my place is a tiny shithole. You'd notice if someone touched or moved something."

"Maybe this isn't about you."

"What do you mean?"

"You don't know any Marines. Maybe this is about the Kings. Hold on." Lucky undid his seat belt and got out of the car. Mason followed, his brows drawn together as Lucky started inspecting the truck.

"What are you doing?"

"Looking for something."

"For what?"

"For anything that shouldn't be there." Lucky sat on the

ground, lay down, and disappeared under the truck. He cursed under his breath, and when he dragged himself out, he had something small and black in his palm.

"Shit. Is that what I think it is?"

"A tracker."

Just as he said the words, King came out of Bibi's, his expression concerned. "What's going on?"

Lucky turned to King and showed him the tracker he'd pulled out from under Mason's truck before apprising him of the situation. King's jaw muscles tightened as he checked the device over. He handed it back to Lucky.

"Put it back where you found it."

Mason arched an eyebrow at that. "Someone's been trailing me, and you just want them to keep on doing it?"

"We'll get Jack to have a look at it when you get to Palm Beach, but in the meantime, we don't want whoever planted it there to suspect you know about it. We'll have a better chance of finding who it belongs to that way. Ace is on his way to pick me up and drive us down to Palm Beach, so I'll do some poking around on the ride over and let you know what I come up with."

"Okay. Shit. I don't get it. If this is about you fellas, why would someone be following *me*? It doesn't make any sense."

"Maybe they are trying to get to me through you," Lucky said, looking thoughtful. "We have been spending most of our time together, so it makes sense."

"Who'd you piss off?" Mason teased.

Lucky let out a snort. "An easier question would be who *didn't* I piss off?"

King shook his head before meeting Mason's gaze. "We can't rule out that you're the intended target. Just because you don't know anyone in the military other than us, doesn't mean whoever this is wasn't hired by someone to keep an eye on you or track you down. You know anyone who might be looking for you?"

Mason let out a heavy sigh. "Yeah. My folks." He was grateful when King didn't ask why his family didn't know where he lived or why he clearly didn't want them knowing.

"Would your parents go as far as hiring someone to find you?"

Mason nodded. If his father wanted it bad enough, there was nothing he wouldn't do to track Mason down. And here he'd thought maybe they'd realized he didn't want to be found and had given up.

"Okay. Head to the hotel, and we'll see what we come up with. If anything out of the ordinary happens, I want to know about it."

They thanked King and got back in the truck, the truck plunged in silence until they got on I-95.

"Do you think it's your father?" Lucky asked. "You said he has money, so he could hire someone experienced to find you."

"I've been thinking about that, but the guy clearly found me, so why hang around? Why not just call my folks and tell them where I am? That coin wasn't there last time I was at my apartment. It's been weeks. Why wait?"

Lucky released a heavy sigh. "I don't know. Maybe I'm just hoping it is your parents."

"Why's that?"

"Because the alternative is not so good."

Lucky had a point. With a grunt, Mason motioned to the radio. "Put some music on, will ya? I'll drive myself crazy thinking about this, and there ain't nothing I can do about it right now."

"Sure." Lucky turned on the radio and snorted at the country music that flooded the car. "Really?"

"What? Come on, darlin', who doesn't love a little Blake Shelton?" Mason started singing "Sure Be Cool If You Did" to Lucky, and Lucky threw his head back and laughed. He snickered, then appeared to be listening to the lyrics, his smile turning soft, and his eyes filling with affection. Mason reached out and laced their fingers together, his heart swelling when Lucky squeezed his hand and left his hand in Mason's. Mason sang along, aware of Lucky tapping his hand to the beat. When Lucky had enough of sappy love songs, he changed the station, and they both sang along to everything from classic rock to Latin pop songs. Well, Lucky sang along to the Latin pop songs, and Mason tried to make sense of the lyrics, making out bits about falling in love, dancing, and music. There were a couple of lyrics in English, which he understood.

"How do you do that?" Mason asked, keeping his focus on the highway, but seeing Lucky from the corner of his eye.

"Do what?"

"Dance like that?"

Lucky was moving his upper body, but it was smooth liquid. Boneless.

"I don't know. I've been dancing since I can remember. I feel the music, and my body responds, and we know how good my body is at responding," Lucky purred.

"Christ." Mason shifted uncomfortably in his seat. "When we get there, how long do we have before we report to King?"

Lucky chuckled. "About three hours or so?"

"Okay, good."

"That so? You have something in mind, Cowboy?"

Mason waggled his eyebrows. "Oh yeah."

The trip to Palm Beach took a little over three and a half hours, and the hotel Jay booked for everyone was just five-minutes down the road from the shindig at the exclusive members-only yacht club they'd be providing security for. No one batted an eye when Lucky informed Jay he and Mason were sharing a room. King roomed on his own, which wasn't a surprise to Mason, and Ace—who normally shared with Lucky—roomed with Red, while Jack and Joker roomed together like they always did.

As soon as they arrived at the hotel, Mason handed his keys over to the valet attendant, grabbed their bags, and headed inside. Thanks to early check-in, they were in their room in record time, and the second Lucky closed the door, Mason pounced.

Lucky laughed as Mason grabbed him, pulled him hard against him, and nipped at his neck. When he kissed Lucky, their playful mood quickly descended into scorching need. They clawed at each other's clothes until they were naked and panting. Lucky stopped trying to consume Mason long enough to grab lube, and then he was all over Mason again, fingers tugging at Mason's hair as they fumbled their way over to the bed. Lucky shoved Mason, and he fell back onto the mattress. With a wicked smile, Mason rolled onto his stomach, and got onto his hands and knees, his ass on offer.

"I think it's time your cowboy rode you, darlin'."

"Oh fuck." Lucky didn't bother asking if Mason was sure, and that sent a shiver of pleasure through Mason. If he hadn't wanted it, he wouldn't have offered, and Lucky knew that, knew *him*.

Lucky climbed onto the bed behind Mason, and he trembled at the feel of Lucky's lube-slicked finger pressed to his hole. His muscles tightened, and he grabbed fistfuls of the duvet as Lucky folded over him, his weight on Mason both comforting and arousing. Mason closed his eyes, allowing himself to be swept away in the maelstrom that was the man he loved. Lucky trailed scorching kisses up Mason's back as he breached him while he reached around with his free hand and palmed Mason's painfully hard leaking cock. A low groan escaped Mason as Lucky stretched him, first with one finger then two, his strokes on Mason's dick matching the rhythm of his fingers as he fucked his hole. By the time he added a third finger, Mason was ready to come apart. Sweat dripped down the side of his brow, and he let out a growl.

"Darlin', I really need you to fuck me."

Lucky took hold of his chin, and turned his face to kiss the breath out of Mason. He gasped for air, and Lucky moved in behind him. Looking over his shoulder, Mason shuddered at the sight of Lucky lining himself up. His skin was flushed as he pushed the head of his cock inside Mason, and Mason let out a string of curses.

"Fuck, that burns so good," Mason breathed.

"You ready for this ride, Cowboy?"

"Hell, yes."

Lucky sank down to the root, his thighs pressed to the back of Mason's, and it felt amazing. He was so damned full. Then Lucky started moving, and Mason was a hot mess.

"Oh fuck. Fuck, yes." Mason groaned long and deep as Lucky dug his fingers into Mason's hips. "That's it, baby. Let me feel you."

Lucky took Mason's words as a personal challenge, and snapped his hips forward, burying himself deep and hard inside Mason. With every thrust, Mason urged Lucky on, begging for harder and deeper. The sound of their skin smacking together filled the room along with Mason's filthy encouragement, not that Lucky needed it. His man was the very picture of ecstasy, his plump lips parted, and his brows furrowed as he pounded into Mason.

"Fuck, Mason, I'm gonna come."

"Fill me up, darlin'. I want to feel your come drip out of me."

Lucky's thrusts turned frantic as he drove himself inside Mason over and over, his movements wild. As Mason pumped his own cock, his orgasm exploded through him when Lucky slammed his hips into him, Lucky's hot come filling Mason. Lucky cried out, his curses in both English and Spanish as he fucked Mason through their release. Mason's arm gave out, and he collapsed on the bed, Lucky sprawled on his back. He didn't even care that he was lying on his own come. He couldn't move, and not because of Lucky's weight on him.

The sound of the air conditioner kicking on accompanied their panting, and Mason smiled at Lucky stroking his hair, his cheek pressed to Mason's back. He let out a contented sigh, and Lucky placed a kiss to his shoulder in response. A hiss escaped Lucky as he pulled out of Mason, but neither of them dared move.

"We should shower," Lucky murmured, but he didn't budge.

Mason hummed, content to stay where he was, Lucky sprawled over him. God, he was so in love with this man. It was a little terrifying. Lucky hadn't said the words, but Mason felt it in Lucky's tenderness, in the way he caressed Mason's side, left sweet kisses on his skin, or murmured lovingly in Spanish. Mason couldn't understand a good deal of it, but he got the most important bits, like "Mi amor," "Cariño," "Mi corazón." *My love, darling, my heart.*

Eventually they got up and showered, where Mason

made love to Lucky all over again because he couldn't get enough of Lucky. Like they were making up for lost time. Then they had to get to work.

As soon as they arrived at their meeting with the rest of the Kings, Jack and Joker, Lucky handed the tracker over to Jack.

"It's not high-end stuff, but not something you can order off Amazon," Jack replied, inspecting the tiny device. "I'll look into it."

Unfortunately, Jack wouldn't be able to really delve into it until after they were done working the case. King did some digging and confirmed Mason's father had indeed hired someone to track Mason down, but the private investigator did not possess a military background. That wasn't to say it couldn't be the same guy; the presence of the coin was odd. When they returned to St. Augustine and Kings headquarters, King would do some more digging, which Mason appreciated. Mason also intended to investigate as soon as he was back at his desk on Monday. For now, he'd concentrate on the job before him.

One of the top executives of a large Fortune 500 company was having a huge anniversary shindig with several hundred guests in attendance, folks who didn't blink at shelling out thousands of dollars a year to park their big fancy boats at the club marina. It was all caviar and dinner jackets. There'd been a mix-up with the security company the client originally hired, leaving the company double booked and the client without security. Pulling a few strings, the client managed to personally get a last-minute contract with the Kings. Considering all the Kings' personnel on site doing a risk assessment and putting together a battle plan, Mason would hazard a guess the client wasn't sweating the cost.

The Palm Paradise Yacht Club and Marina at Lake Worth Lagoon was huge, with two floors and several rows of yachts of various sizes docked at the marina, starting from smallest to the bigger ones farthest out. The lagoon ran parallel to the coast, separated from the Atlantic Ocean by barrier beaches, one of them being West Palm Beach. The somewhat cooler late November air was accompanied by the breeze coming off the ocean, and it whipped at Mason's face, the feel of it wet and salty. They were surrounded by the smell of the ocean and the not so subtle aroma of fresh fish.

Mason leaned into Lucky, his voice low as he motioned to one of the yachts they walked by. "I'm surprised you don't have one of those."

Lucky let out a snort. "Yes, because when you look at me, you think 'guy who likes to fish.'"

Mason chuckled. He scanned the area around them, and with the coast clear, grabbed a handful of Lucky's ass and murmured in his ear. "I was thinking more, 'guy who likes to get fucked on the deck.'"

Lucky groaned and shoved him playfully. "I may have to reconsider this not-having-a-boat thing."

"Are Colton and I that embarrassingly sweet when we flirt?" Ace asked Red, his voice loud enough for Mason and Lucky to hear.

"No, bro, you're way more embarrassing," Lucky teased, earning the middle finger from Ace.

The Kings brought everyone in for a meeting before the guests were due to start arriving, and all personnel were assigned specific posts. Equipment was distributed, and they all wore white vests beneath their suits, though no firearms were on the premises. The security teams were divided up with two team members checking the guest list, bags, purses, and pockets, while others stood stationed at doorways, exits, and entrances. Jack and Joker remained inside Jack's truck parked in the club's parking lot where they'd monitor the security feed. Mason, Lucky, and Ace were on the ground floor, while Red and King were on the second floor. Their job was to make the rounds and check in with the rest of the security team.

The party was spread out across several rooms in the club, one for cocktails and "the good stuff" as one guest stated while looking longingly at the shelves lined with whiskey and brandies. After the schmoozing and aperitifs, a three-course meal would be served in the dining room, followed by more drinks and schmoozing in the Commodores Room. Mason made sure to drool all over Lucky in his tux back at the hotel. Damn, the man looked fine. No wonder guests kept mistaking him for one of their own. At least until they saw the black earpiece in his ear.

Mason made his rounds, smiling politely when a guest greeted him or smiled at him. He realized then how comfortable he felt in his own skin. How had it taken him forty-one years to figure himself out? He liked who he was with Lucky, working for Four Kings. Thinking about his life as a cop, as a detective for Major Crimes, it felt like a lifetime ago. Like he'd been a different person, which was kinda crazy, considering that life he felt so far removed from had been a few short weeks ago. Was he crazy for feeling like a chapter of his life was ending and a new one was beginning? This was certainly one hell of a time to have an epiphany.

"Mason Cooper?"

"Yes?" Mason turned, expecting to find one of his fellow security officers there, but instead a man he'd never met stepped up beside him, his smile familiar. Mason tilted his head, studying the guy. "You look familiar. Have we met?" The man was about Lucky's height, his build similar. Mason would estimate he was roughly the same age as Lucky. His jaw was chiseled, his hair pitch-black to match his thick eyebrows, and his eyes were stunning. They were gray with amber around the iris, except for the left one, which appeared half amber, half gray. He was very handsome, dressed in a tailored gray suit. Something in the way he stood seemed familiar as well, a stiffness Mason had seen before, the way he carried himself.

"We should chat."

"I'm sorry, but I'm part of tonight's security detail. I can't leave my post."

"I think you can." The man leaned in, the barrel of a gun pushing against Mason's hip. "Why don't you escort me outside?"

"You don't want to do this."

"It's in your best interest, and the interest of those you care about, to come with me. If your boyfriend or any of his friends come near us, I will put a bullet in them. You try something, anything, and someone is going to get hurt. Don't fuck with me, Mason. I know who you are and what you're capable of. One wrong move, and someone else is going to die. Do you really want another man's blood on your hands?"

Mason froze, something about the way he'd said the words alluded to so much more. "You really think no one's going to come looking for me?"

"I'm sure they will, but by then it's going to be too late for you."

The guy meant to kill him.

Mason snorted. "If you think I'm just gonna follow you to my death, you're dumber than a box of rocks."

"Oh, you're going to come with me, all right."

"How do you reckon that?" Mason sneered. He subtly scanned the room as he put together a plan of action.

"Because you killed my father."

Mason's blood turned to ice, his heart in his throat as he realized who held the gun to his side. "Ryden?"

"Oh, so you *do* remember me," Ryden hissed, grabbing hold of Mason's arm in a tight grip, his gun jabbing into Mason's hip again. "You're going to escort me out to the marina like we're a couple of pals catching up on old times. I know you want to hear what I have to say."

Mason slowly walked with Ryden toward the door, turning his back on the floor of guests. "Of course I remember you. Not a day goes by where I haven't thought about you or your family."

"Bullshit!" Ryden's voice was low but filled with venom. He stayed close to Mason as Mason escorted him from the room and out into the hall. Mason couldn't believe Ryden was here. Last time he saw the guy, Ryden had been a scrawny teenager. "You never gave a fuck about me, Mason. If you had, you wouldn't have done what you did!"

"I'm so sorry, Ryden. I am. I know what I did was unforgivable, but I swear to you, it was—"

"Shut up!"

They were starting to get odd looks, making Ryden more and more agitated, and that was the last thing they needed. There was no telling what he would do. Mason needed to get Ryden away from the guests, and a foolish part of him wanted to hear what he had to say. The guy had every right to loathe him, but maybe Mason could help him in some way.

"You've been following me," Mason said, keeping his tone quiet and steady.

"Nice work, Detective." Ryden walked him down the hall and downstairs toward the yacht club's side doors that led out to the docks. They stepped out into the cool night air, the marina lit up beautifully, the lights reflecting on the water. It was a gorgeous night for a stroll—not so much for dying. Lucky was going to be so pissed at him, but he needed to talk to Ryden. After years of trying to outrun the ghost of his past, it had finally caught up with him.

As they headed toward the end of the dock, Mason's earpiece came to life, Lucky's concerned voice on the other end.

"Everything okay? Jack says you're outside."

Mason pressed his PTT button, his heart squeezing at the lie he was about to tell the man he loved. "Yeah. Just escorting a guest to his boat. I'm okay."

"You should have let one of us know," Lucky informed him, his tone laced with suspicion. His instincts were probably kicking into overdrive, and Mason couldn't let Lucky run out here. He might be a former soldier, but he was unarmed, and Mason wouldn't take that risk. Lucky would probably call him an idiot. Like the guy had never faced off against someone with a weapon having been unarmed, but the thought of Lucky getting hurt because of Mason's actions was not acceptable to him.

"I know," Mason replied. "I'm sorry. I'll be right back, and then you can yell at me some more." Tears welled in his eyes, but he blinked them back. They reached one of the huge yachts at the very end of the dock, the door of which was open at the top of the stairs.

"Get on the boat," Ryden grumbled, his voice rough, and Mason had to wonder if maybe Ryden wasn't as prepared to kill a man as he thought. If he wanted Mason dead, why hadn't he done it already?

Mason climbed the stairs, Ryden at his back. The luxury yacht they were entering was at least a hundred and fifty feet. Hey, at least if he bit the bullet, he'd be doing so in style. Yeah, Lucky was so going to kick his ass. Ryden led him into what looked like a living room area, a dining room off to one side. He'd made sure to secure the doors on the way in, and the blinds on the windows were closed. It was all polished cherry wood, marble tabletops, and expensive upholstery.

"So this is how the other half lives, huh? This your boat?"

Ryden scoffed. "Yeah, all us homeless vets have a two-hundred-foot yacht docked near the park bench we sleep on."

"Jesus, Ryden." Mason shook his head, his heart hurting for the guy. "I'm so sorry. Let me help you."

"Help me?" Ryden laughed before he started pacing, the gun held at his side. "My whole life has been a lie, and it's all because of you. Because of you, I spent my life hating him."

"Hating who?"

"My father. I blamed him for destroying our family. If he hadn't died by falling asleep at the wheel, his career would have been over anyway. No one was going to hire a ranch hand who'd been fired for negligence, for getting a kid hurt. I hated him for setting me on the path I ended up on, when in reality he was an innocent victim. That was my welcome home gift, you know. Discovering that *you* were the one responsible for the clusterfuck that is my life."

Ryden thrust the gun in his direction, and Mason slowly put his hands up, his tone soothing when he spoke.

"Ryden, put the gun down and let's talk about this."

"Fuck you, Mason! You have no idea what I've been through! What *you* set in motion!"

"Why don't you tell me?"

"Why? So, you can buy yourself enough time for your Green Beret to save your ass? Ain't no one coming to save you, Mason. Fucking snake eaters think they're hot shit."

"You seem to know a bit about them."

"Only because they think they're so much better than us when everyone knows we're better."

"You're a Marine?"

"Was," Ryden murmured, his bottom lip trembling. He sniffed and blinked away the wetness in his eyes, his expression quickly turning to stone. "Can't fly for Uncle Sam if you only got one eye." He pointed to his left eye, the one that was half amber and half gray. "Trauma, they said. Complete loss of vision. Flying was all I had left, and then I lost that along with everything else."

"I'm so sorry, Ryden."

"Don't you dare fucking pity me," Ryden spat out. "Do you know why I joined the Marines? So I wouldn't be a piece-of-shit fuckup like my daddy. At least that's what I kept telling myself. Then it was all over. I came home, only to find out my momma had passed away while I was on a RECON mission. She left me a letter. A goddamn letter." He reached into his pocket and pulled out a letter that had been folded and unfolded so many times it was on the verge of falling apart. Ryden's face crumpled, but he pulled himself together. "You know what her dying words to me were? '*Forgive me.*' She died thinking I would hate her for what she did, but how could I?"

Ryden was filled with so much fury and hate that Mason wanted to do something for him. The way he paced, how he fought to keep the tears from his eyes. Ryden was a man on the verge of breaking. He believed he had nothing left to lose, and that made him dangerous.

"Of course you couldn't hate her," Mason offered gently. "She was your mother, and a good woman."

"A good woman who sold her soul to the devil for her son," Ryden spat.

Mason stilled. "What are you talking about?"

"Don't act like you don't know. Your whole goddamn family's made up of liars, especially you and your bastard father. It wasn't bad enough you fired my father knowing he was innocent, and then got him killed, but then your father uses my mother's grief against her, buying her silence."

"That... that's not...." Mason felt sick to his stomach. He shook his head, but deep down he knew Ryden was speaking the truth.

"My mother was distraught and grieving. She went to your father to give him a chance to come clean, and what does he do? He convinces her to take his blood money. How else was she going to take care of her son as a single mother with no income coming in? Who would pay for the funeral expenses? For my education? All she had to do was say nothing."

Mason swallowed past the bile in his throat. He would apologize again, but his words held no weight. They wouldn't undo what had been done to Ryden and his family. Did his father's ruthlessness know no bounds?

"My entire life since that night has been one miserable circumstance after another, like I'm fucking cursed. You know the saying, if it weren't for bad luck, I'd have no luck at all? That's me. After I read her letter, I was so fucking *angry*! I told myself, I'm going to hunt that son of a bitch down and make him pay. So I did. I found you." Ryden shook his head before spinning and aiming the gun at Mason. It shook in his hand.

"You did find me, but I'm not the man you think I am. What I did was unforgiveable, but I've spent every day since trying to make up for it, trying to be a better man. It's why I left, why I changed my name. If I'd have stayed, I would have ended up like him, and I *never* wanted to be like him. Your father was a good man, and I did him wrong. My father did this to us. He's hurt us both, but are we going to let him keep hurting us like this, Ryden? Don't we deserve to heal and be happy?"

"You were supposed to be a monster! You should have been a dirty cop, or a fucking addict, or drunk, or something! It aint' right. You ended up with everything. A career to be proud of, people who love you, a boyfriend who's crazy about you. Me? I lost *everything*, Mason. My family, my career, my apartment, my fucking eye!" Tears streamed down Ryden's cheeks, his resolve faltering as his hand shook.

Movement behind Ryden caught Mason's eye, and he screamed for Lucky just as Ryden spun, gun in hand.

"No!"

TWELVE

LUCKY IGNORED MASON, launching himself at the man with the gun in his hand, making sure to grab the guy's wrist and jerk it to one side to avoid getting shot. He had no idea why the guy hadn't fired, but Lucky wasn't about to wait around to find out.

"Lucky, don't hurt him," Mason called out from somewhere behind the guy. Whoever this man was, he was obviously trained in combat, evident by the way he blocked each of Lucky's blows, his grip firm on his weapon.

"Now is not the time, Mason."

"You two need to stop this right now."

"Are you crazy?" Had Mason lost his mind? "This guy kidnapped you at gunpoint and dragged you out onto a boat to kill you." Lucky managed to land a punch in the guy's ribs, but he didn't go down. It only made him more pissed.

"Ryden's not gonna kill me. He's not a bad guy."

"The fuck he isn't. Give me the gun, Ryden, and I won't fucking shoot you with it," Lucky snarled, bringing his knee up to block Ryden's kick. Fucker knew what he was doing.

"Bring it, snake eater," Ryden growled.

"Fucking jarhead." Okay, now Lucky was even more pissed. Fighting with one hand was certainly a challenge, but nothing Lucky hadn't done before. He called on his training, keeping an iron grip on the wrist of the hand holding the gun. Close quarter combat was one of his proficiencies, and he was going to use every move in his arsenal to bring this guy down.

"For fuck's sake, will you two quit it already? Use your damn words."

"I have a few words for you," Lucky told Ryden. "Hijo de puta." He slammed his head against Ryden's, and the guy stumbled back. Without hesitation, Lucky tackled him to the ground, knocking the gun out of his grip, and punching him in the jaw. How the fuck did he dare kidnap Mason? And point a gun at him? Try to hurt him. "Motherfucker!"

"Lucky, stop!"

Lucky pulled back a fist, only to have Mason grab his arm.

"Baby, please."

That split second of hesitation was enough for Ryden to land a punch square across Lucky's jaw, followed by a kick that knocked the wind out of Lucky, and he fell to the floor, wheezing for breath. Lucky cursed under his breath, and quickly scrambled to his feet just as Ryden swiped the gun off the floor, but not before Lucky lunged at him, the gun going off when the two of them slammed into each other. A gasp jerked Lucky's attention away from Ryden.

"No, oh God. No, no, no," Ryden cried, falling to his knees as Lucky darted over to Mason, catching him before he crumpled to the floor.

"No. Mason, love. Look at me." Lucky pressed his hand

to Mason's left shoulder and the pool of crimson spreading across Mason's white shirt.

"I'm so sorry," Ryden cried, his hands on his head. "I didn't want to hurt him. I swear to God I didn't. I mean, I wanted him hurt, but I didn't want—oh fuck."

Lucky ignored Ryden, too busy assessing Mason's injury. He lay Mason's head on his lap and pressed his PTT button. "I need Red and a fucking ambulance! The last yacht in the marina, Paradise Island. *Now*." Lucky shook his head, blinking back the tears. "It's going to be okay, mi amor. Tranquilo, todo va a estar bien."

"On my way," Red replied through the earpiece. "Ambulance is en route."

"Lucky," Mason said through a groan. He sucked in a sharp breath as he tried to get up.

"What are you doing? Stay down."

"You have to help him."

"What?" Lucky ran a hand over Mason's hair. "The bullet went straight through, thank God, but you're bleeding very heavily. Just don't move."

"He's distraught, and God knows what he's been through. He needs our help."

"He needs to be in jail," Lucky hissed. "And I'm going to make sure he ends up there."

Mason shook his head, tears in his eyes. "I won't let you do that."

"Mason, the man shot you." Lucky's eyes went to the guy in question. Ryden didn't seem aware of his surroundings as he paced, talking to himself, his fingers in his hair, and tears rolling down his cheeks.

"Darlin', look at me."

Lucky dropped his gaze to Mason's beautiful face. He placed a kiss to his brow. "I'm listening."

"I know every man forges his own path, but I started something that night. His father died because of me, because of my actions, and what he's been through? Baby, he's a man at the end of his rope. He has nothing and no one. I won't be a part of his destruction. Please, darlin'. For me. Do this for me."

Lucky was on the verge of arguing, but Red came running into the room with his medical kit. He froze when he saw Ryden and the gun in his hand.

"Red, take care of Mason."

Red walked slowly over, his eyes never leaving Ryden as the guy continued to pace, unaware of anyone else around him. Suddenly, Ryden took off toward the stairs at the end of the room, and Mason grabbed Lucky's lapel.

"Go after him. He's gonna do something stupid. You gotta stop him from hurting himself, Lucky."

Unable to deny Mason anything, Lucky kissed him. It was a sweet but quick kiss before Lucky slipped out from under Mason and took off after Ryden. The guy might not have meant to shoot Mason, but there was no telling what he'd do if he came across one of the Kings or one of their security personnel. Lucky wouldn't let him hurt anyone else. Everything in him screamed to take the guy down, but Lucky listened to his heart instead. To Mason.

He found Ryden upstairs on the deck near the front of the boat. He stood with his back to Lucky, the gun in his hand at his side as he stared out at the ocean.

"I know you have no reason to believe me, but I really didn't mean to shoot him." Ryden snorted softly. "Ironic, huh? I came all this way thinking I'd be able to pull the trigger, but when the time came, I couldn't. I wanted him to pay for what he'd done. Then I end up shooting him, and he wants to fucking help me."

Ryden turned, the pain and self-loathing squeezing Lucky's heart. He knew that look. He'd seen it in the mirror every day for weeks on end when he'd returned, after losing his brothers.

"I'm so sorry," Ryden said through a sob. "You're a good man, Eduardo. Even if you are a snake eater." Ryden laughed, then sniffed. "He's a good man too. You take care of each other."

Oh fuck no. Lucky sprang forward, grabbing Ryden's arm before he pointed the gun to his own head and shot. He knocked the gun out of Ryden's hand, and it fell into the dark water below. Ryden broke then.

Lucky threw his arms around him, grabbing him before he slipped to the floor. He wrapped Ryden in his embrace as he wept into Lucky's chest, his body racking from the sobs.

"It's going to be okay," Lucky said softly. He swallowed hard. "Mason and I, we're going to help you, but right now, I need you to come with me. I need to know Mason is okay."

Ryden nodded. He stood, and Lucky wrapped an arm around him, leading him back downstairs, the sound of sirens in the distance made Ryden flinch. When they got downstairs, Mason sat on the couch, shirtless, an IV attached to him, and a bandage around his shoulder. When he looked up at Lucky and smiled, it was the most beautiful thing Lucky had ever seen. He told Ryden to sit, then joined Mason on the couch, ignoring the questioning looks from his brothers, who were gathered to one side, their eyes filled with concern. They were not happy right now. Lucky guessed Mason had told them about Ryden.

King stepped forward, his arms crossed over his chest as he addressed the room, his narrowed eyes on Ryden. "The official story is one of our own thought he saw someone sneaking onto the boat, and when he came to investigate, mistook Mason for a thief. The shoddy lighting made it seem like Mason had a gun, so Ryden was defending himself. Mr. Foster, consider yourself very lucky that Mason Cooper is a good man and that his boyfriend actually listens to him, or your ass would either be at the bottom of the lagoon or on your way to jail."

Ryden nodded. The guy couldn't look any smaller. "Yes, sir."

King walked over to Ryden and took a seat beside him. "I hear you were a Marine."

As King spoke with Ryden, Lucky turned his attention back to Mason. "How are you feeling?"

"Like I've been shot."

Lucky scowled at him, and Mason chuckled. He took Lucky's hand in his and brought it to his lips for a kiss.

"Thank you, darlin', for giving me the benefit of the doubt. I know your every instinct was screaming otherwise."

Lucky grunted. "You're a little crazy, you know?"

Mason's deep rumble of a laugh made the butterflies in Lucky's stomach go wild. "I think I am. I'm certainly crazy about you."

Lucky swallowed hard. He put a hand to Mason's cheek. "Don't do that again. Por favor. Nunca quiero perderte, Cariño. Te amo mucho."

Mason's smile was blinding. "I'm, uh, I'm gonna need you to say that one more time. In English, please."

With a soft laugh, Lucky leaned in and brushed his lips over Mason's. "I said, I don't want to ever lose you, sweetheart. I love you too much."

Mason's contented sigh lifted the heaviness in Lucky's heart. Being mindful of Mason's wound, Lucky kissed him until the ambulance arrived. Red had stitched him up, but they needed to examine him. Lucky rode with him after King promised he'd look after Ryden. As much as the rest of the guys wanted to join them, they had a job to finish. Ace promised they'd be there as soon as the event was over.

Lucky sat at Mason's bedside in the private recovery room at the hospital. The doctor had all kinds of tests run and checked Mason's wound, stitches, and ordered his bandages changed. The doctor told Mason he'd been very fortunate to have walked away with only a flesh wound. Lucky shrugged at Mason's scowl when the doctor left.

"Eh, just a flesh wound. It's not like you lost a limb or anything."

Mason narrowed his gaze at the door the doctor had left through. "I feel like I was being judged. Was he judging me? Like, a 'don't waste my time with your pathetic little holes' kinda judgment?"

"This is Florida. Who knows?"

"Something tells me unless I show up here with a gator wrapped around my head, he won't be impressed."

"I would not recommend it. Green is not a good color for you." Lucky chuckled at Mason's pout, his smile fading when Mason checked his bandage. He was a big man, and he looked big in the inclined hospital bed, but the white bandages against his tanned skin were a stark reminder of what almost happened. "I could have lost you."

Mason held out his hand, and Lucky scooted closer, lacing their fingers together. "None of that now. No what-ifs. I could have easily been shot on the street while on patrol or working a homicide."

"That… is not helping." Lucky let out a shuddering breath, and Mason squeezed his hand.

"My point is, we can't start down that path, darlin'. We both work dangerous jobs, and we knew that going in."

"Yes, I know." But it was different now, wasn't it? Mason was a part of his life. They had given their hearts to each other. He supposed it was something he would have to get used to. He'd never loved someone the way he loved Mason. Never worried for them, feared for them. "I'll try," he promised.

"Thank you." Mason shifted over and patted the bed beside him. Lucky took a seat, perching on the edge facing Mason. He brushed Mason's hair away from his brow. It was getting long in the front, but the long strands drew attention to his brilliant blue eyes. He was such a beautiful man. And he was all Lucky's.

"What are you thanking me for?"

"For saving him. I know it went against everything you were trained to do."

"I'm still very pissed he hurt you, but I understand it was an accident." Lucky worried his bottom lip, and Mason arched an eyebrow at him.

"You're not gonna get all shy on me now, are ya?"

"No. Ass. I'm worried. Ryden has a lot of issues to work through. I think maybe he is suffering from some PTSD, but I don't think he's getting treatment. He was going to shoot himself, Mason. Maybe he should be in a hospital."

Mason met Lucky's eyes. "Is that what you fellas did when you got back?"

"Fuck." Lucky shook his head and let out a heavy sigh. "No. It's not what we did, but even with Red, King was able to convince him to get treatment."

"How do you know Ryden won't? Maybe he can't afford

it or whatever they'd been providing him with wasn't the right treatment for him. Who knows? Ryden deserves to heal, to have a happy life. He deserves a second chance, Lucky. I don't know much when it comes to military veterans, but maybe you can help me learn? I want to do more. Not just to help Ryden, but others like him, like you." Mason put his hand to Lucky's cheek. "Baby, he's got no one and nowhere to go."

"He does have someone," Lucky said, smiling tenderly at Mason. He was such a good man with so much love in his heart. Lucky was so proud to have him in his life. An idea occurred to him, and he brightened. "Maybe he could have somewhere to stay also."

"What do you mean?"

"Maybe you move in with me, and we can move Ryden into your apartment?"

Mason's smile was huge. "That so? You gonna take care of me, Eduardo?"

Lucky rolled his eyes and huffed, pretending to be put out. "Yes, well, someone clearly has to. Besides, your apartment is not as bad as you make it out to be. I think it would be perfect for Ryden."

"It's small."

"Only because you are a wall of muscle. Ryden is my size. He'll do fine. I think having his own place will help him feel like he's on a new path, and he'll be close by so we can check on him."

"And you think he's gonna say yes? If you fellas were that easy to persuade, I reckon you wouldn't have joined the military in the first place. Any of those mottos say anything about stubbornness? Seems to be a prerequisite for joining."

Lucky crossed his arms over his chest. "You know, I could move Ryden in with me instead."

"No, sir. That will not be necessary." Mason tapped his cheek. "C'mere and give me a kiss."

Lucky arched an eyebrow at him, and Mason held his shoulder.

"Ooh, being shot sure does hurt."

"Oh my God," Lucky said with a laugh. "You're really going to play that card?"

"You bet that fine ass I am. I will milk this for all it's worth. Now come here, Eduardo, and kiss me."

Lucky leaned in and kissed Mason, joy flooding through him as Mason deepened the kiss, his strong arm wrapping around Lucky and holding him close. Lucky put his hand to Mason's chest, caressing his soft skin as he opened up for Mason, smiling against Mason's lips when his man let out a little hum.

"Tell me again."

Lucky smiled. "I." He punctuated the word with a kiss. "Love." *Kiss.* "You." *Kiss.*

Mason brushed his fingers down Lucky's jaw. "And I love you too, darlin'. Te amo."

"Now it's your turn," Lucky insisted. He wasn't normally so needy, but it had been a very eventful few weeks, and Mason had scared the hell out of him, so he'd earned the right to ask for additional reassurance.

Mason smiled warmly before kissing Lucky's palm. "I'm not going anywhere, darlin'. I will follow you like a lovesick fool to the ends of the earth."

Someone cleared their throat, and they turned to the door. Ryden stood there, his face flushed.

"I'm sorry for interrupting. I came by to see how Mason was doing." He quickly put his hands up. "But I understand if you want me to get lost."

"It's okay," Lucky said as he got up and returned to his chair beside the bed. "Actually, we wanted to talk to you."

"Oh?" Ryden nodded and waited patiently.

Looking at Ryden now, Lucky's heart went out to him. In the black Kings hoodie that was too big for him and baggy sweatpants, he looked so small. He was thinner than a man his height and build should be. His black hair was a mess, and there were dark circles around his eyes. It seemed fate had put Ryden in their path at just the right moment.

"Yeah." Mason motioned over to the empty chair next to Lucky, and Ryden quietly shuffled over. He took a seat, and Lucky was forced to look away. It pained him to see a fellow brother-in-arms so broken. Ryden had been a Marine, a soldier who prided himself on being the best, a pillar of strength, will, and determination. Lucky might not know Ryden's history, but it took a hell of a lot for him to make it as a Marine. Something told Lucky there was more to Ryden's story, more to how he'd lost his vision, in addition to the confessions of his mother.

"Lucky and I have been talking, and we'd really like it if you moved into my old apartment after I move in with Lucky."

Ryden laced his fingers together on his lap, his leg bouncing. "That's really kind of you both, but I... I don't have any money, so I can't pay rent."

Lucky had a feeling Ryden couldn't pay for most of the basics he needed, like food, clothing, and shelter.

"Ryden, don't worry about the rent. We can take care of that until you get back on your feet."

Ryden's head shot up, and he jumped from the chair before he began to pace nervously. "I can't do that. I mean, I shoot you, and you want to pay my rent? That's just... no. I appreciate the gesture, I do, but I'll work something out. I've survived this long, right?" He meant it to be a joke, but it fell flat.

"Looks like the gang's all here," King said as he walked into the room, the rest of the guys behind him.

"I should go," Ryden mumbled, heading for the door.

"Easy there." King held out a hand to stop Ryden. "Red and I would like to have a word, if that's all right."

Ryden looked worried, but visibly relaxed when Red came to stand next to him, his smile reassuring. If anyone could find a way to reach Ryden, it was Red. No one was better at putting people at ease than he was.

"It's okay, Ryden. Why don't you let me buy you a coffee, and we can talk? King will join us in a bit."

Ryden returned Red's smile and followed him out of the room. He paused outside the door and gave Mason a nod of thanks. Once they were gone, King took the seat Ryden had vacated.

"He's got a long, tough road ahead of him," King said, sitting back with a sigh. "But we'll do everything we can to help."

Mason sniffed and blinked back the wetness in his eyes. "Thank you, King. I really appreciate that."

"I know you want to help him," King stated carefully, "but if you're doing this out of some sense of guilt—"

"Let me stop you right there." Mason put a hand up and shook his head. "It may have started out that way, but that's not what this is. Working with Lucky, seeing what you fellas do, how you help people. I realized there's so much more I can do. I know come Monday, I won't be a member of Four Kings Security anymore—"

"You could be."

Mason stared at King. "I'm sorry?"

King shrugged. "I still need a team leader."

Mason opened his mouth to reply, then closed it. Lucky had to put a fist to his lips to keep from laughing at Mason's expression.

"But I thought you said you've already found someone to fill the position?"

King nodded. "I did, and I have."

Mason blinked, and this time Lucky couldn't help but laugh, especially when King arched an eyebrow at Lucky.

"Does it always take your boyfriend this long to figure things out, or is it the painkillers?"

"Screw you, King," Mason grumbled before peering at him. "Are you offering me a job?"

King squinted back. "Is that not what I said?"

"No, it ain't. You did not say, 'Hey, Mason, do you want a job?' You were doing that thing you do where you say something and everyone else has to read between the lines, solve the fucking Rubik's cube, beat the Minotaur or some shit!"

Lucky blinked at Mason before he let out a bark of laughter that startled both King and Mason. He doubled over laughing, tears in his eyes. King shook his head at Mason.

"Jesus Christ, Cowboy. I think you broke him."

"Oh fuck." Lucky wiped a tear from his eye. "I love you guys." Man, he really needed that. And he thought King and Ace were entertaining. Ace had nothing on Mason.

King sighed like they were both too exhausting for words. Hmm, his expression was very similar to the one his tía—Ace's mother—got all the time when he and Ace were younger.

"Mason Cooper, I have a team leader position open at Four Kings Security that I think would make a great fit for you. I am extending you a job offer. Should you accept said offer, I will give you a new contract, and we'll discuss your training."

"You're a dick," Mason told King.

"I was looking for more of a yes or no answer."

"Yes."

"Good." King stood and headed for the door. "I'll draw up the contract, and you can come to the office tomorrow morning."

With that he was gone.

Mason tilted his head to one side. "What just happened?"

"I think you have a new job," Lucky said with a snicker.

"Holy shit."

Much to Lucky's amusement, Mason repeated the words several times during their drive back to Lucky's house in St. Augustine Beach. The doctor had cleared him for the drive, but they were instructed to stop a few times so Mason could walk around and not get stiff. His handsome cowboy seemed to be having trouble wrapping his head around his very sudden shift in employment.

"Maybe you want to take some time to think about everything?" Lucky asked as he pulled into the driveway of his house. He worried Mason had been hasty in his decisions and might come to regret them sooner rather than later.

"Stop."

Lucky frowned at him. "Stop what?"

"Stop thinking I'm going to regret saying yes to moving in with you." Mason pushed the truck door open, and Lucky quickly took off his seat belt, jumping down and closing the door. He walked around the truck to meet Mason.

"Why don't we go upstairs and have some of Red's sweet tea out on that pretty balcony of ours."

Lucky hadn't missed the "ours," and his heart beat a little quicker at that, but he'd wait until Mason said whatever it was he wanted to say. They headed round the front, following the white concrete step stone path that cut through the front garden, the three palms offering great shade in the summer, along with the veranda that stretched from one side of the house to the other. They climbed the stairs to the front door, the spotless white pillars and railing giving everything a quaint touch. Lucky loved his house. His cousins teased him about the pink siding, purple window shutters, and the four white rocking chairs lined up outside, calling it a "doll house," but he didn't care. He took pride in his home, paid a gardener to keep his grass and shrubbery perfectly trimmed and bright green. Someone came once a week to dust and clean.

The back of the house faced the beach, with a balcony stretching along the length of the second floor. It was peaceful, private, and Lucky often sat outside on the comfortable lounge chair just watching the ocean. Inside, they dropped their bags by the door, and left their shoes there as well. Mason had learned quickly about not walking through his immaculate tiled floor with his dirty boots. Shoes by the door. His madrecita's rules were now also his rules.

"You go upstairs. I'll bring the drinks," Lucky told Mason.

With a kiss to his cheek, Mason left, and Lucky smiled like a fool. He poured them each a glass of Red's sweet tea, then went upstairs to the den and the doors that led out onto the balcony. He stopped in the doorway, admiring the view. Not of the ocean, but the beautiful man stretched out on one of the patio chaise lounge chairs like he'd been there all along.

Lucky placed the glasses on the table between the two chaise lounges, smiling when Mason spread his legs and patted the chair.

"No, you're injured." He held his hand out to Mason. "*You* should be leaning on *me*."

"Twist my arm," Mason drawled, allowing Lucky to help him sit up. He slid forward, and Lucky squeezed in behind him. There was enough room for both of them, Mason stretched out between Lucky's legs, his back to Lucky's chest. Lucky wrapped his arms around Mason and let his chin rest on Mason's shoulder.

"This is nice," Lucky said, feeling the breeze of the cool November air and hearing only the sounds of the waves crashing against the shore off in the distance.

"And just think, we can do this anytime we like."

"Mason, are you sure? It's not too fast?"

Mason sat up with a grunt, ignoring Lucky's protest for him to take it easy. This man was going to be the death of him. Lucky sat up, and Mason shifted so he was straddling the chaise as well and they were facing each other. He took Lucky's hands in his, giving each palm a kiss.

"Darlin', if you want me here, I want me here. Quite frankly, even if you didn't want me here, I'd want me here, so it's up to you. It's your home. You're inviting this grumpy-ass cowboy to live in. I can't guarantee that by the end of the month you won't wanna feed me to the sharks."

Lucky snorted. "I have better ways to torture you."

Mason waggled his eyebrows. "Sexy ways?" Lucky laughed, and Mason smiled warmly at him. "I love your laugh. I love everything about you."

"Even when I drive you crazy?"

"Especially when you drive me crazy. It took me a stupidly long time to find where I belonged, and now that I know it's at your side, I'm not going anywhere. You're stuck with me, darlin'."

"Promise?" Lucky asked, his voice quiet. He wasn't so naïve as to believe in forever, or even a lifetime, but the way Mason was looking at him, the way he brushed his fingers down Lucky's jaw, was enough for Lucky to believe in them.

"Promise." Mason brought their lips together, and Lucky surrendered to Mason's kiss, to his strong arms, and the promise of adventures ahead.

Lucky thought back to everything he'd been through, to the man he'd once been and the man he was now. When he'd been given the nickname Lucky by the youngest of their brothers in arms, Lucky and Spider joked that it was because Lucky was always boasting about all the men and women he'd gotten lucky with, but Pip had gotten this knowing smirk, like he knew the real reason. He'd been right. It had nothing to do with getting laid. He *was* lucky.

Maybe nothing was forever, but what mattered was right here in front of him right now, and Lucky would cherish that for however long he had it, because although the stakes were high, love was worth the risk, and whatever challenges they faced, he was all in.

EPILOGUE

KING TOOK a sip of his coffee, watching the pedestrians hurry from one place to another. The café was busy, but then it usually was during this time of year. There was a sharp chill in the air, what with the weather in the high forties during the day, but it was nice. He finally got to wear some winter clothes, but soon it would be fucking freezing, and King wouldn't mind being back in sunny Florida. His phone rang, and he answered.

"How's the weather in jolly old England?" Ace asked, his English accent making King grunt.

"That was terrifying. Please, don't ever do it again. It's not raining."

"I love your sunny disposition and positive outlook on life."

King held back a smile. "How's Mason taking to his new role?"

"He's happy as a hog in mud."

"You're exhausting."

"Seriously, though. The man was born to lead. The team loves him."

"I knew they would."

"Did you? Hmm." Ace's exaggerated gasp made King smile. He could always count on his best friend to give him something to smile about.

"What?"

"Holy shit!"

"Don't hurt yourself."

"Ha-ha. You, sir, are a dick. That's why we could never agree on any of the applicants and why you kept vetoing our choices. You were holding the team leader position open for a certain cowboy. How long were you going to wait?"

King shrugged even though Ace couldn't see him. "Not much longer. I was waiting for the right opportunity."

"Like an investigation from IA, a freelance job, and him getting shot? Did you know he was going to ask you for work?"

"I may have planted the seed."

"How?"

"Remember the fliers?"

"I wondered why you insisted on having fliers distributed at the sheriff's office. Ooh, sneaky. Right place, right time. Mason ran, and then you stuck him with Lucky."

King grunted. "Their inability to see how crazy they were about each other was frustrating. Forced proximity. They were either going to end up killing each other or sleeping together. My money was on the latter. After that, it was only a matter of time until one or both gave in." King finished his coffee and nodded a thank-you to the barista who cleaned off his table.

"Damn. You orchestrated this whole thing."

"I helped things along."

"You're a little terrifying. I love it."

"How's Ryden doing?" King had been worried about the guy, but Red had a long talk with Ryden at the hospital, and the two had bonded. Red, Mason, and Lucky had taken the guy under their wing, and King was glad Ryden had let them.

"Dr. Bradbury said he's doing great. He's in a place now where he knows he needs help and is willing to accept it. He hasn't missed any sessions, and we take turns checking on him. He and Santos have become best buds."

"Oh yeah?"

"Yep. Ryden says he doesn't feel so outnumbered now by the snake eaters on the floor," Ace said with a laugh. "I'm glad you found a job for Ryden, King. It's really boosted his confidence."

"Risk assessment is a good fit for him. He's out in the field and using his skills to asses for danger." It was a safe role for Ryden. "We'll see how he does further down the line." Security wasn't in the cards. As much as King hated saying it, they couldn't have an armed security officer with impaired vision. Not when people's lives were on the line, but that didn't mean Ryden couldn't fill a host of other life-altering roles. The man was sharp, smart as a whip, and a genuinely sweet guy. He was a bit hotheaded, but the Kings worked with their fair share of hotheads every day.

Ace went quiet, which was never good. When he spoke up, his tone was void of its usual playfulness. "How much longer?"

"As long as it takes."

"King, it's almost Thanksgiving. Can't you just knock him out and shove him on the plane?"

"That's kidnapping."

"Like that fucker hasn't done worse?"

"If we're doing this, it has to be done right. You know that as well as I do."

Ace sighed. "Yeah, I do."

A man in a brown suede jacket, black scarf, gloves, and hat left the coffee shop, and King stood.

"I need to go."

"Stay safe."

"Always." King hung up and returned his phone to his coat pocket. He paid the bill, and left the café. Baseball cap pulled low, he crossed the street, keeping a safe distance between him and his target. With his gloved hands shoved in his jacket pockets, he walked at a steady clip. His clothes, messenger bag, and brisk pace, along with his knowledge of the city, allowed him to blend in with the London crowd. With the holidays approaching, Oxford Street was busier than usual. His target stopped at the newsagent, and King slowed, pulling out his cell phone like he was taking a call. He turned to the older lady selling flowers and purchased a small bouquet of roses.

"That'll be twenty-one pounds."

King smiled pleasantly and handed her twenty-five pounds. "Cheers, love. Keep the change," he replied in his perfect West London accent. She thanked him, and he turned in time to see his target leave the newsagent. King remained in pursuit, heading toward the Oxford Circus tube station. He tapped his Oyster card to the reader, the barrier barely having a chance to close between him and the person in front. His target headed for the Central Line Westbound platform and King stayed close yet kept enough distance between them so as not to arouse suspicion. His target walked to the end of the platform, and King stopped near the center, using the flowers to keep his face partially hidden.

Air whipped around him, the sound of sparks and clacking filled the underground followed by a whoosh, as if a plane was landing. A very old, rickety plane. Pedestrians moved closer to the yellow line as the brakes shrieked, slowing the train before it came to a stop. The doors slid open, and the early afternoon crowd stepped off. King stepped up and moved to the end of the car, then propped himself against the small, high seat next to the emergency exit to keep an eye on his target.

The repetitive beep sounded a warning that the doors were sliding closed before the train started rolling forward, the sticky brakes causing the train to lurch before it smoothed out. A woman not hanging on stumbled, and King caught her before she hit the floor. He steadied her with a smile, accepting her soft-spoken "cheers" as she sat, and then he resumed his seat.

Despite the crowded car, the only noise came from the train itself and a group of teenagers standing by the doors chatting and laughing. His target sat at the far end, as far away from everyone as possible. He lifted his gaze occasionally to look around before he went back to texting. After removing his cell phone from his pocket, King pressed his thumb to the screen and unlocked it, and the man's text appeared on his phone as he composed it.

They loved it! I'll tell you all about it when I see you.

King's fists tightened around the flowers, the painful prick of the thorns digging into his palm reminding him to recenter himself. *Patience.* The manila envelope beneath his coat tucked into the waistband of his jeans burned at his back, or at least it felt that way. A reply text came through the cloned phone, appearing on King's screen.

Are you sure you don't want to meet at the pub or something? I can come by the studio during the day, no worries.

King heard the desperation and fear in the young man's voice. The response was expected, but it still turned King's blood to ice.

You trust me, right? I just want to help you. There are only two spots left.

Several heartbeats later....

Okay. I'll be there.

King turned away, his jaw muscles working as he gritted his teeth. The lights flickered, the wires and cables outside the windows flying by as the train sped through the tunnel. When the train pulled into Notting Hill Gate station, King stood. He casually left, stepping down just as the sick bastard passed by. King lost himself in the crowd despite his size and height. He stood on the right side of the escalator as his quarry stood several steps ahead of him. When they left the station, King crossed the street while his target made a right. He walked opposite him, the trees and parked cars along the street of the posh neighborhood helping to conceal him, not that the guy would have noticed. He was too busy thinking about what he was going to do to the innocent young man waiting for him.

The converted Victorian house was worth a mint, much like the rest of the homes in this neighborhood, the rent of which was on par with any apartment in New York City, but price didn't matter to this guy. He had the cash to burn. Depraved monsters often did. The guy jogged up the steps to the front door, his smile wide as he greeted the pretty blond man standing by the door. The kid was in his early twenties—twenty-one or two at most. King crossed the street, and even from this distance, he saw the young man's fair skin flushed a bright pink, and not from shyness or pleasure. He flinched when the older man put a hand on his shoulder. King slowed down, waiting for his target to close the door. As soon as he did, King went up the stairs.

It was a little after three when King slipped inside the house. He listened to the sounds around him, took note of the mail on the floor outside people's doors. It was a Friday afternoon. In this neighborhood, most people would still be at work or out shopping, meeting up with friends, or having a few pints at a pub. No one was home in this house. He'd made sure of it. A voucher for a free meal at the five-star Thai restaurant on the High Street wasn't something folks would pass up.

Taking the steps two at a time, King reached the top floor. He stepped up to the door and leaned in to listen.

"Please, don't."

"You want to make it in this business? This is what it takes. It's par for the course, babe. Just relax."

King took a few steps back, ran his gaze over the door-frame, then slammed his boot against the door with all the strength he possessed, splintering the frame and ripping the door off one of the hinges.

"What the fuck?"

King moved his gaze from the asshole to the young man with his jeans unzipped and tears in his eyes. He smiled softly at the kid. "It's okay, love," King said, his fake accent laid on thick. "You're okay now. Why don't you come here, away from him?"

The young man looked at the predator beside him, then at King. He scrambled off the couch and darted over, launching himself at King, who gently wrapped an arm around the trembling boy.

"It's okay. You're okay. He's never going to lay another hand on you. I promise."

The young man nodded and pulled back with a sniff. He quickly zipped his pants, then folded his arms over his chest as if trying to cover himself up despite the layers of clothes he was wearing.

"Why don't you go home. Do you need me to call you a cab?"

"No. I'm okay." The young man looked hesitantly over his shoulder at the man glaring daggers at King.

"Go on now," King urged gently, walking him to the door. The young man nodded, then was off. Picking up the door, King pushed it into its frame and locked it, or rather unlocked it, then locked it, considering the lock part of the door had been ripped off.

"Who the fuck are you?"

"I'm your new ghost." King joined the guy on his couch, taking a seat at the end of it. "I'm here to haunt your every waking moment."

"Get the fuck out of my flat before I call the cops," the guy spat, ready to get up when King held a hand up, stilling him.

"I would love for you to call the cops, Barry. In fact, I'm hoping you will. You can tell them about these." King reached under his coat to the back of his waistband and removed the manila envelope. He opened it and took out the glossy eight by tens. He took the top one and flicked it at Barry. "Let's start with Kory." He took the second photo and flicked that one. "Then you can tell them about Arty." He flicked the third one. "Then Billy." *Flick.* "Sandy." *Flick.* "Chris." *Flick.* "David. Eric. Travis. Von." *Flick, flick, flick, flick.* He whipped the rest of the stack at Barry.

Barry stared down at the dozens of scattered pictures.

"Where the hell did you get these?"

"That's not your concern."

"Who sent you? Whatever they're paying you, I'll double it. Triple it. Whatever you want. You want girls? I can get you some gorgeous ones with huge tits and soft lips."

King narrowed his eyes. "You're not very bright, are you?"

"Oh, I see. You like guys? I can get you some beautiful fucking guys who would love to suck cock."

King reached into his front pocket and pulled out a four-by-six photo. He showed it to Barry. "Like him?"

Barry squinted at the photo. "I remember him. Oh yeah, I can track him down for you. You'll love him. He acts like he doesn't want it, but the twinks are easy. They like the pain."

"Right." King returned the photo of Laz to his pocket. He smiled at Barry and dropped the roses to the floor. The guy returned his smile, then found himself on his stomach with King's hand around his throat and his knee to Barry's back. "What about you, Barry? Do you like pain?"

"Please."

"That's what they say, isn't it? When you threaten to ruin them if they don't go along with it?"

"What the fuck do you want?"

King hauled him to his feet by his neck. "What I want, other than to cause you an excruciating amount of pain, is for you to pay for your crimes." He led Barry into the kitchen, pulled out one of the chairs, and forced him into it. "Don't move." Barry's gaze darted to the doorway, and King shook his head as he walked over to one of the kitchen drawers. "You don't listen very well, do you?"

"Wait, what happened to your accent? You're American?"

King ignored him, opening the drawers until he found what he was looking for. "Ah. Perfect." He lifted the roll of duct tape. "I love this stuff."

Barry's eyes went wide, and he bolted out of the chair. King was in the doorway before the guy got there. He threw his hand out, snatching hold of his neck and squeezing. Barry made a gurgling noise as he tried to pry King's fingers off him.

"What did I say about listening?"

"I'm sorry," Barry wheezed as King shoved him down into the chair again. He secured Barry to the chair, his arms trapped against his sides. As soon as the top was done, King taped his ankles to the chair's legs. Returning the tape to the drawer, King moved the kitchen table out of the way. He checked under the sink and found a roll of trash bags. Tearing two off, he found a pair of scissors and cut them open. He lay the cut bags flat on the floor, took hold of Barry's chair with him in it, lifted it, then slammed him down in the center.

"Fuck! What the hell are you doing? Are you fucking insane?"

King picked up a second chair and placed it directly in front of Barry.

"What... what are you going to do?"

"I try not to judge people," King said as he took a seat. "Who am I to lay judgment on another human being after the things I've done? Yes, I could argue that I was following orders, that I was doing it for my country, that war hurts everyone, not just those on the frontlines, but when all is said and done, I made a choice. I chose to take lives to save others. Granted, they were murderers, rapists, and terrorists, but they were human lives. The thing is, I've made peace with my demons. We cohabit somewhat amicably. I feed them on occasion, and they appreciate it."

"What the *fuck*?"

"You're right. That's neither here nor there."

"Are you going to kill me?"

"There are things out there scarier than death, believe me. Let's get started, shall we?" King leaned forward.

"What the fuck are you doing?" Barry struggled, but he didn't so much as budge.

"I'm going to give you something to think about." King took hold of Barry's lower arm, squeezing a pressure point that had Barry crying out at the pain, which King knew from firsthand experience was particularly excruciating.

"Oh God! Please don't do this! What the fuck do you want from me?"

"You have this terrible habit of not listening, Barry. You need to pay for your crimes. I have a private plane waiting for me. You're going to join me. We'll fly back to the States, where you will promptly turn yourself in and confess to your crimes."

Barry let out a bark of laughter. "Are you fucking kidding me? I'm not going to prison for a bunch of little sluts who were happy to get fucked to save their job."

The human body was incredible. With just the right pressure, one could either alleviate pain or cause a great amount of it, all without leaving a mark. King pressed his thumb into a sweet little spot on the inside of Barry's right knee.

"Oh fuck!" Barry cried out, tears pooling in his eyes. "Stop. Please!"

"See, the thing is, those young men weren't *happy* to have you fuck them. They were scared, vulnerable, and intimidated. You took advantage of them because that's what predators like you do, and you raped them. You're a rapist, Barry."

"No, that's not—"

King took hold of Barry's wrist and squeezed, making Barry howl. With a sigh, King stood and went to the drawer, cut off a piece of duct tape, and slapped it over Barry's mouth. He placed his thumbs to the same spot on Barry's other wrist. "I have plenty more pressure points to choose from, and every time you lie to me, the pain is going to get worse and worse until you eventually pass out. I'll then wake you up, and we'll start all over. Now, let's try this again. You threatened young men with ruining their fledgling careers and coerced them into having sex with you, and the ones who tried to refuse, you forced. You're a rapist, Barry."

Tears streamed down Barry's face as King pressed his thumbs into Barry's wrist. It wasn't the kind of torture technique he'd use on a trained enemy, but it was more than enough for this bastard. King continued to exploit Barry's pressure points, from his inner thigh to his neck. A little less than an hour in, and Barry nodded furiously. King removed one side of the tape, peeling it back, and waited.

"Okay, yes. I forced them. I took advantage of them. But please. I worked too long and too hard on my career to—"

"Wrong answer." King flipped the tape back. "A lot of people when they fight go for the quickest, most effective points to bring someone down. The groin, the shin, the kidneys, the eyes. Me? I like a good solid punch to the solar plexus." He placed two fingers to the center of Barry's torso just below his heart and lungs. "This little bundle of nerves in here is great, because when it gets hit, and I mean *hit*, your organs go into shock and you go down. Breathing will become difficult, and the pain is, well, why don't I show you?" King pulled back his fist and snarled, no intention of hitting the guy, but Barry didn't know that.

Barry's eyes went wide, and he convulsed against the chair in an effort to get away. Tears mixed with snot as he sobbed. He shook his head furiously, mumbling against the tape. King pulled back the silver strip, then sat back.

"Yes?"

"Who the fuck are you?" Barry asked through sobs.

"I'm a man with a mission, and until I complete my mission, I won't stop. I've been following you for over a month. You know what the great thing about CCTV is? You're around it long enough, you forget it's there. I didn't forget."

"Please, man. I don't want to go to jail. I won't survive."

"Should have thought of that before you sexually assaulted fifty-three young men over the course of fifteen years. You're going away for a very, *very* long time. I'm going to make sure of it."

The loathing in Barry's eyes was impressive, and then his expression turned smug. "None of them will testify."

King reached into his pocket and pulled out a small stack of airline ticket receipts. "These boys are. They're at home packing as we speak." The shock on Barry's face made King smile. "See, it only took one very brave young man to come forward to inspire others. Plus, they have me, my men, and my company to support them. They don't have to worry about legal fees, intimidation, or threats to their lives because protecting people is what we do."

"I have money," Barry spat out.

"I have more." King leaned forward, his eyes meeting

Barry's. "I know how men like you operate. You think you have money and friends in high places? Well, so do I. If I need to use every contact in my arsenal to take you down, then I will, and if it comes to that, I promise you that I will bury you in a hole so deep no one will ever remember you even existed."

"What do you care? They're nobodies to you."

"Wrong again. See, one of these young men is family, and because of him and what you did to him, I know about you, and what you did to them. For a long time, you've been the monster haunting his dreams. I'm here to put an end to that."

"And what does that make you? You think torturing me into a confession makes you a hero?"

King snorted. "You think I'm doing this to be a hero?" He leaned forward and pressed a thumb to the pressure point on the inside of Barry's knee, tearing another scream from him. "This isn't about heroics, Barry. This is about me protecting my family."

"What makes you think I won't tell them *you* coerced *me* into confessing?"

"Because that would really upset me, and then you'd upset my brothers, and they won't take kindly to that. Did I mention they're all very talented individuals? Oh, and one's the boyfriend of one of the young men you raped. With you on US soil, how do you think he'll feel if you go back on your word and end up free on the streets? I'm the calm, rational one. There's only so much I'll be able to do to keep these guys from hunting you down, and, well, you seem to have a pretty good imagination." King sat back and folded his arms over his chest. "Take your time. Think about it. I have all the time in the world."

"You're not going to kill me," Barry challenged.

"No. But wherever you go, I'll go. Consider me your new shadow. I'll show up at your job, the pub, Tesco's, and when someone asks who I am, I'll just tell them the truth. I wonder what your industry friends and contacts will think when they hear about what you've done? You think this is torture?" King sat forward, his stare hard. "I haven't even started, and I won't have to lay a finger on you."

Barry didn't move his gaze from King's, but King saw the wheels turning behind the man's shrewd brown eyes. He sat up, and Barry flinched.

"Okay."

King held a hand up to his ear. "What was that? I didn't hear you."

"Okay. I'll turn myself in, confess to everything. I'll cooperate."

"Smart choice. Here's what's going to happen." King stood, walked to the kitchen counter, and pulled a knife from the knife block. "I'm going to cut you free, make a call, and then we're going to get into the black cab that'll be waiting outside to take us to the private airfield. We'll get on my plane, and as soon as we land in sunny Florida, you'll be taken away in handcuffs by the FBI." He stood over Barry, knife in hand. "If at any point in time you try to do something stupid, I will not hesitate to correct you on your grievous error of judgment." King cut Barry loose. He pointed to the side of the kitchen. "Stand there and don't move."

Barry rushed to do as King asked, resignation written all over him. He was done. King hadn't been kidding when he said he'd become the man's shadow. He knew the hells of torture well, and any man strong enough to survive even the worst physical torture rarely stood a chance against his own mind. The human brain could only take so much before it broke, no matter the training.

Escorting Barry to his bedroom to fetch his passport and any necessary documents—since he would not be returning to his luxury London flat, or to the country, for that matter, considering he was a US citizen—he then led Barry outside to the cab waiting by the curb. He opened the backdoor and waited. A heartbeat later, Barry climbed in, and King slid in beside him.

Less than an hour later, King escorted Barry up the stairs and into the plane. He shoved him down into the seat across from him, then fastened Barry's seat belt a little tighter than necessary. "In case there's turbulence," King said with a smile. He took a seat, thanking the stewardess for the drink. She turned to their guest, and King shook his head. "He won't be having any. Airsickness."

The stewardess nodded. "Just let me know if you need anything."

"Thank you." King removed his phone from his pocket and entered the code into his speed dial.

"Yeah?"

"The package is en route."

"Affirmative."

King hung up and got comfortable. It was going to be a long eight hours. Thankfully, Barry didn't feel the need to fill the silence. King sent a text to Ace, who'd inform Red. The only one who knew he was even in London was Ace. They'd agreed it would be best to wait until King had Barry in his custody before they got Laz's hopes up. Ever since the incident with Elena and Bryan, Laz had been determined to see justice done, so King set out to make sure it happened.

The PLANE LANDED at Northeast Florida Regional Airport, and as soon as they were given the all-clear, King removed his seat belt and stood. He stretched, then showed Barry to the door. Having swapped his winter outerwear for a light jacket halfway through the flight, King removed his sunglasses from his front breast pocket and waited for the exit door to be opened. He stepped out onto the stairs and let out a heavy sigh. *Wonderful.*

"Move," King ordered, following Barry down the stairs to the tarmac, where a small team of federal agents and several men and women in suits stood to his right, while a small group of Army soldiers stood to the left, three large black Suburbans with pitch-black tinted windows parked close by. King turned to one of the women to his right wearing a sharp tailored suit.

"Ms. Cunningham, this is Mr. Barry Wheeldon."

"Thank you, Mr. Kingston. We'll take it from here."

King handed Barry over, not sparing him another glance before he turned and walked over to the soldiers, one of whom stepped forward.

"Sir, please come with us."

King motioned for the private to lead the way, and he followed close behind to the middle Suburban, the back door of which was opened for him when he approached. The private saluted the man inside the vehicle and was then dismissed.

King poked his head in and shook it. "And here I thought you'd be out on some golf course working on your backswing." He climbed in beside the handsome man in his early sixties, closing the door behind him. "General."

The General chuckled and shook King's outstretched

hand. "Long time, Ward." The general tapped the glass divider, and the engine roared to life.

"I'm guessing this isn't a social visit."

"No. You look well, by the way. I hear you and the boys are doing real good. I'm proud of you, son."

King swallowed past the lump in his throat. "Thank you, sir." They had a history together, an unbreakable bond forged in loss, grief, and secrets. If anyone found out the real reason their unit was sent to Syria, they'd all be arrested. The only people who knew were the General, the Kings, Jack, Joker, and the men who never made it back.

"I need your advice."

King wasn't easily surprised, but that certainly did it. The man had the whole of the US government and its military at his disposal. What the hell would he need King for?

"I have this high-level asset who's working on something crucial for our government. Thing is, he's not... how do I put this? He's unique. A genius. When it comes to coding, there's no one better, but he's not so good with everything else. We've got him in a secure facility with a team in place, some of the brightest minds in our country, but he's... well, it's a goddamn mess. We have a small army in place to ensure his safety, and somehow he keeps giving them the slip. It boggles my mind. We have tried everything."

"He's got to know the security is there for his protection. Is he putting up a fight?"

"No. I don't know how he does it, but he disappears. We need him to finish this project, but he's struggling bad, and I've reached the end of my rope. Washington's expecting results, and if they don't get it, they're going to force it, and you and I both know what that means, but that won't work with him. They'll end up killing him, Ward."

"You have to find someone who can work within the

parameters of his needs as well as ensure that their priority remains his safety. It's a balancing act. It's about creating the ideal environment, one in which he can function, but also serves as a place of comfort, security."

"You're absolutely right," the General replied, letting out a steady breath. "I knew talking to you was the right thing to do. You'll do great."

King blinked at him. "I'm sorry?" He let out a laugh. "Oh no. I'm done."

"Ward, I need you on this. It *has* to be you."

"No." King crossed his arms over his chest, his stomach feeling like it was full of lead. "I played by the rules, did my part. I've sacrificed enough."

"And I haven't?" the General growled, the car plunging into silence.

King turned his attention out the window, hating that this conversation was taking him back to that place. It was supposed to be over. He was proud to have served, but he was done.

"I'm sorry. I know what I'm asking of you."

"Do you? Because it seems to me like you're asking me to take on Washington again."

"No." The General's soft tone had King turning to look at him. The fear in his eyes caught King off guard. "I'm asking you to protect my son."

King sat frozen to the spot, unsure he'd heard correctly.

"He means the world to me, Ward. If one of those bastards gets their hands on him, I don't need to tell you what would happen."

They'd make him disappear, and the General would never see his son again, or if he did, it wouldn't be alive.

"Ward, please."

King closed his eyes and inhaled in a long steady breath

before releasing it slowly. He lifted his gaze to meet the General's.

"Okay. I'll protect your son."

CHECK OUT KING'S STORY, *Diamond in the Rough*, the fourth book in the Four Kings Security series on Amazon and KindleUnlimited.

A NOTE FROM THE AUTHOR

Thank you so much for reading *Join the Club*, the third book in the Four Kings Security series. I hope you enjoyed Lucky and Mason's story, and if you did, please consider leaving a review on Amazon. Reviews can have a significant impact on a book's visibility on Amazon, so any support you show these fellas would be amazing. King's book, *Diamond in the Rough* is now available from Amazon and KindleUnlimited.

Want to stay up-to-date on my releases and receive exclusive content? Sign up for my newsletter.

Follow me on Amazon to be notified of a new releases, and connect with me on social media, including my fun Facebook group, Donuts, Dog Tags, and Day Dreams, where we chat books, post pictures, have giveaways, and more!

Looking for inspirational photos of my books? Visit my book boards on Pinterest.

Thank you again for joining the Kings on their adventures. We hope to see you again soon!

ALSO BY CHARLIE COCHET

Shifter Scoundrels Series

Co-written with Macy Blake

FOUR KINGS SECURITY UNIVERSE SERIES

Four King Security

Four Kings Security Boxed Set

Black Ops: Operation Orion's Belt

The Kings: Wild Cards

The Kings: Wild Cards Boxed Set

Runaway Grooms

THIRDS UNIVERSE SERIES

THIRDS

THIRDS Beyond the Books

THIRDS: Rebels

TIN

THIRDS Boxed Sets

OTHER SERIES

Paranormal Princes

Soldati Hearts Series

North Pole City Tales Series

DID YOU KNOW?

If you own a book or borrow it through Kindle Unlimited, you can get Whispersynced audiobooks at a discounted price. Interested in audio? Check out the Charlie Cochet titles available on Audible.

ABOUT THE AUTHOR

Charlie Cochet is the international bestselling author of the THIRDS series. Born in Cuba and raised in the US, Charlie enjoys the best of both worlds, from her daily Cuban latte to her passion for classic rock.

Currently residing in Central Florida, Charlie is at the beck and call of a highly opinionated sable German Shepherd and a rascally Doxiepoo bent on world domination. When she isn't writing, she can usually be found devouring a book, releasing her creativity through art, or binge watching a new TV series. She runs on coffee, thrives on music, and loves to hear from readers.

www.charliecochet.com

Sign up for Charlie's newsletter:
https://newsletter.charliecochet.com

amazon.com/author/charliecochet

facebook.com/charliecochet

instagram.com/charliecochet

bookbub.com/authors/charliecochet

goodreads.com/CharlieCochet

pinterest.com/charliecochet

Made in the USA
Las Vegas, NV
13 January 2024

84313760R00173